SHADOWS OF THE BADGE

SHADOWS OF THE BADGE

Introducing Detective Jake Harper

J.K. WOLFE

SHADOWS OF THE BADGE

Published by Deep Watch Press

Copyright © 2025 by J.K. Wolfe

Cover Design by Ambient Pixel Design

https://JKWolfeBooks.com

All Rights Reserved.

This is a work of fiction. Names, characters, businesses, places, events, locales, and incidents are either the products of the author's imagination or used in a fictitious manner. Any resemblance to actual persons, living or dead, or actual events is purely coincidental.

No part of this book may be used or reproduced in any manner whatsoever without written permission from the author except in the case of brief quotations embodied in critical articles or reviews.

ISBN: 979-8-9990159-2-1

DEDICATION

To my beautiful wife, my love,

who taught me about redemption,

who believed in me when few others did.

Thank you.

Author's Foreword

This is a work of fiction. But the truth lives between the lines.

Many of the events in *Shadows of the Badge* are drawn from real experiences. The things I've seen with my own eyes, and the things my colleagues have carried with them long after the shift ended. From adrenaline-fueled patrol calls where split-second decisions change lives forever, to the quiet, soul-crushing weight of investigating abuse, loss, and the destruction people inflict on one another; these stories are rooted in the real work, the real pain, and the real choices behind the badge.

I didn't write this book to tell my story. I wrote it to make sense of what I've lived through, and to honor those who walk the same line every day. This story is for the cops who stood their ground when it would have been easier to look away. For the ones who were knocked down, written off, and got back up anyway. For anyone who has ever been judged by their worst moment and fought to become something more.

At its core, this is a story about redemption. About the weight of the past, and the strength it takes to rise above it. Detective Jake Harper isn't perfect. But like many of us, he keeps showing up. He keeps trying. And he understands something I believe deeply: integrity means doing the right thing not when it is easy, but when it costs you everything.

In Harper's words: *"Right is right. No matter the cost."*

Thank you for reading.

— J.K. Wolfe

<u>**CONTENTS**</u>

"The evil that men do lives after them; the good is oft interred with their bones." - William Shakespeare.

PROLOGUE

The glass was crystal, hand-blown and weighted perfectly in his palm. The scotch inside it, dark amber and smooth, cost more than most people's mortgages.

He stood in front of the floor-to-ceiling windows, the city skyline glittering beneath like scattered diamonds on black velvet. This was his kingdom. His empire. And tomorrow, it would grow even larger.

The deal was done. Only the final paperwork and a few carefully orchestrated press releases remained. His company, his vision, was about to go global. The kind of move that made kings. The kind of move that made presidents.

He allowed himself a smile, tilting the glass toward his reflection. A toast to himself.

He could see it all. A few more years in tech, then the pivot: public service. A run for state office. Congress. Maybe even Governor. He had the money. The charisma. The story. He was everything the public wanted, a self-made man with a clean record and a dazzling smile.

Not to mention his looks. Tall, broad-shouldered, the kind of build that came with both a personal trainer and a nutritionist. A sharp jawline, clean-shaven. A mouth that knew how to smile with just the right hint of humility. His thick, jet-black hair, styled but never stiff, held just enough gray at the temples to suggest maturity without age. His tanned skin glowed with the health of high-end retreats in Sedona or Tulum. His steely blue eyes had convinced more than one investor to sign on the dotted line.

In short, he looked exactly like what he believed himself to be—a man destined for more.

He set the glass down with a soft clink and loosened the cuffs of his tailored shirt. The imported fabric fit perfectly to his lean frame. Holly said he looked powerful in it.

He poured another finger of scotch, letting his mind drift. To the things she let him do to her. How their bodies fit. Maybe he'd call her. He frowned, recalling her breathy "I love you" during their last late-night tryst. Lately, that had become a pattern. Emotional conversations, subtle pleas for something real. It bored him. Maybe he wouldn't. He didn't want complicated. He didn't need love.

Holly had been a fun distraction. Beautiful, mature, willing. But lately she'd started showing up unannounced. Asking questions. Wanting a future. She didn't understand the rules of the game. And for a man like him, sentimentality was a liability.

His thoughts shifted to the new intern. Twenty-two, fresh out of college, all curves and ambition.

She had that hungry look, the one he recognized instantly. Eager to prove herself. Eager to please. Long legs, a tiny waist, and eyes that sparkled with a blend of innocence and drive. Her blouses were a little too tight. Her heels, and hemlines, a little too high. She laughed at his jokes and lingered too long after meetings. She didn't know it yet, but she wanted him.

And soon, she'd have him. Or rather, he'd have her.

He smiled, imagining the surprise on her lips, the way she'd gasp when he guided her into his office. The way she'd whisper "sir."

Grinning at his reflection, he basked in it. Brilliant. Desired. Untouchable.

Then came the knock.

He frowned. Unexpected. He padded across the hardwood, glass in hand, and peeked through the peephole.

Surprise flickered across his face.

He opened the door halfway. "What the hell are you doing here? I told you never to come—"

The figure didn't answer.

A hand shoved the door wide. He stumbled backward as the intruder entered, fast and purposeful.

"Is this about the money?" he asked, voice sharp now. "Because I told you, everything's handled. I have safeguards. You can't tie anything to me. If this is a scare tactic—your employer's not going to be happy—"

The intruder, with a tilted head, was calm. Cold.

"Who do you think sent me?"

He didn't see the knife until it flashed beneath the hallway light.

The first stab sank into his abdomen, deep and paralyzing. His scotch glass shattered, fragments dancing across the hardwood as he fell to one knee.

"Wait," he gasped. "We can talk—"

The second cut severed the words.

He reached instinctively for his neck, stunned by the sudden warmth there. Blood poured through his fingers. The pain surged with the third cut. Then a fourth.

Vision blurred. His world turned red. Then black.

He collapsed, limbs twitching. Blood spread across the floor like spilled ink.

His final thoughts were not of women or wealth, but of the press release he would never approve. The company he would never expand. The legacy he would never leave.

Darkness claimed him.

And the kingdom fell silent.

• • • • •

"It is not the critic who counts; not the man who points out how the strong man stumbles, or where the doer of deeds could have done them better. The credit belongs to the man who is actually in the arena, whose face is marred by dust and sweat and blood..." - Theodore Roosevelt

CHAPTER 1: MURDER IN THE FIRST

The city of Stonehaven had always been relatively quiet, despite its growth in recent years. Nestled between the rolling hills of Oregon's Willamette Valley, a place where neighbors waved at each other, children played in the streets without fear, and the police radio was usually limited to drunken fights, the odd bar brawl, or petty theft. But murder? That was something out of the headlines, something that happened in surrounding, larger cities and out in the county. There hadn't been a homicide in Stonehaven in almost two decades.

Detective Jake Harper had lived here most of his life, save for his time in the Coast Guard. He knew its streets, its politics, its people, even the ones who lurked in the shadows. And this wasn't lawless Blackridge County, where Harper had patrolled the streets for the Sheriff's Office. This place had a rhythm, a hum, an unspoken promise of safety.

His phone buzzed, cutting through Sunday evening's quiet.

"Harper. We got a body. It's bad."

Harper's grip tightened around the phone, his pulse quickening. Foster hesitated just long enough for Harper to notice. It was a rare pause from a man who usually spoke with unwavering certainty. Detective Sergeant Craig Foster didn't use words like 'bad' lightly.

"What do you mean, bad?"

"Brutal. It's a mess. Get down here."

After giving Harper the address, the line clicked dead.

Here we go. Harper had seen his share of violence, both overseas and on the streets, but something about this call twisted in his gut. Maybe it was the tone in Foster's voice. Maybe it was the silence that followed. Either way, it didn't feel like just another case.

Harper sighed, setting his coffee mug down. The warmth did nothing to steady his nerves. He'd been a detective for six months, long enough to know this call was different. Six months in a job that felt equal parts fulfilling and exhausting, where cases like child abuse and financial fraud had kept him busy. Tedious at times, but at least predictable. So far, his biggest break had been helping solve a string of car break-ins. Now, all of a sudden, he was getting called to a murder. He wasn't sure if that was a sign of things to come, or just a cruel reminder of how quickly things could spiral out of control.

Harper grabbed his jacket, shrugged it on and stepped outside, where the last traces of daylight bled into the purple-black of night.

• • • • •

The air outside was crisp with the falling night. Harper's detective rig, an unmarked gunmetal gray Dodge Durango, cut through the city, its engine humming softly as the headlights sliced through the streets. Familiar neighborhoods passed in a blur. Suburban streets lined with tidy homes, each one more mundane than the last. But this would not be a mundane night.

Harper's fingers tapped restlessly against the steering wheel, eyes flickering to the clock for the third time in as many minutes. Each streetlight flashed rhythmically across the windshield, illuminating fleeting glimpses of empty sidewalks and curtained windows. A city asleep, unaware its quiet had already been broken.

He didn't know the name of the victim yet—he'd get briefed when he arrived—but the familiar dread of a body filled his gut. He couldn't shake the image of a lifeless corpse, cold and unfeeling, waiting to be uncovered, to be explained. By the time he pulled up to the condo, red and blue strobes bathed the street in an eerie glow.

Harper pulled into a parking spot, the tires of his car scraping against the curb, and stepped out. Harper's green sneakers touched lightly on the blacktop, belying the heavy thoughts swirling through his mind. The place was upscale. Modern. Not the kind of place for a bloodbath. But the crime scene tape snaking across the entrance told him otherwise.

As Harper walked under the tape, the sounds of the city were swallowed up. The cool breeze, thick with the scent of pine and damp earth, now mingled with the faint metallic tang of blood. It was a scent that made Harper's stomach tighten.

Officer Linda Moore stood near the door, arms crossed. Her uniform was rumpled, her boots scuffed with years of wear. Like her, they'd seen it all. Her face was unreadable, but her eyes were harder than usual. She gave Harper a brief nod as he approached, the grim set of her features telling him everything he needed to know. Moore wasn't some rookie. She'd been on the job for over two decades, and whatever she saw tonight had shaken even her steady resolve.

"Michael Grant. Forty-two. Tech entrepreneur. Big in local politics." Her voice was steady, but there was tension beneath it. "We got the 911 call around six. Neighbors heard a crash, didn't know what it was at first. By the time the EMTs arrived, he was already gone. Slashed throat. And the place is a mess."

"Grant?" Harper repeated, though he didn't need a reminder.

The tech mogul, Harper thought. The name fell into place. Michael Grant. Founder of a local software company. He was always in the news, talking about his rags-to-riches story, his push for community development, his position in local business circles. Harper didn't recognize him personally, but this was no small-time victim. Harper's brain was already cataloging motive possibilities, political enemies, corporate espionage, a jilted lover maybe. A man like Grant made waves. *And waves always left someone drowning.*

Harper stepped inside. The world seemed to slow, the noise of the street fading as his senses adjusted to the new reality of the space. The room was dim, the only light coming from a single table lamp near the front door. The metallic scent of blood hung in the air, mingling with the sterile tang of forensic powder. The condo was sleek, all sharp angles and expensive taste, but disorder had ripped through it like a storm.

And then he saw it.

The body.

Michael Grant lay sprawled across the polished hardwood floor, his tailored black suit soaked with blood from several stab wounds. His throat had been cut deep—too deep for hesitation. His hands were clenched, eyes frozen in wide-eyed horror. The blood pooling beneath him had already begun to congeal, dark and sticky against the floor's pristine surface. He hadn't even been dead long enough to start smelling. *The killer took time to finish the job.* Or at the very least, hadn't rushed. That said something. Rage, yes, but controlled. Purposeful.

What really caught his attention wasn't just the brutality of the wound, it was the mess.

A shattered coffee table sprawled across the floor, glass shards glinting beneath the dim light. Picture frames lay broken, their contents strewn in disarray. Fragments from an expensive crystal glass, the kind for fine liquor, were scattered near Grant's hands. The sleek leather couch had been viciously slashed, white stuffing spilling from the wounds like exposed entrails. Decorative pillows were torn apart, their shredded fabric fluttering in the faint draft. This wasn't destruction, it was something far more deliberate. Intentional.

And yet, the valuables remained untouched. A high-end speaker system, a sleek laptop, an open liquor cabinet stocked with bottles worth more than Harper's paycheck. And then there was the watch on Grant's wrist.

"Rolex Daytona" Moore muttered, catching his gaze. "Worth over a hundred grand."

Harper raised an eyebrow.

"My dad was into watches," Moore said by way of explanation, shrugging.

Harper let out a slow breath. The watch was the kind of thing that could fund someone's escape, or could cost them everything.

"This wasn't a robbery," he said. *This was something else. The killer was searching for something.*

Moore nodded. "No forced entry. No sign of anything missing."

Harper knelt beside the body, studying the slash across his throat. It was precise, confident, deep. This wasn't an accident, and it wasn't the kind of wound inflicted in a panicked struggle. Whoever had done this had meant to do it.

"It was personal," he muttered. "He knew his killer."

Moore crossed her arms. "That's what we think too. The mayor's already sniffing around. The chief wants answers. And the press…" she exhaled. "Everyone's going to be watching this one."

Harper sighed, his hands slipping into his jacket pockets. His gaze lingered on the body, on the chaos of the room, on the fractured pieces of someone's life. "Figures," he said under his breath, more to himself than to Moore. He'd been here before, in the thick of a high-pressure case. But this one felt different. He could feel it deep in his bones.

"Any witnesses?" he asked, trying to focus, trying to reel in his thoughts.

Moore shook her head, eyes narrowed in thought. "No one saw anything. Home Security was turned off." Harper raised his eyebrows.

Moore stared at Harper, her face drawn. "You'd better buckle up, Jake. This one's going to get ugly."

Harper's mind was already spinning. As he stood there, looking at the broken glass near Grant's body, one thing was crystal clear: The city's quiet pulse had been fractured.

And it was his job to put the pieces back together.

•••••

CHAPTER 2: THE WEIGHT OF THE BADGE

Harper had been running on fumes long before the murder of Michael Grant. Now, after an entire night of processing the crime scene, collecting statements, canvassing for witnesses, and piecing together a preliminary report, exhaustion clung to him like a second skin. His eyes burned as he rubbed them roughly, blinking hard against the gritty feeling that had settled there. His shoulder sagged, heavy with fatigue, each step from his car feeling like a mile.

Justice doesn't sleep, Harper thought. *And apparently, neither do I.*

Three hours. That was all he had managed before dragging himself back to the office, his car still smelling like stale coffee and last night's takeout. He'd barely made it through a shower before shoving himself into fresh clothes, brewing a pot of coffee strong enough to cut through the fog in his skull, and heading back to the station. His wife, Alyssa, had been asleep when he got home, and was still slumbering when his alarm went off before dawn. He'd kissed the forehead of his three-year-old daughter, Adelyn, *Addie.* Brushing soft curls from her forehead, feeling her gentle breathing beneath his fingertips, he'd wished silently that this quiet moment could last longer before he stepped back into the storm.

The Stonehaven Police Department wasn't large, with forty-six sworn officers total split between patrol, detectives, and admin. Harper stepped into the Detective's bullpen, greeted by the familiar symphony of typing keys, the hum of tired computers, and the stale aroma of burnt coffee that clung stubbornly to every surface. His desk, scratched and worn from years of use, felt welcoming as he dropped into the chair, which creaked from the stress. Around him, cluttered notes, empty coffee cups, and hastily scribbled case files were scattered, a chaotic comfort only a cop would understand. It wasn't glamorous, but it was home.

Across from him, Detective Sergeant Foster leaned against a whiteboard, pinning crime scene photos and initial reports haphazardly. The older man appeared as rested as Harper felt, rubbing the salt-and-pepper beard along his jaw. Foster had worked major crimes in Portland for nearly two decades before semi-retiring to Stonehaven. He didn't talk much about those years, but the slow, deliberate way he moved told Harper everything. A broad-shouldered man who carried the job in the slope of his spine, Foster had the voice of someone used to being listened to, and the patience of a man who'd raised four kids, two of whom had followed him into law enforcement.

He rapped a marker against the board. "Alright," Foster said. "Let's run through what we have."

Detectives Carrie Hurst and Ryan Cho sat nearby, notebooks open.

Hurst perched at the edge of her chair, posture perfect, pen already in motion. Her blonde ponytail was pulled tight, stretching faint lines across her brow. Eight years in patrol had taught her the value of precision, and six years as a detective had sharpened her instincts to a razor's edge. She was meticulous, rarely missed a detail, and never hesitated to give a report or an opinion. Married, with a toddler at home, she and Harper had traded more than a few stories of sleepless nights and sticky-fingered chaos.

Cho, seated beside her, looked like he'd slept even less than Harper, but he carried it better. The youngest detective on the team, Korean-American and lean with sharp eyes behind thick-rimmed designer glasses, he radiated frenetic energy. Irreverent, foul-mouthed under pressure, and was fast on his feet, Foster had once called him a bloodhound in glasses. Single, often casually charming, Cho approached every case like it was a puzzle designed just for him.

"Michael Grant. Forty-two," Foster began. "Found dead in his condo. Throat slashed, multiple stab wounds. Overturned furniture, broken glass, but no signs of a struggle. But valuables untouched. Watch still on his wrist. No forced entry."

"That apartment was a mess," Cho said, tapping his pen. "Looked like a damn hurricane rolled through. But they didn't take anything."

"Right," Foster replied. "Which makes this feel personal. Harper?"

Harper took a sip of coffee, eyes fixed on the crime scene photos. "This wasn't a smash-and-grab. Whoever did it came there to hurt him. Badly. Rage, but controlled. And the security system was disabled before the attack. That's not random."

"Definitely not," Hurst said. "I pulled his financials this morning. No red flags. No gambling debts, no sign of financial desperation. He wasn't sitting on a pile of unpaid loans. I've got a warrant request in to dig deeper into his personal and business accounts. Should have it signed before lunch."

Cho nodded. "One neighbor heard yelling around six. Thought it was a domestic fight. Another mentioned a black sedan idling outside earlier that afternoon. Figured it was an Uber. I'm pulling street cam footage to confirm."

Harper leaned back in his chair. "Tech CEO, political ties. That means enemies. Maybe former employees. Disgruntled investors. We need to check call logs, emails, meeting records. Anyone he pissed off in the last six months."

Foster's phone buzzed. He checked the screen, scowled.

"City Hall again?" Harper asked.

"Third time this morning," Foster said. "They want a narrative before we've even got a motive."

"That sounds about right," Hurst said, flipping her notebook. "Politics loves a clean headline."

Foster pushed off the board. "Cho, talk to the family and inner circle. Anyone close to him. Hurst, take his finances. Every wire, account, holding company. Find me something."

Cho saluted lazily. "On it."

"Oh," Hurst added, scribbling something, "and his foundation sent over a year of donation records. I'll start there. Sometimes these charities are more laundering than giving."

"Harper," Foster said, eyes steady. "You're heading to the ME's office for the autopsy. Sit in, take notes. Then swing by Grant Technologies. Start digging into his professional life. Rivals. Lawsuits. People who hated him in a suit and smiled at him in public."

Harper nodded slowly. "Copy that."

A quiet settled over the room for a moment. Harper looked back at the board, letting the coffee settle in his gut. Something about the weight of this case was different. Maybe it was because it had been so many years since Stonehaven saw a murder. Or maybe it was the crime scene itself, too deliberate, too controlled.

This isn't random. Someone did this with intent. Precision.

But beneath that, something deeper stirred. A quiet echo of a past he couldn't quite silence.

Harper's gaze landed on the photos of the crime scene. His vision blurred, exhaustion seeping into every muscle. He closed his eyes, the murmur of conversation fading to a distant hum, his mind slipping into unwelcome memories: a shadowed alley, accusations whispered, trust fractured. He blinked it away, tightening his jaw.

Or maybe it's just me. Maybe it's the part of me that never really let go of Blackridge.

A sharp cough from Foster yanked him back. Harper straightened in his chair, rubbing his temples roughly, chasing the ghosts away. Foster's gaze lingered, briefly sympathetic.

"Grant wasn't random," Hurst finally said, her voice breaking the tension. "Whoever did this wanted to send a message. Question is, to whom?"

Harper took another sip of his coffee, swallowing down the bitter taste. He wasn't about to let his past dictate his present. Not now. Not on this case.

• • • • •

Harper had always wanted to be a cop.

He could still recall the feeling of plastic handcuffs hooked to his belt as a kid, chasing his friends around. Whenever they played a neighborhood game of "cops and robbers," Harper was always the cop. Even then, it felt like a calling, not just a game.

Harper paused, eyes lingering on his reflection in the precinct's glass doors. At thirty-seven, he still looked the part: five foot ten, lean but muscular build, sharp blue eyes. Hints of silver now threaded through his thick brown hair. His jaw etched with a short stubble beard, the kind that hovered between intentional and forgetful, adding to the weathered edge he'd earned over the years. The job had taken its toll, the years leaving their signatures across his body. A faint scar curling along his forearm, a stiff shoulder that never healed right, and calloused hands that no amount of soap could soften. But the intensity in his gaze remained, the same stubborn fire that had burned in him as a rookie still smoldered behind his eyes, undimmed by time.

As a patrol officer, Harper's uniform had always been pressed to perfection, his boots shined to a mirror polish. Now, as a detective, he opted for practical professionalism: jeans, a fitted polo that showed the hours he spent at the gym, and his well-worn Chuck Taylors. Every morning, he clipped his badge to his belt and holstered his Glock on his left hip, a southpaw. Gone were the stiff suits and dress shoes; detective work required clothing he could move in, chase someone down in if needed. And Harper never forgot that.

He could still remember the pride of pinning on his first badge at the Blackridge County Sheriff's Office that summer after graduating college. The crisp lines ironed into his charcoal gray and tan uniform, the spit shine on his boots every morning. His first pursuit, a stolen pickup truck barreling through a neighborhood, his adrenaline surging as he and his field training officer chased it down, the thrill of the sirens competing with the radio for attention.

His parents had been so proud, beaming as they snapped photos of him in uniform. His mother squeezed his shoulder, pride shining in her eyes, tears threatening. Erin's fingers intertwined with his, her warmth grounding him in that overwhelming moment, her eyes filled with excitement for their future. He remembered vividly the cold metal of the star, the weight of it on his chest, heavier than he expected, but in the best possible way: a symbol of everything he'd worked for.

There had been long nights hunting fugitives, the brutal cold of winter stakeouts, the camaraderie of sharing bad coffee and worse jokes with his fellow deputies. He'd loved the job. Loved the purpose it gave him.

Until they betrayed him.

Framed him.

Upended his whole life, all because he asked the wrong questions to the wrong people. Because he couldn't let a case go. Because doing the right thing meant stepping on the wrong toes.

He hadn't been reckless. Just thorough. Persistent. The kind of cop who double-checked reports and followed trails others ignored. But in Blackridge County, digging too deep came with consequences.

And Harper learned that the hard way.

One day he was chasing down leads and earning praise from his supervisors. The next, he was being hauled into an office, accused of misconduct, stripped of his badge and silenced, for the good of the department.

Fall in line. Walk away. Take the hit and move on.

But Harper didn't walk away. He fought. And in doing so, he had lost everything.

• • • • •

The morgue at the county medical examiner's office was colder than Harper expected.

He'd arrived shortly before ten, a travel mug of coffee in hand and a hard knot in his stomach. Sterile, quiet, and humming with the faint buzz of overhead lights, the space smelled faintly of disinfectant and stainless steel. The odor wasn't pleasant—formaldehyde, antiseptic, something faintly sweet and chemical—but it wasn't what Harper had feared.

His footsteps echoed faintly on polished tile, the sterile chill prickling his skin through his jacket. The hum of fluorescent lights pressed in from above, their flickering nearly imperceptible yet somehow oppressive. He breathed in cautiously, sharp antiseptic stinging his nose, mingling with an unsettling sweetness that tightened his throat. He clutched his travel mug tighter, feeling the heat seeping through the metal, grounding him as the knot in his stomach tightened. Each breath came deliberately slow, measured to stave off the faint nausea simmering just beneath his control.

Better than puking on your first one, he thought, taking a steady breath. *Small victories.*

He stood in the observation area, clipboard in hand, trying not to focus too hard on the body laid out beneath the surgical lights.

This was his first autopsy as a detective. He heard stories of detectives turning green, excusing themselves, even vomiting mid-exam. Harper had braced himself for the same, but to his surprise, composure held. The nausea from earlier was gone, with no sudden wave of discomfort. Just a steady, clinical curiosity settling in as the pathologist worked.

Michael Grant's body lay on the steel table, pale and stiff. A far cry from the polished tech mogul who grinned in newspaper headlines. The Y-incision had already been made. Harsh lines crossed his chest. Dried blood ringed his throat. Harper's breath hitched—just for a moment—but he steadied himself. The Y-incision gaped starkly, flesh peeled open in harsh, clinical precision. He forced himself to exhale slowly, pushing back the image of Grant's smiling, confident face from headlines now replaced by this stark reality.

This was a man with power. With plans. And now he's meat on a table.

Dr. Kevin Ellis, a tall, narrow-faced man with half-moon glasses perched on the end of his nose, moved with practiced precision. His gloved hands moved fluidly, each motion exact, effortless. He peeled back layers of tissue without hesitation, eyes narrowed slightly behind half-moon glasses as he observed the wounds. His voice remained calm, almost clinical to the point of disinterest as he narrated his work, a stark contrast to the violent reality beneath his fingers.

Harper jotted notes, mentally filing each detail into the framework of the case.

"Cause of death is the incised wound to the neck," Ellis said, gesturing to the brutal slash across Grant's throat. "The depth of the wound severed the carotid artery and jugular vein on the left side. Death would've been rapid, in seconds, not minutes."

Harper's eyes lingered on the gash.

That wasn't panic. That was confidence. Control.

Ellis pointed to several additional wounds along the torso and upper arms. "Ten stab wounds, give or take. Mostly shallow. Defensive. He fought."

Harper leaned in slightly. "Weapon profile?"

Ellis nodded, removed his gloves, and picked up a tablet with cross-sectional images. "Blade was likely around seven inches long. Fixed. Clean edge. Twenty-degree bevel. Looks like a full tang handle, could've been serrated along the spine."

Harper's eyes narrowed.

He knew that blade.

Not exactly, but close. The specs were burned into memory. Long, sturdy, military-style with a 20-degree edge. It matched the profile of a Kabar knife. Standard issue for Marines. Harper had carried one himself during his time with the Coast Guard. And back in Blackridge County, several deputies—Marine vets—kept their service-issued Kabars tucked into patrol bags. It was practically a badge of honor.

He filed the detail away. Probably nothing. But possibly everything.

Ellis continued, gesturing toward faint bruising along the knuckles and subtle ligature marks on the wrists. "He fought, but whoever did this gained control fast. There was rage here, but it wasn't sloppy. This was calculated."

Harper's jaw tightened as he studied the scattered wounds along Grant's torso, carefully placed and controlled. His grip on his notebook stiffened involuntarily, fingers pressing against the leather edge until it bit into his palm, a stark realization settling over him. Whoever had done this wasn't just angry, they were methodical, calculated, lethal.

Rage with restraint, Harper thought. *That's worse. Means they knew exactly what they were doing.*

Harper nodded, expression unreadable. He stared down at what remained of Michael Grant and felt something shift. The pieces of the case were scattered, but they were starting to form an outline.

"Thanks, Doc," Harper said, tucking his notes into the clipboard.

Ellis peeled off his gloves. "If anything turns up in tox, I'll give you a ring. But I'd be surprised if it changes much. This was a clean kill. Cold. Personal."

Harper left the autopsy suite with a better picture of the murder.

And a worse feeling about the killer behind it.

• • • • •

CHAPTER 3: FIRST THREADS

The city skyline blurred behind the streaked windshield of Harper's Durango as he navigated through afternoon traffic toward Grant Technologies. The sleek office tower stood in the heart of Stonehaven's business district, all glass and steel, mirroring the muted gray sky above. Harper pulled into the visitor parking lot and killed the engine, fingers drumming against the steering wheel as he studied the building's polished, corporate perfection. It looked like the kind of place where ambition wore a suit and secrets hid behind frosted glass. He wasn't expecting a confession, but something about Alan Whitaker, Grant's Vice President, had rubbed him the wrong way from the moment they spoke on the phone.

Too polished. Too rehearsed. The kind of man who answered every question with just enough truth to obscure the lie.

Inside, a receptionist directed Harper to a corner office. Whitaker stood as he entered, flashing a smile that didn't reach his eyes. He was mid-forties, with a receding hairline, plump features, and skin pulled a little too tight, the sort of face that looked like it had spent time and money fighting gravity. His suit was expensive, his shoes immaculate, but Harper clocked the nervous tic in the man's left hand as it tapped the glass surface of his desk.

"Detective Harper," Whitaker said smoothly, extending a manicured hand. "Terrible circumstances. We're all still reeling."

Harper shook his hand briefly, noting the dry, clammy skin. "Appreciate you making time."

Whitaker gestured toward the chair across from him. "Please, have a seat."

Harper remained standing for a moment, letting his gaze drift over the sterile office. White walls. Minimalist furniture. No family photos. No clutter. No warmth. It felt less like an office and more like a showroom, a carefully curated image.

"Nice place," Harper said. "Feels like a dentist's office."

Whitaker blinked, then chuckled, as though unsure whether it was a joke. "We try to maintain a clean, efficient environment."

Harper finally sat, settling into the chair like he had all the time in the world. "Let's start with something simple. What was Michael Grant like to work with?"

Whitaker folded his hands, adopting the air of someone giving a TED Talk. "Visionary. Brilliant. Demanding, of course, but visionaries often are."

"Demanding how?"

"High standards," Whitaker replied. "Michael didn't tolerate mediocrity."

"Any friction with the staff?"

Whitaker smiled thinly. "Well, some people aren't cut out for excellence. But I wouldn't call it friction."

Harper nodded slowly. "I imagine running a company this size creates enemies."

"Competitors, certainly," Whitaker said. "But enemies? That's melodramatic."

"Humor me. Anyone come to mind?"

"Detective, I run operations, not security."

"So you weren't looped in on any threats, complaints, angry emails?"

Whitaker exhaled with a touch of theatrical patience. "If we took every disgruntled email seriously, we'd never get anything done."

Harper smiled faintly. "Right. But now Grant's dead, so humor me a little more. Any high-stakes deals recently? Mergers, acquisitions, anything that would've made waves?"

A flicker of irritation crossed Whitaker's face. "That's proprietary. I'm afraid you'll need a warrant."

"Thought you might say that."

Harper let the silence stretch. Watched Whitaker fidget.

"What about his personal life? Any known stressors? Marriage? Affairs?"

Whitaker's jaw tensed. "Michael kept his personal matters private."

"Sure. But you two worked together for over a decade. You're telling me he never confided in you?"

"Michael valued discretion. We weren't drinking buddies, Detective. We ran a business."

Harper let that hang, then shifted gears. "And the rest of the staff? Anyone he was particularly close to?"

Whitaker hesitated, eyes flicking toward the hallway. "He maintained professional boundaries. We all did."

"Of course," Harper said, voice neutral. "Still, I'll need to speak with HR. Review emails, messages, internal memos. Anything from the last thirty days."

Whitaker's smile vanished. "You'll need to go through our legal team. Our servers contain sensitive intellectual property. You know, product roadmaps, investor communications."

"And interviews?"

"We'd prefer to schedule them through counsel. I'm sure you understand."

Harper gave him a long look. "I do. Doesn't mean I like it."

Whitaker said nothing.

Harper stood, pocketing his notepad. "Thanks for the warm hospitality."

"Detective," Whitaker said, voice low, "just be careful where you dig. Some things are better left alone."

Harper paused at the door. "Yeah. And some things are better dragged into the light."

"One more thing," Harper said, voice quieter now, more deliberate. "You said Michael had no enemies. But the scene in that condo said otherwise. Someone hated him enough to kill him up close. Sloppy, emotional, personal. And whoever did it? They knew how to get in without triggering the alarm."

Whitaker stared, hand held out, patience with Harper clearly at an end.

As he stepped into the hallway, a movement near reception caught his eye. A woman—early forties, brunette, gym-toned figure, striking features and watchful eyes—was watching him. Her name tag read: Holly Caldwell. Executive Assistant.

The second their eyes met, she turned and disappeared around the corner.

Harper frowned. What was that about?

Behind him, Whitaker cleared his throat. "If there's nothing else, Detective?"

Harper glanced back once. "Oh, there's more. Count on it."

He walked out without another word, already replaying the flicker of fear he'd seen in Caldwell's eyes.

Whatever Whitaker was hiding, she knew about it. And Harper was damn sure going to find out.

• • • • •

The city lights faded in Harper's rearview mirror as he guided his car through the quieter, tree-lined streets leading toward Holly Caldwell's home. His fingers tapped idly against the steering wheel, the low hum of the engine the only sound filling the space. The drive should have been routine, but his mind drifted to Blackridge, to the past he could never quite outrun.

The last time he'd dug too far into a case, it had cost him everything.

Blackridge County, a decade ago. He'd been young, ambitious, still fueled by the belief that being a good cop was enough to make a difference. The case had started as a simple drug bust involving misplaced evidence and whispers of dirty money exchanging hands. He'd followed the trail like any good cop would, connecting dots that weren't meant to be connected. Then, the warnings started. The whispers that the dealer might be a cop. The sideways glances from fellow deputies, the sudden reassignment of cases, the pressure from his superiors to "let it go."

But Harper had never been the type to let things go.

Then came the setup. The false accusations. The internal investigation and supervisors that turned their back on him. The media had run with the story, painting him as a disgraced deputy caught tampering with evidence and using excessive force. By the time he cleared his name, his career in Blackridge was long over, his personal life and marriage in shambles. The badge he had once worn with pride had become an albatross around his neck. He'd spent years clawing his way back, rebuilding his reputation in Stonehaven, but some wounds never fully healed.

Harper exhaled slowly, dragging his focus back to the road. The past could wait - *this* was the present, and Holly Caldwell had answers he needed. Whitaker might've been playing gatekeeper, insisting that all interviews go through corporate counsel, but that didn't carry any legal weight outside of the building. Harper wasn't investigating a data breach or a hostile takeover; he was working a murder. People didn't get to lawyer up on behalf of an entire building. He could knock on any door he damn well pleased, and if someone had something to hide, that was their problem.

This is a homicide case, he thought. *Not a goddamn corporate merger.*

Caldwell's house sat at the end of a quiet cul-de-sac, a modest but well-kept single-story home with a neatly trimmed lawn. The porch light cast a soft glow across the driveway, illuminating a silver sedan parked with precision near the walkway. Harper pulled up to the curb, shut off the engine, and stepped into the stillness. The air held that clean dusk scent—grass, concrete, something faintly floral.

As he stepped out, his shoes crunched over the loose gravel edge of the sidewalk. He took his time walking up. Curtains fluttered, too smooth to be accidental. Someone had been watching. The peephole darkened as he reached the steps.

He knocked. Two solid raps, not aggressive, but with weight.

A second passed, then the soft slide of a deadbolt. The door creaked open a few inches.

Holly Caldwell peered out. She looked different here, still striking, early forties, golden-brown hair pulled back, but less polished than she had been at Grant Technologies. She looked like someone carrying too much. Exhausted but trying not to show it.

"Detective," she said, voice steady but cautious. "What are you doing here?"

Harper offered a slight nod. "Just a few questions. Mind if I come in?"

A beat. Her eyes flicked past him toward the empty street. She hesitated, then stepped aside.

The inside of the house was stylish, controlled, neatly staged with cool grays, curated lighting, and the scent of lavender laced with something less pleasant underneath, something stale. The curtains were drawn. He took in the space, noting the framed photos on the wall. A boy in a baseball jersey. A man in a golf polo beside her at some family function. Smiles caught in time.

Divorced or separated, Harper thought.

Harper glanced at the photos. "Your son?"

"Eli," she said, leading him toward the living room. "Thirteen now. He lives with his dad most of the time."

Harper gave a small smile. "Tough age."

Her mouth twitched. "Tougher when you've got two houses to bounce between."

He nodded but didn't press. The way she said it carried more than the words.

She gestured toward a chair. He took it. She stayed standing a moment too long before lowering herself to the edge of the couch, arms crossed over her chest.

"I already told HR everything I know," she said, voice taut.

"You did," Harper said. "But I'm not here for a statement."

She said nothing.

"I'm trying to solve a homicide. And I think you know more than you were comfortable sharing in front of your boss."

"I don't—"

"—Not asking you to incriminate yourself," Harper said calmly. "Just asking for honesty. For Michael's sake, if nothing else."

That landed. Her eyes flicked away.

Harper gave it a few seconds, then shifted in his seat, letting the tone ease.

Harper didn't rush it. "You've got a great setup here," he said, glancing around. "Been here long?"

"Six years," she said automatically, then caught herself. "We bought it just after Eli started school. It was supposed to be a fresh start."

Harper nodded slightly. "Nice neighborhood. Quiet. You decorate it yourself?"

She gave a tired smile. "Most of it. I used to care more about all that."

He let that linger.

Then, gently: "So. Michael Grant. Tell me about the last time you saw him."

She straightened slightly. "At the office," she said. Too quickly. "Earlier that day. We talked about a few things he needed to prepare for his trip."

"Trip?" Harper tilted his head.

"He mentioned going off the grid. Said he needed to think. To clear his head."

Harper made a small note. "You two were close?"

She hesitated. "He was my boss."

"That's not what I asked."

Her eyes dropped to the carpet.

"Michael ever come here?" he asked, casually.

Her eyes hardened slightly. "No."

"You sure?"

She exhaled. "Yes."

Harper made a small note in his pad, though it didn't matter. He was watching her hands now. The way her fingers wouldn't stop pressing into her skirt.

"So, the day he was killed, that was the last time you saw him?"

She glanced toward the window like she wanted to be somewhere else. "Yes."

"Was that the last time… or just the last time in public?"

Her jaw flexed. "You're not going to be subtle about this, are you?"

"I can be," Harper said. "But I'm also not going to dance around something that matters."

Another silence. She looked down at her lap, then back up at him. "It wasn't what people think. I didn't throw my marriage away on a whim."

"I didn't say you did."

Holly continued to stare a hole in the carpet.

"I'm not here to judge," Harper added. "Just trying to understand what kind of person he was… and what kind of secrets he was keeping."

Another pause.

Then, soft but steady: "We were… involved."

"How long?"

"A little over a year."

"Anyone know?"

"No. Not really. Maybe Alan suspected. But Michael was careful. We both were."

"You left your husband for him?"

Her breath caught. "Yes."

Harper nodded slowly. "And was he worth it?"

That stopped her. The mask cracked. She swallowed, her fingers curling into the fabric of her skirt.

"It's not that simple."

Harper leaned forward. "It never is."

She swallowed. "It wasn't an affair. Not to me."

Harper leaned back slightly, giving her space. "What was it?"

"I thought it was real," she said. "Michael had this way of… making the rest of the world go quiet. Like he saw me, not just what I did for him." Her voice cracked. "I know it was a mess. But when we were together, it wasn't about sex or sneaking around. I loved him."

"And now he's dead," Harper said softly.

She nodded, tears threatening in the corner of her eyes. "And now he's dead."

Harper didn't rush in with a question. He let it hang there, thick with what she hadn't said yet. He'd seen it before—the sharp edge of guilt dulled by the ache of something that had once felt honest.

"When did it change?"

She swallowed hard. "Last month."

"What happened?"

Silence stretched between them, pressing in from all sides. Finally, she let out a slow breath, and her posture softened just a little.

"Last month, Michael changed. Got quiet. Distant. I could feel him slipping away… like I was already a loose end."

Harper studied her carefully. "Loose end for what?"

She stood up, crossed to the armchair across from him, and sat on the edge like she was ready to bolt. Her hands twisted together.

"Something he was involved in. A deal. He wouldn't give me details, but he said it would make everything different. Said it would secure his legacy, put Grant Tech at the top."

"Did he say who was involved?"

"No names. Just… people with money. Influence. Government contracts. He said that if anything went wrong, no one would be able to trace it back to him. That once it was finalized, nothing would be the same. At first, he was excited. Almost giddy."

"And then?"

"Then he got scared."

Harper leaned forward, eyes narrowing slightly. "Did he tell you what changed?"

"He said I didn't want to know," she whispered. "Told me to stay out of it. To pretend none of it existed. He got paranoid. Edgy. He said there were risks, that not everyone was playing clean. That if it blew up, he had a way to protect himself."

Harper leaned in a little. "What kind of protection?"

She hesitated. "I don't know. Files, maybe. He said if anything happened, the truth would still come out."

"But you saw something."

Her lips pressed together. A flicker of fear crossed her face.

"I don't know what you mean."

"It means," Harper said evenly, "that you looked scared at the office. You wouldn't look at me. And Whitaker shut me down the second I started asking about Grant's recent projects."

He let that sit.

"There's something you're not telling me. Something you're afraid of."

Her chest rose and fell, shallow and fast. Her gaze darted to the window. Her voice came out thin.

"I—I can't."

"You can," Harper said, calm but firm. "You're already in this, Holly. If someone wanted to hurt you, staying quiet won't save you. But talking might."

Her composure broke. She turned away and covered her face for a moment. Her voice shook when she spoke.

"There's a cabin," she said, barely audible. "Near Mt. Hood. We used to go there… for privacy. Just us. But the last time, about a week before he died, he was different, on edge, wouldn't sleep."

Harper didn't move. Just listened.

"I woke up in the middle of the night," she said. "He wasn't in bed. I found him in the office, crouched near the desk. He was tucking something into a small metal box. Then he slid it into a hidden safe in the floor."

"Did you see what it was?"

She shook her head. "No. He slammed it shut before I could. Told me I didn't want to know. That it was better for me that way."

Harper jotted the location. "You know where the safe is?"

"In the floor, under the desk in the office. Hidden by a rug."

Harper jotted something down, then looked back at her. "Where's the cabin?"

"Just outside Welches. Off a side road. It's secluded, no neighbors for miles."

He nodded, already considering the warrant, the logistics. The timeline.

"Do you really think someone killed him over that deal?" she asked, her voice barely more than a breath.

Harper met her eyes.

"I think whoever killed him, it had something to do with what you just told me. We need to find out what he left behind."

•••••

"If you gaze long enough into the abyss, the abyss gazes back into you." - Friedrich Neitzsche

CHAPTER 4: GHOSTS IN THE MACHINE

Harper kept his eyes on the dark stretch of highway ahead, the rhythmic hum of the tires on the asphalt the only sound filling the car. Holly had fallen asleep in the passenger seat, her head resting lightly against the window. The soft glow of the dashboard cast faint shadows on her face, making her look more vulnerable than she had back at her house.

The drive to Welches would take about an hour and a half. Harper had already called Cho, instructing him to meet them at a gas station just outside town. Cho hadn't asked many questions, just a clipped acknowledgment before the line disconnected. That was one of the things Harper liked about Cho, he didn't waste words, just got things done.

With Holly asleep, Harper's thoughts drifted. An affair. On the surface, it was a tired cliché - an executive assistant swept up in a power dynamic, trading stability for ambition. It would've been easy to judge her, to write her off as just another cautionary tale. But Harper knew better than most that life was rarely that simple. People didn't fall apart all at once - they unraveled slowly, thread by thread. Everyone carried their own ghosts, their own regrets. Sometimes it was love that led them astray. Sometimes it was desperation. And sometimes, perhaps in Holly's case, they just wanted to feel something real in a life that had grown hollow.

I'm the last one to judge anyone, Harper thought, his grip tightening on the wheel. Holly had her affair, sure, but he had his own ghosts. His own regrets.

His mind pulled him backward, past the years on patrol at Stonehaven, past the slow, painful work of reclaiming his name, past the bitter collapse of his marriage. All the way back to Blackridge County. Back to those first hollow days after his termination, when everything he thought he'd built crumbled in his hands. The badge was gone. The job, the future, the purpose, it had all vanished in a single sweep. And in the silence that followed, the anger had come. The shame. The unraveling.

•••••

Then.

The day Harper lost his badge, the weight of the moment didn't hit him all at once. It settled in slowly, like a creeping sickness, a dull ache that tightened around his chest with each step he took. When he walked out of the Blackridge County Sheriff's Office for the last time that cold January afternoon, it had begun to settle in deep. The building looked the same, the same chipped tile floors, same hum of overhead fluorescents, but things had just changed irrevocably for Harper.

The uniform that had once meant everything to him - the same he'd bled in, sweated in, and taken pride in - was gone. Stripped away, just like the trust, just like the future and career he'd spent years building. In its place was a plain manilla envelope clutched in his hands, filled with paperwork and silence. Termination forms. HR disclaimers. A notice of suspension for his police certification. The polite, procedural language of a system washing its hands.

Handing over his badge and service weapon to the lieutenant had felt surreal, like acting out someone else's nightmare. The badge was heavier than he remembered, solid brass and shame. The lieutenant didn't say a word. Didn't meet his eyes, just reached out and took it like he was collecting a library book.

And then the final indignity: the escort. Policy, they said. Standard procedure. Harper didn't resist. Didn't speak. Barely holding back tears as he walked past desks and hallways that had once felt like a second home. Past lockers bearing names he used to know like family.

No one said a word.

The ones who had once called him brother—shared meals, shifts, danger—now kept their heads down. A few turned away. Others just stared blankly at their screens, pretending not to notice. Not a single pair of eyes met his. Not even a nod. He didn't know what was worse - the silence or the rejection.

By the time the heavy security door clicked shut behind him, the air outside felt too sharp, too real. The cold wind bit at his face, but he didn't flinch. He just stood there, holding that damn envelope, staring at nothing.

That afternoon, he had walked in a deputy. He walked out a ghost.

By the time he pulled into the driveway of the house he and Erin had bought together, the house they had poured their dreams into, she was already waiting. The way she stood on the porch, arms crossed, told him everything he needed to know. At first, she had been supportive, standing by him when the accusations first surfaced. She believed in him. They would fight it together.

But belief had an expiration date. And so did patience.

"We have to sell," Erin had said one night a few weeks later at the kitchen table. Her voice was level, but her eyes were hard. "We can't afford this place on just my salary."

Harper had barely touched his dinner. The tightness in his chest worsened. "Erin, I'll find something else."

"Doing what? No department is going to hire you, Jake."

"I'll clear my name," he insisted. "I'll get back in."

She scoffed. "And what, we just hold our breath until then?"

The house went on the market a week later. They packed their lives into boxes and moved into Erin's parents' home—temporary, she had promised, but he had seen the resentment brewing behind her forced smile. The man she had married, the man with a bright future in law enforcement, was now a liability. The nights became longer, filled with arguments that stretched into the early hours.

One particular argument was burned into his memory.

"Why couldn't you have just kept your goddamn mouth shut, Jake?" Erin had asked. "Why did you have to go and poke the bear?"

Harper had felt the shame rising, a flush creeping up his neck as he tried to defend his actions, and his integrity, for what had felt like the hundredth time. But Erin wouldn't even let him get a word in.

"No, Jake. I *know*," Erin snapped, her voice sharp enough to cut. "You just *had* to do the right thing. You couldn't let it go. And now look where that got us."

She gestured around the cramped kitchen of her parents' house like it was Exhibit A.

"We're living with my parents. We lost our house. Our plans. Our *future*. All thanks to your precious fucking *integrity*." She spit the last word like venom, then turned away before he could answer.

That night, Harper had wandered down the hall, numb and sleepless, only to hear her voice through the half-closed door of the den, low, bitter, and tired.

"I should've never married Jake," she told her parents. "I should've found someone… normal. Someone who wasn't such a fucking idiot."

Her father scolded her for the language. Her mother tried to remind her that marriage was about weathering storms. But Harper heard the truth in Erin's voice, clear as a gunshot.

And in that moment, he felt the cracks between them split wide—no longer fractures.

A canyon.

But it hadn't always been this way.

Before the shouting, before the slammed doors and the silence that followed, there had been something good. Something worth holding onto. And at the very beginning of it all—before the wedding, before the fallout—there had been Quentin Everstone.

Quentin had been more than a roommate. More than a best man at the wedding. He was the brother Harper had chosen. Through hangovers and heartbreaks, late-night calls and long silences, they'd been in each other's corner. A second voice in Harper's head. A second home when his first started falling apart.

Losing Erin had broken his heart.
Losing Quentin had made him question whether there was anything left worth rebuilding.

● ● ● ● ●

Then.

The dorm commons smelled like burnt coffee, cold takeout, and whatever Quentin was burning through on his guitar amp. Jake Harper sat hunched over a legal pad, absently chewing the cap of his pen as he stared through the numbers he'd scribbled. Econ formulas blurred into nothing while a low blues riff drifted through the cracked door to their room.

It was always like this, Harper grinding through textbooks, Quentin playing the kind of melodies that made girls linger outside their door and professors forgive late papers.

The music stopped mid-note, and a moment later, Quentin Everstone stepped into view, Red Bull in one hand, guitar pick still wedged between his fingers. He was barefoot, as usual, with one pant leg rolled up slightly, the cuffs frayed. His reddish-blond hair stuck up like he'd forgotten what a comb was, and his oversized T-shirt hung loose over a frame that was just a little too soft around the edges. He wasn't fat, just comfortably unbothered by a little extra weight. Blue eyes that always looked half a thought ahead of everyone else.

There was something about him, though. An ease. A charisma that couldn't be taught.

"You're wasting a perfectly good Friday night on microeconomics?"

Harper looked up, pen between his teeth. "Some of us have to pass to graduate, Quinn."

"Some of us are planning to tour after graduation," Quentin shot back with a grin, sliding into the opposite chair. "This degree is just a backup plan."

That had always been Quentin. Brilliant. Magnetic. The kind of guy who could charm a lecture hall or a late-night crowd at the local bar, then come home and talk philosophy until sunrise. And his voice, God, his voice. Smooth and aching with just enough rasp to make it feel lived-in. When he sang, heads turned. Professors paused mid-lecture. Girls who were out of his league found their way into the front row, into his arms, into his bed. It wasn't just talent, it was gravity.

Harper remembered one night in particular. A little dive bar just off campus. Quentin was onstage with nothing but his battered acoustic and a whiskey on the stool beside him. The lights were low, the chatter had died down by the second verse. He played *Poison and Wine,* slow and deliberate, dragging out each word like he'd lived it.

Harper had his arm draped around Erin, who leaned against him at their usual corner table. But she wasn't touching her drink. Wasn't talking. Wasn't smiling.

She was watching Quentin. Watching him *sing.*

And Quentin, just as the chorus broke, looked straight at her.

"I don't love you…but I always will."

Just a glance. A beat too long.

But it landed.

Quentin looked right back at her. Just for a second. But it was there.

Harper hadn't thought anything of it at the time. Chalked it up to the song. The moment. Quentin was a performer, after all, he *lived* for a room that hung on his every word. That's what Harper told himself.

But now, years later, that look stayed with him.

It hadn't been just a moment. It had been a warning.

Quentin had been there when Harper met Erin. He was the one who nudged him forward when Harper almost let her walk out of that bookstore. Harper had been standing near the clearance table, pretending to browse a beat-up paperback, trying to work up the nerve to say something. Quentin leaned in and said, "If you let her leave without getting her number, I'm staging an intervention."

So Harper spoke. And the rest unfolded like fate.

As Harper and Erin grew serious, Quentin was always around. He was always welcome. Back then, Harper and Quentin were inseparable. Study partners. Drinking buddies. Bandmates, briefly. Brothers in everything but blood.

Quentin often joined them on double dates, usually with whatever short-lived flame he was into at the time. He was the kind of guy who fell fast. By the end of the first week, he'd swear this one was different, that she was the one. And then a few weeks later, he'd break it off because she didn't like Springsteen or didn't "get" Bukowski. Harper used to laugh about it. Erin would roll her eyes and tease him for being a romantic masochist.

Still, Quentin kept showing up. Even when his own relationships fizzled out, he'd hang around. Game nights. Coffee runs. Sunday brunch. Sometimes, Harper would catch him watching Erin with a strange expression, like he was trying to figure her out. Trying to understand what made her different. What made their relationship work.

At the time, Harper thought it was just jealousy. Not the bitter kind. More like the ache of someone who hadn't found his person yet.

Looking back, it felt like something else entirely.

Quentin had played *I'm Yours* at their wedding. He even joked, just before he started the song, "Don't blame me if she changes her mind halfway through the ceremony."

Everyone laughed. Harper. Erin. And Quentin.

He had cheered when Harper said he wanted to be a cop. Threw him a party after he graduated from the academy. Showed up at his swearing-in at Blackridge County with a flask in his jacket and a lopsided grin, saying he had never been prouder.

They celebrated each other's wins like they were shared victories. That was what friendship meant, or at least what Harper believed. They had stayed up drinking cheap bourbon when Harper got into the academy, and again when Quentin booked his first solo gig. They pushed each other through college exams, laughed through heartbreaks, crashed on each other's couches, and took midnight road trips just to chase silence.

If one of them fell, the other was supposed to help him back up.

And Harper did. Again and again.

When Quentin dropped out of school to pursue music full-time, Harper showed up to every gig he could. Even when the crowds were thin. Even when the music wasn't good. When Quentin packed up and moved to Nashville to live in a van, it was Harper who helped him buy the van. When it broke down barely a month later and Quentin came home broke and burned out, Harper talked Erin into letting him crash on their couch. He found him a beater car to get around and fronted the cash when Quentin couldn't afford insurance.

When the music finally failed him, Harper didn't judge him. He didn't say "I told you so." He shared his own story about the Coast Guard. About structure. About brotherhood. About starting over.

Quentin listened. For once, he really listened.

He had been soft then. Out of shape. Lacking purpose. Harper started running with him every morning, coached him through workouts, helped him clean up his diet. Slowly, Quentin found discipline. He dropped the weight. Found his edge. By the time he swore into the Army, he looked and sounded like a new man.

Harper was there for that too. Standing in the back of the MEPS center while Quentin raised his right hand and repeated the oath.

And when he came back from Basic, he was someone else. Gone was the barefoot philosopher-musician. In his place was a man carved from hard lines and silent calculation. The reddish hair was clipped close to regulation, the jaw newly squared and set, eyes colder now behind the same brilliant blue. He wore his uniform like it had always belonged to him.

After Quentin made Corporal, Harper celebrated with him. They cracked open beers on Harper's back deck, just the two of them, watching the sun set behind the trees like the world might actually be going their way for once.

Six months later, Quentin proposed to Amy. Harper stood beside him again, this time in a tux.

Looking back, Harper realized he had been there for every rise and every fall. Every restart. Every broken plan. And Quentin? He had always been happy to let him carry the weight.

• • • • •

CHAPTER 5: THE UNRAVELING

Then.

It had only taken Harper a few months after his termination to land a job as an insurance investigator; a desk-bound purgatory spent sorting through staged car crashes, fraudulent fire claims, and endless paperwork. It was honest work, but it felt like penance. A way to prove, at least to himself, that he could still do something right. The paycheck was steady enough to stabilize them, to get them out of her parents' house and into a decent rental. But the damage had already been done. The trust, the partnership, the belief that they were in it together... it had all eroded under the weight of their new reality.

Still, Harper hadn't let go, not at first. Nights after work, he quietly filled out applications, updated his résumé, chased background packets with something close to desperation. Departments across the state. Big agencies, small towns, even tribal police. But every interview ended the same way.

We appreciate your interest. We've gone with another candidate.

No one said it outright, but he could read between the lines. The stink of Blackridge hadn't washed off.

He tried to hide the rejections, but Erin knew. She saw the unopened envelopes, the stiff silence after phone calls, the way his shoulders sagged when he thought she wasn't looking. And over time, something between them calcified. Her patience thinned. His guilt hardened into silence. What used to be a partnership felt more like a performance, each pretending they still believed things might return to how they were.

Then came the fights about the Coast Guard.

Re-enlisting in the Coast Guard Reserve was the only thing that kept him sane. If he couldn't wear the badge, at least he could still wear a uniform. Still serve. Still cling to some shred of structure, of identity. The Reserve didn't ask questions. It didn't care about rumors or reputations. It gave him a purpose, however small, and a reason to keep getting out of bed.

Erin hated it.

"You're gone one weekend a month, sometimes more for training," she snapped one night, the words ragged with exhaustion. She was still in her hospital scrubs, dark circles under her eyes, her hair twisted in a hasty bun. "We need you here. I need you here. And for what? To go play soldier?"

He remembered the way she'd said it, flat and biting. Not just angry, but hollow. Like something had died in her months ago, and this was all that remained.

"I don't want to do this again," she added, voice quieter now, laced with old wounds. She was referring to the early years of their marriage, when Harper had just transitioned from active duty to the Reserve, juggling college classes with weekend drills, deployment standby always looming. She'd said she understood back then. Maybe she had.

But now?

Now the uniform no longer made her proud. It only reminded her of all the ways he wasn't home.

"I serve because it's all I have left," Harper said that night, barely above a whisper.

She stared at him like she didn't recognize the man in front of her. "It's not about service, Jake. It's about *us*. About responsibility. About being here. About starting the family we always talked about."

But there was no "us" left to save. Not really.

The final fight had never been about the Coast Guard—not really. It was about everything else. About all the resentment, the missed chances, the quiet guilt neither of them knew how to name. She accused him of clinging to a past that no longer existed. He accused her of giving up on him the moment things got hard.

And in the end, neither of them had been wrong.

Before that night—before the final split—there had been distance. Not all at once, but piece by piece. Conversations that used to run long into the night were replaced by short texts and unfinished sentences. Eye contact turned to sidelong glances. Touch turned to tension.

Erin felt it before she could put it into words: the sense of drifting. That slow erosion of closeness. He talked about service and sacrifice, about honor and pride. She talked about building a life, about stability, about starting a family.

He still believed in the mission. She just wanted a future.

She ached for children. Not someday. Now. She wanted to hold something that belonged to both of them, to make all the chaos mean something. But Jake couldn't see past the wreckage of what he'd lost. His badge. His purpose. Himself.

He was too busy chasing ghosts to see what was right in front of him.

She wanted a man who had his life figured out. He wanted a woman who still believed he was worth figuring out.

Neither of them could give the other what they needed.

And in that gap between hope and resignation, something broke.

What came next was anger.

At first, Erin's rage was verbal. Words sharpened like blades, wielded to wound. Their arguments, once rooted in frustration, turned venomous. Her voice echoed through the halls of their too-small house. Every scream, every insult, every curse was a reminder of just how far they'd fallen.

She told him he'd ruined their lives. That she should've married someone *normal*. A banker. An accountant, like some of his friends from college. A man who wore khakis and went to barbecues, who didn't chase the ghosts of justice through badge and uniform.

And then came the moments that crossed the line. She didn't just yell. She lashed out.

More than once, Harper had dodged a flying plate. A mug. A book. One night, she threw a glass tumbler with such force it struck him square in the forehead and shattered, slicing his skin open.

He remembered the sting of the glass, the warmth of the blood trickling down his face. But it wasn't the pain that stuck with him.

It was the shame. The shame of standing there and taking it. Of not yelling back. Of not walking out. Of staying.

Because the truth was, he *couldn't* bring himself to say the word. Divorce. He couldn't admit that his marriage—this thing he'd once fought so hard for—was just another failure. One more black mark on a list that already felt endless. The house. The job. The badge. His name. And now, Erin.

So he stayed.

Maybe out of loyalty. Maybe out of habit. Maybe because he remembered who they used to be. When they were two kids who fell in love over late-night drives and shared dreams. Maybe because she'd once believed in him when no one else did.

Or maybe because he still believed he deserved it. That somewhere deep down, this was punishment. For failing. For falling. For dragging her into his mess.

She always apologized after. Called it an accident. Said she hadn't meant to throw it *at* him. Just *near* him. That she was overwhelmed. Exhausted. At her limit.

And maybe part of him believed that. But another part knew better. Because it had happened before. Years ago, in the first apartment. When they were broke and tired and trying to make it work. A slap during a fight. A plate that cracked against the wall. They never talked about it afterward. Just buried it. Moved forward.

Until Blackridge happened. Until everything they buried came roaring back. And this time, there was no promotion around the corner. No new beginning. No sunrise on the other side of the storm. Just the slow collapse of a marriage built on silence and the things they didn't say. So he took it. The blame. The fury. The glass. Because part of him believed he had it coming.

But it wasn't just her anger that drove them apart.

It was what came next.

Jordyn.

She had come into his life when things were already unraveling, when the edges were fraying faster than he could hold them together. She worked a few desks down in the claims division. Same floor, different energy.

Jordyn was impossible not to notice. Blonde, with loose waves that framed her face like something out of a shampoo commercial, effortless, sunlit, and alive. Her eyes were a striking green, bright and mischievous, the kind that made him lean in without thinking, just to see what she'd say next. Full lips always glossed in soft rose, tilted in a knowing smirk like she already had him figured out.

And then there were the curves. She didn't strut or flaunt, she moved like someone who *knew* the power of her body. Tight jeans that gripped her hips, pencil skirts that invited a second glance, silk blouses that exposed just enough to stir the imagination but not quite enough to draw a complaint.

She wore heels when no one else did. Leaned across Harper's desk just a little too far, giving him a view he couldn't unsee. Laughed too long at his driest jokes. Let her hand linger on his arm a beat too long. Her perfume, jasmine and something darker, clung to the air like memory, refusing to let go.

There was nothing accidental about Jordyn. And Harper, for all his restraint, was already circling the edge before he realized there was no line left to draw.

She was magnetic. Charming. Sharp. Dangerous in that quiet, deliberate way that sneaks up. The kind of woman who didn't just turn heads, she made men forget what they were doing.

And Harper? He noticed. Of course he noticed. Everyone noticed. But unlike everyone else, Jordyn noticed him back. She listened. Laughed at his jokes. Asked about his past like it mattered. She believed in him, or at least, made him feel that way. Made him feel *seen*. Desired. Like maybe he wasn't a broken man clawing through the wreckage of a ruined life. Like maybe he wasn't a disgraced cop buried under paperwork, coming home to a wife who couldn't look him in the eye. A year after Blackridge, Harper's marriage was held together by routine, obligation, and the memory of who they used to be. Erin had stopped touching him. The kisses had gone cold and they hadn't made love in months. Conversations turned to arguments, and arguments turned to silence. Some days, she didn't look at him at all.

But Jordyn?

Around her, he didn't feel like a liability. He felt like a man again. She saw him. Or maybe just the version of himself he wanted to be again.

He'd gone from wearing a badge with pride to investigating fraudulent claims behind a desk. He drank too much. Avoided mirrors. Drifted through days like a man trying not to be seen. But Jordyn leaned into the wreckage. She listened, but more than that, she *pushed*. Told him he wasn't broken. That Erin didn't understand what it meant to love a man with a mission.

Jordyn knew he was married. She just didn't care. She was a woman on a mission, relentless, calculated, and unapologetic. From the beginning, she set her sights on him, not out of affection, but lust wrapped in ego. He was attractive, *too* attractive, in her mind, to be wasted on a woman like Erin. Jordyn saw him as a trophy. Something she could take. Something she *deserved*.

She didn't think Erin appreciated him. Said it without saying it, through pointed glances, offhand comments, and the way she always made sure Harper knew she noticed. Erin had let herself go. She didn't take care of him, not the way Jordyn would. That was the story Jordyn told herself. The one she sold with every smirk, every suggestive laugh, every carefully timed lean across his desk.

Her flirtation crossed the line early and often. A touch that lingered a beat too long. A look across the office that didn't ask, it *promised* dark sensuality. A bite of her lip when no one else was watching. Late-night texts after happy hour, her clothes tighter, or missing altogether. Nude photos. Whispered promises of a night Erin couldn't, or wouldn't, give him.

Jordyn didn't ask permission. She created the opportunity. And then waited for Harper to make the mistake she knew he would.

Harper, bitter and exhausted and tired of feeling invisible, didn't stop her. Because when you're drowning, you don't question the hand that pulls you up, even if it's not the one you're supposed to reach for.

And the worst part? He *knew* what she was doing. Knew with every glance, every touch, every late-night message was bait. He saw it coming, felt the hook set, but let it happen anyway.

Because it felt good to be wanted. To be chosen. Even if the reasons were all wrong. He told himself it was harmless. Just emotional. That her pursuit was just flattery. Nothing physical.

Until it was.

One night, drunk, raw and at his lowest, he let the loneliness win.

The kiss started in the parking lot. Hot. Uninvited. Irresistible. She kissed him like she meant it, like he mattered, like he was still worth wanting. Her hands tangled in his hair, pulling him close, her mouth urgent against his. And for the first time in what felt like years, he let himself believe that was true.

He didn't pull away. He kissed her back.

The sex wasn't just a release. It was resurrection. For a moment, just one, he wasn't a disgraced cop or a broken husband. He was a man again. Seen, desired, whole.

Until the guilt came.

It didn't take long. The shame crept in before he even left her apartment, cold and relentless. It crawled up his spine, coiled in his gut, and wrapped around his throat like a noose. The justifications—*Erin doesn't love you anymore. The marriage is already over*—crumbled under the weight of what he'd done.

Harper barely made it to the edge of the parking lot before he doubled over and vomited, bracing a hand against the concrete wall behind her apartment. He choked on the taste of his own disgust, bile and guilt burning in the back of his throat.

Jordyn had made him feel whole. But it wasn't real. It was borrowed, not earned. A momentary escape dressed up as a connection. And it came at the cost of what little remained of his marriage.

And worse than that, he'd sold out his own integrity. Piece by piece. Not all at once, but slowly. The first glance. The first reply. The first lie he told himself to make it feel okay.

He ended it not long after. Told Jordyn it was a mistake. That it couldn't happen again. But by then, it was too late. The damage had been done. And Erin wasn't stupid. She had felt him slipping long before she ever had proof.

When he finally confessed, Harper expected anger. Part of him even welcomed it. Maybe her rage would be the release valve they both needed, some twisted kind of catharsis to crack the cold silence between them. Maybe it would finally bring something *real* back into the house, even if that something was fire.

But what he got was *primal*, unfiltered, and unrelenting.

It was like a dam burst. All the resentment, all the bitterness that had been festering behind clenched jaws and cold shoulders came pouring out in a torrent of fury. Her voice rose to a pitch he'd never heard before, shrill and trembling with contempt, like every second of her suppressed rage was now sharpened to a blade.

"You're pathetic," she spat. "You ruined everything. And now you think *you* get to play the victim?"

She slapped him. Not once. Multiple times. Across the face. Open handed. Closed fist. She hit him like she'd been waiting for the excuse. Told him he wasn't a man. That groveling was the *least* he owed her. That his betrayal had *validated* every cruel thing she'd ever said or done. In her mind, the affair didn't just explain the past, it justified it, rewrote it. Now, she was the aggrieved party. And he was the monster who had pushed her to it.

But the truth? The truth was, the abuse had started long before Jordyn.

The glass across the room. The plates. The screaming. The way she twisted his guilt into obedience. The way her love turned transactional—conditional on his complete surrender. She didn't just want fidelity. She wanted *control.*

She told him to quit his job. That it was beneath him anyway. That he wasn't cut out for it. That he should take something *menial.* Something she could be proud of him for actually holding down.

She told him to cut off his friends. Said they were "toxic." Said they were feeding his delusions about being a cop again. That they enabled him. That *she* was the only one he needed.

She even suggested, casually and cruelly, that since she hated the Coast Guard Reserve so much, he should just get himself kicked out. "Piss hot," she said. "Pop for weed. It's Oregon. They can't do much to you for that."

And she was serious.

She didn't want a partner. She wanted a man on his knees. Reliant on her income, her approval. Grateful just to be allowed in her house. She wanted submission disguised as penance. And when she didn't get it, the pressure turned to threats.

Any hesitation he had about kids needed to end, she said. She wanted a baby, *now.* And he would provide that. Immediately.

But something broke in Harper when she said it. Because he realized in that moment—absolutely, irrevocably—that he could not raise children in that house. Not with that rage. Not around *her.*

That was the straw.

Not the glass. Not the screaming. Not even the affair.
It was the idea of passing this rot to the next generation that made him finally, finally draw the line.

They tried counseling. Erin's idea. A last-ditch effort, a show of trying. Harper agreed, more out of inertia than hope.

The therapist was a clean-cut man in his early fifties. Wore horn-rimmed glasses and talked like a middle manager at a megachurch. His words were slow, deliberate, laced with a forced gentleness that felt more condescending than comforting.

Harper felt the imbalance immediately.

From the start, the therapist wasn't neutral. He talked about "authority" like it was a dirty word. "Control" became a diagnosis. Harper's career in law enforcement, his military background, his very *identity*, were framed not as experiences, but as *problems*.

Erin, meanwhile, leaned back smugly, arms folded. Vindicated.

Every session turned into a crucifixion. Harper's failings were paraded out like evidence in a trial. The therapist dissected him piece by piece. Emotionally unavailable, rigid, suppressive. A man who didn't understand vulnerability. A man who had *forced* Erin into emotional extremes.

When Harper brought up the abuse, the broken glass, the screaming, the tumbler that had split his forehead open, the therapist waved it off.

"She's reacting to feeling powerless," the man said calmly. "You're a former police officer. You understand power dynamics. Maybe it's time to let her have *her moment*. Even if it's physical."

Harper froze. "You're saying it's okay that she hit me?"

"I'm saying," the therapist replied, folding his hands, "that sometimes, when a person has been wronged deeply, they need space to express their pain. And maybe you need to be *strong enough* to absorb that. She's the one carrying the real burden here."

Harper stared at him in stunned silence.

No mention of the bruises.
No mention of the blood.
Just a soft, smiling mandate:
Take it.
You deserve it.

And in that moment, Harper knew two things. The marriage was over. And if he stayed, it would only get worse. Even after he ended things with Jordyn, long before the sessions started, the damage had already been done. Not just by the affair, but by the years of anger, neglect, and emotional decay that had come before it. His affair was a symptom, a desperate gasp for air in a house that had long since filled with smoke.

There was nothing left to salvage. In the end, *he* was the one who left.

Not in some cinematic rush, not with a suitcase in the rain. Just a quiet summer morning. A note on the kitchen counter. A single duffel in the trunk. The front door closing with a soft finality.

Erin didn't chase him. Didn't scream. Didn't cry.

Maybe she had finally run out of rage.

Maybe he had finally run out of reasons to stay.

And when the dust settled, when the silence became louder than the fights, he realized he and Erin hadn't been the only one to walk away.

Some betrayals didn't come with screaming.
Some came with a drink on the porch and a hand on your shoulder.

Quentin Everstone had been his brother in every way but blood. And when everything else was collapsing, Harper had thought, hoped, he could still count on him.

He was wrong.

• • • • •

CHAPTER 6: BROTHER'S KEEPER

Then.

When Harper's world began to fall apart, Quentin was right there.

He brought whiskey and sympathetic nods. Listened like a friend was supposed to.

They sat out on the porch long after the sun dipped below the treeline, Harper talking through what happened at Blackridge while Quentin swirled his drink and muttered things like "Those bastards were always crooked" and "You were too good for that place anyway."

It felt like loyalty. It looked like friendship.
But there was something else beneath the surface.

There had been a time, not so long ago, when Harper had been the one keeping Quentin afloat. One of his many firings, this time from a landscaping gig he never really took seriously, had left Quentin spiraling. His parents, already fed up with his stalled music career and revolving door of jobs, threatened to cut him off. Quentin had called Harper in a panic, voice low and ragged, saying he had nowhere else to go.

Harper didn't hesitate. He smoothed things over with Quentin's folks, said all the right things, made promises Quentin wouldn't. Then he let him crash on the pull-out for a week, maybe two, maybe longer. It all blurred together in those days.

They spent one of those nights sitting on the dock behind Harper's rental, legs hanging over the water, a six pack between them. The river moved slow and dark beneath the stars, and Quentin had finally dropped the sarcasm long enough to say, "I don't know what I'm doing anymore, man."

"You're stuck," Harper had said. "That's fine. Happens to everyone. What matters is what you do next."

That next week, Harper called in a favor. A buddy from the Coast Guard had opened a small craft brewery across town. Needed someone to pour samples and keep things light with customers. Harper put in a recommendation, and the job was Quentin's by Friday.

"You're good with people," Harper told him. "Start there. Build something."

Harper had always been there for Quentin. But a few years later, the roles had reversed.

Quentin had been thriving. The Army had given him structure, a mission, a sense of pride he had never found chasing open mics and half-written songs. And for once, he was standing taller than Harper. The dynamic had shifted, and Harper hadn't noticed it at first.

He didn't notice the way Quentin's eyes lit up, not with concern, but something closer to satisfaction, when Harper talked about how bad things had gotten. How his police career was a dead end, all his applications rejected. How Erin barely looked at him anymore.

"You've gotta find yourself again, Jake. She's not your anchor. Maybe she never was."

Harper hadn't seen it at the time; the way Quentin's eyes lingered when he spoke of Erin, the subtle edge in his voice when he said, "You deserve better."

When Harper finally opened up about the darker parts—the shouting, the insults, the times Erin shoved him in anger and then turned it around to accuse *him* of instability—Quentin leaned in, eager.

"You need to get out," he said. "You should've left her yesterday."

Harper hesitated. Said he still wanted to fix it. That he hadn't been perfect either. He talked about his own failings. His mistakes. The cracks he'd helped cause.

And then, reluctantly, he told Quentin about Jordyn. He didn't go into detail, just enough to make it clear that she was pursuing him. Hard. And that part of him, ashamed as he was, wanted to give in.

That's when Quentin changed. The friend who once looked up to Harper saw his moment to flip the script. To take the moral high ground, not by example, but by ego.

"Jesus, man," Quentin said, shaking his head with a grin. "You've got a goddamn goddess trying to climb into your lap, and you're *hesitating?* You think Erin would do the same for you? Come on. You're a man, you've got needs."

Then he leaned back in his chair and added, "Tell you what. First time you finally fuck her, I'm buying you a hundred-dollar bottle of whiskey. Hell, I'll *engrave it.*"

Harper recoiled. Said he wasn't sure. That Jordyn felt like trouble. Harper wasn't blind to what Jordyn offered, or what she represented. She was everything Erin no longer was. Warm. Present. Wanting him. But there was something too precise about her seduction. Too practiced. Like she was playing a game and already knew she'd won. Deep down, Harper knew it wasn't love. It wasn't even lust. It was escape.

Quentin laughed, loud, crude, and dismissive. "They're *all* trouble, brother. That's the fun part. You need to get laid, bro. Get it where you can."

Then he started giving him tips. Names of divorce attorneys. Told him to drain half the joint account and make a clean break.

"Take the money and the girl, man. Start over. You're already halfway out the door anyway."

And the worst part? Quentin made it sound like *freedom.* Like Harper's pain was a punchline he'd been waiting to deliver. He never gloated. He didn't need to. But the way he poured the next round felt too casual, like Harper's failure made the whiskey taste better.

He had kept Harper on a pedestal for years, built up in his mind as the one who always had it together. The one who chased the right path, made the right choices, carried the weight. But now, with Quentin standing in a better place for once, Harper's stumble wasn't something to forgive.

It was something to discard.

Instead of reaching down like Harper had done for him so many times, Quentin tossed him aside. Not with rage, not with grief, but with *indifference*. The kind that cuts deeper than either.

To Quentin, Harper was no longer the brother who helped him through his darkest seasons. He was beneath him.

And Quentin didn't keep it quiet. It was a full, public execution.

As soon as Erin found out about the affair, Quentin took a side, and made damn sure everyone knew which one. The same man Harper had picked up drunk from parking lots, defended to superiors, fed when he was broke, housed when he was homeless, *that* man suddenly became Harper's loudest critic.

Quentin sent long, self-righteous emails. Page after page of thinly veiled contempt wrapped in faux-spiritual insight and ego. He copied his wife, Amy, like he was auditioning for sainthood.

"You claim you loved me like a brother," Quentin wrote, "but the love you offer people is transactional, toxic. You love what serves you, what makes you feel powerful, desired, dangerous. You mistake loyalty for usefulness."

"You're not broken, Jake. You're hollow. A man who feeds on pity and burns every good thing given to him."

He went further.

"I would never do what you did," Quentin wrote. "I could never betray my wife like that. Because my marriage vows actually mean something. You're not just broken, you're a waste of breath."

He didn't stop there. He fed Erin lies, fabrications about Harper's past, twisting truths into poison. Claimed Harper had cheated before, that he'd always been that way. That Jordyn wasn't the first. That he had a pattern.

It didn't matter that Harper had been there for him, *every damn time*. Didn't matter that he'd defended him, housed him, talked him off the ledge.

Quentin didn't just walk away. He lit a match, dropped it in the wreckage of Harper's life, and walked out feeling righteous.

"I'm a man of integrity," he wrote in his final message. "And I won't tarnish my life by staying in relationship with someone like you, Jake. Don't contact me again. Ever."

After that, it all unraveled.

When Harper and Erin tried counseling, things only got worse. Erin had been blaming the Coast Guard, saying Harper's absences were tearing them apart. When she demanded during one session that he get himself kicked out of the Coast Guard by failing a drug test, it took months for Harper to realize that hadn't come from her.

It came from Quentin.

He heard it later. Offhand. Through someone who didn't know better. That had been Quentin's idea. His advice.

When Harper finally left, when he took off the ring and walked away, Erin didn't spiral.
She moved in with Quentin and Amy before the month was over.

Officially, it was temporary. Just a friend helping a friend. But Harper had his suspicions. The late nights. The silence. The things that didn't add up. He never asked. Never confronted either of them.

He saw them once. At a gas station off I-5. Erin in the passenger seat of Quentin's Tacoma, laughing at something he said. Her head tilted back, hair brushing her shoulders the way it used to when she laughed at Harper's jokes. Quentin didn't see him. Or pretended not to.

Harper stood there, holding a cup of burnt coffee, watching them pull away. He didn't speak. Didn't follow. He just went back to his car, set the coffee down, and sat behind the wheel until the ache in his chest dulled enough to drive. Some nights, lying awake in the dark, he could still see the way Quentin looked at her across that bar stage. He could still hear those lyrics echoing back.

He didn't need proof. Not anymore. Because in the end, it wasn't just another failure, it was betrayal. And it wore the face of the man he used to call his brother.

Quentin had stood on Harper's neck to make himself taller.

And the worst part? Harper had *rescued* that man from drowning. Not once. But so many times. Picked him up off the floor when his own parents wouldn't.

Talked him off the ledge with nothing but patience, cheap beer, and the promise that it would get better. He had sat beside him on that dock, the river stretching out below them, and told him he still had time to get it right.

Quentin hadn't just turned his back, he'd walked away holding everything Harper had ever given, and never once looked back.

He never got closure. Never asked for it. But some nights, when the house was quiet and his thoughts started circling, Quentin's name still surfaced like a bad taste he couldn't spit out.

The friendship was gone. The trust, shattered. And yet the echo of it all still haunted the quiet moments. Harper carried that silence like a scar—not bleeding, not fresh, but there. A reminder. Of who he was. Of who he refused to become. Of the betrayals that cut the deepest.

He never spoke Quentin's name again.
But he never forgot it either.

He used to believe in the idea of brotherhood. Loyalty. That unspoken bond forged in fire and trust. But Quentin had twisted it. Used it. And now, whenever Harper heard those words, *brother's keeper,* he didn't think of loyalty. He thought of knives in the dark.

• • • • •

"Just because you're paranoid doesn't mean they aren't after you."
- Joseph Heller

CHAPTER 7: RULES OF ENGAGEMENT

Now.

The glow of fluorescent lights cut through the late evening darkness as Harper pulled into the gas station parking lot. The drive to Welches had been mostly silent, save for the occasional rustle of Holly shifting in her sleep. Now, she stirred awake as Harper shut off the engine.

"We're here," he said, glancing at her.

Holly blinked, stretching slightly before rubbing her eyes. "We're here already?"

Harper nodded. "I'm grabbing coffee. You want anything?"

She hesitated, then gave a small nod. "Coffee, um—two creams, one sugar. Please."

Harper stepped out of the Durango, the crisp mountain air biting against his skin. The gas station was mostly empty, save for a semi idling near the diesel pumps. The flickering neon sign cast a pale, uneven glow across the lot.

Inside, the air smelled of stale coffee and microwaved burritos. He was filling two cups when the door jingled.

Cho.

"Made good time," Cho said, strolling in like they were meeting for lunch. His coat was open, untucked button-up visible beneath.

"Figured you'd be here first," Harper replied, handing the cashier a few crumpled bills.

Cho glanced toward the parking lot. "That her?" he asked, nodding in Holly's direction.

"Yeah." Harper passed him a cup. "That's her. She's shaken, but she opened up."

"Shaken's better than silent." He took a sip from the cup Harper passed him, then grimaced. "Christ. You sure this is coffee and not transmission fluid?"

They stepped outside into the mountain air.

"So?" Cho tilted his head toward the SUV. "You get anything worth the drive, or just more I'm-scared-and-confused?"

"Cabin in the woods. Said Grant hid something. Gave me a code."

Cho raised an eyebrow. "All we need now is creepy fog and a guy with a chainsaw."

Harper glanced toward the forest. "Let's hope we're not that lucky."

● ● ● ● ●

Twenty minutes deeper into the trees, the cabin emerged, quiet, tucked away, and secluded. The headlights of Harper's Durango cut through the darkness, Cho's unmarked silver Bronco following silently behind, its beams trailing like a shadow.

As they rolled to a stop on the gravel drive, Harper eyed the modest structure. It sat on a half-acre clearing, flanked by thick timber on all sides. A stone-lined firepit sat out front, ringed by a few plastic chairs. Beyond the tree line, the snow capped peak of Mount Hood loomed in the distance, visible beneath the pale wash of the full moon.

Harper noted the electronic keypad mounted beside the front door. "Stay in the car," he told Holly. Calm but firm.

She nodded, fingers white-knuckled around her coat sleeve.

Harper stepped out into the cold night air, Cho joining him a moment later.

"Let's walk it," Harper said, voice low.

The two moved in silence, fanning out as they made a slow, cautious circuit around the cabin. Gravel crunched under Harper's sneakers. The forest pressed close, quiet but alive with the faint sounds of wind through branches and something small scurrying in the underbrush.

The place looked undisturbed. No tire tracks beyond their own, no sign of forced entry or recent activity. Just an empty hideaway nestled in the woods, still and waiting.

When they circled back to the front, Cho gave a small nod. "Looks clear."

Harped exhaled and turned back towards the car, where Holly watched from the passenger seat, tension written across her face.

Cho squinted at the keypad beside the door. "She give you the digits?"

Harper nodded. "Four-five-eight-two."

Cho smirked. "Probably their anniversary. Or the combo to his gym locker."

Harper gave him a look.

"Hey, I call it like I see it."

Harper rolled his eyes as they walked up to the door.

Cho eyed the cabin, then glanced at Harper. "So, we going in or just gonna keep standing around with our dicks in our hands?"

Harper shook his head. "Not without a warrant."

Cho sighed. "Figures. I'll grab some shots."

He moved around the perimeter, snapping photos with methodical care.

Back at the SUV, Holly sat rigid in the passenger seat, her arms crossed tightly over her chest. Her knee bounced restlessly, the rhythm of it betraying her nerves. Every so often, she glanced towards the cabin, then back at Harper, her eyes searching his face for some kind of reassurance that he wasn't sure he could give.

Harper flipped open his laptop and started the warrant application. The cabin looked deceptively peaceful, just another quiet escape in the woods. But Harper had seen enough in his career to know better. Evil didn't always announce itself. Sometimes it wore flannel and pine. He began typing, drafting the search warrant request with methodical precision. The affidavit had to be airtight. No loose ends, no assumptions. If there was anything inside that cabin worth finding, they had to do it by the book.

One step at a time. One foot in front of the other.

He detailed the timeline, the connection between Grant and Whitaker, the shell companies, the burner phone, the maps. He outlined Holly's testimony, her statement about the cabin and the code. Every sentence mattered. Every line could be scrutinized by a judge. He was just finishing the paragraph about exigency when—

Crack.

Then, glass shattered across gravel, the rear passenger window of the Bronco exploding.

"Fucking shit!" Cho dropped to a crouch, gun out. "That was suppressed."

Harper dropped his laptop, reaching for his weapon as he pressed his back against the Durango. Holly let out a startled gasp, ducking low inside the vehicle. "Move! Get inside the cabin!" he barked.

Cho reached Holly in three strides. "Let's go—down! Stay small!" he shouted, grabbing her wrist and pulling her low. "Eyes on your feet, not the bullets." Cho grabbed Holly's arm and pushed her down low, half-guiding, half-dragging her as they sprinted for the cabin door. Another shot rang out, hitting wood just inches from the keypad lock. Harper fired two rounds blindly into the trees, enough to force a hesitation in their attacker's aim, before lunging toward the cabin himself.

Holly fumbled at the keypad, hands shaking as she punched in the code. The lock beeped, then disengaged.

"Go-go-go!" Harper barked.

Cho moved first, shoving the door open, yanking Holly inside just as Harper slammed the door behind them.

Crack. Crack.

Two more gunshots exploded through the air, the sharp reports deafening at close range. Splinters burst from the doorframe, wood flying into the entryway in jagged chunks. One fragment ricocheted off the wall, another hit the floor near Harper's feet.

Holly screamed and dropped to her knees, hands over her head.

"No visual," Cho said, crouched beneath a window, voice tight. "Asshole's smart, they know their angles."

Harper edged to the side, checked the lock. "Secure. Stay low."

Holly sobbed from the floor, rocking slightly. "Wh-who the hell would *do* this? I thought we were just—we're just—"

"They're not shooting for fun," Harper said. "That means something here's worth killing over."

Harper stood still, listening, heart pounding, breath tight in his chest.

Then, nothing.

Silence.

Harper's chest rose and fell with each controlled breath, ears straining for any sign of movement outside. His grip tightened around his gun.

The woods outside were eerily still, as if the forest itself was holding its breath. No rustling. No footsteps. Just the sound of Holly sobbing softly on the floor and the faint tick of the wall clock in the kitchen.

We aren't alone out here.

Harper turned to Cho. "Clear the house."

Cho nodded, gun raised as he moved cautiously deeper into the cabin, clearing each room with practiced efficiency. A few tense minutes passed before he returned, his expression firm. "Clear. Just us"

Harper gave a slow nod, exhaling. "Alright. We sit tight and wait for backup."

Harper pulled out his phone, dialing the local sheriff's office. When the dispatcher answered, he kept his voice low and firm. "This is Detective Harper, Stonehaven PD. Shots fired. Cabin outside Welches. Suspect still at large. Send backup."

Harper crouched low, instincts kicking in as his military training took over. He looked to Cho. "Stay off the windows."

He moved carefully toward one of the cabin windows, angling himself to peek without exposing his head. His eyes scanned the darkness, searching for any movement, any break in the stillness.

Then,

Crack.

Closer this time.

Glass shattered a heartbeat later as a round tore through the window beside him. Holly yelped, instinctively ducking and covering her head. Another bullet slammed into the wooden wall behind them, cratering with a violent thunk.

Harper flinched but didn't retreat. Instead, his eyes caught a brief, stuttering flicker deep in the dense treeline.

Got you.

He adjusted his grip on his pistol, the red dot sight catching the faintest glow as he tracked the treeline. Harper tracked the muzzle flash. Fired, cutting through the night. Quiet followed for a breath.

A split second later, a cry echoed. Then silence.

The three of them hunkered down, staying low and away from the windows. The only sound was Holly's uneven breathing as she tried to steady herself. The adrenaline was still pumping, heartbeats jolting painfully against ribs, but thankfully, no more shots rang out.

Then, in the distance, the faint but unmistakable wail of approaching sirens cut through the night. Relief settled over Harper, his grip finally easing on his pistol. Cho exhaled sharply, glancing toward him. "You think you hit him?"

Harper didn't take his eyes off the treeline. Harper didn't blink. "Yeah."

"You *think*, or you *know*?"

Harper's jaw set. "I hit him."

"Okay then," Cho muttered, brushing glass from his shoulder. "One for the good guys."

Holly let out a shaky breath. "Is…is it over?"

Harper nodded. "Not even close." Relief settled over Harper, but it was thin. Whoever had fired on them was still out there, watching.

• • • • •

A Clackamas County deputy approached Harper as the flashing lights of patrol units illuminated the trees around them. They searched the area, but there was no sign of their attacker.

"We swept the perimeter," the deputy said. "Found shell casings from a .308 rifle about a hundred yards out. There's a blood trail leading into the woods."

Harper exchanged a glance with Cho. "And?"

The deputy exhaled sharply. "Trail went cold. Whoever they are, they knew how to cover their tracks. We lost them."

Harper clenched his jaw, frustration settling in his chest. They had been close, so damn close. But their shooter was still out there, and that meant this wasn't over.

"We'll widen the search grid at first light," the deputy continued. "But with this terrain, it's gonna be tough."

Harper gave a tight nod. "Understood. We'll coordinate with you."

As the deputies continued their search, Harper turned back to the cabin, his mind already working through their next steps.

The distant crunch of gravel signaled another arrival, and Harper turned to see the rest of his team pulling up, their vehicles lining the dirt path leading to the cabin. Detective Sergeant Foster stepped out first, his gaze scanning the scene before locking onto Harper. His expression was unreadable, but Harper knew what was coming.

"Harper, Cho. Hell of a mess," he said before meeting Harper's gaze. "What'd I miss? Other than someone trying to shoot half my team."

"Shooter's mobile, suppressed rifle, smart positioning," Harper said. "He wanted us dead but didn't stick around to finish the job."

Foster glanced at the shattered Bronco window. "Nice aim."

"Not nice enough." Harper's voice was low. "He bled. Then he vanished."

Foster nodded toward the cabin. "Looks like you kept everyone breathing. But Harper—you know the drill. Officer-involved shooting. You're benched."

Harper exhaled sharply, his frustration barely contained. "Come on, Sarge. We both know this was by the book."

Foster gave a small nod. "I don't make the rules, Jake Harper. I just enforce them. Two, maybe three days. That's all."

Harper clenched his jaw, looking toward the cabin. "What about the search?"

"Hurst is already on her way," Foster said. "She'll take point until you're cleared."

Harper exhaled slowly. "Understood."

Cho gave him a sidelong look. "Try not to shoot anyone on your way out."

"No promises."

Foster placed a hand on Harper's shoulder. "You did good work tonight. But for now, go home. Get some rest."

Harper didn't answer, just glanced at Cho, who offered a small shrug. They both knew this wasn't over.

Not by a long shot.

Harper kept his grip steady on the wheel as he drove back down the Mountain, his mind working over the pieces of the case. The ambush at the cabin only proved what he already suspected, that someone didn't want them digging into Michael Grant's secrets. But why? And who? The missing puzzle pieces gnawed at him, frustration building as the answers continued to slip through his fingers.

As much as he wanted to stay focused on the present, his mind pulled him backward—back to Blackridge County. Back to the last days before his career had come crashing down.

• • • • •

"The saddest thing about betrayal is that it never comes from your enemies." - Unknown

CHAPTER 8: PARTING SHOTS

Then.

Before he was a Lieutenant, Thomas Alvarez had been a detective, the kind young deputies wanted to become. Clean-cut, sharp in both suit and tongue, he carried himself with quiet authority. And Harper, still green with only two years on, admired the hell out of him.

Alvarez had a reputation for solving cases quickly, with clean arrests and clear suspects, good for the press. He made it look easy. To Harper, who was just starting to cut his teeth on patrol, the man was a blueprint: rise through the ranks, do good work, earn respect.

So he'd gone to Alvarez for advice. Asked questions. Took notes. And Alvarez welcomed it, with a smile that never quite reached his eyes.

He poured Harper a cup of stale breakroom coffee and told him stories about the "good ole days," about easy wins and slam-dunk arrests. He even pulled out old case files, showing Harper how a real detective wrote reports, how to frame a narrative cleanly for a DA.

"This one?" Alvarez said, tapping the folder. "Guy left his prints on the doorknob and confessed within ten minutes. Textbook. They still gave me a commendation for it."

Harper had nodded along, impressed. He didn't see the ego behind the performance, not yet.

Alvarez picked up the phone and called over to the detective bureau.

"Got a sharp kid here. Give him something low-stakes, let him get his feet wet."

It felt like mentorship.

It felt like being seen.

What Harper didn't realize—what he wouldn't see until it was too late—was that Alvarez didn't see potential in him. He saw a mirror.

And like all men who thrive on image, Alvarez loved nothing more than seeing himself reflected in someone else's ambition.

So when the detectives finally tossed Harper a case, he jumped at the chance. It wasn't much, just a lead from Detective Josh Marks on a small-time drug dealer rumored to be moving pills out of a rundown neighborhood on the east side of the county. Low stakes, perfect for a rookie hungry to prove himself.

Harper had teamed up with fellow deputy Nolan Warren, a fellow protégé of Alvarez's, and just as eager to impress. The two had been hired together, gone to the police academy side by side, and had each earned a reputation as sharp, ambitious, and willing to put in the extra hours. They worked their contacts, leaned on their informants, and set up a controlled buy. The target was said to drive a white pickup, no confirmed ID, no photos, just word of mouth and a location for the meet.

The plan was simple: Harper and Warren would stake out the drop site, get photographic evidence of the deal, and radio for backup to make the arrest once the deal was done. Simple. Clean.

They arrived early, parking blocks away and making their way into position behind a vacant lot that offered a clear view of the target house. The neighborhood was quiet, still waking up. Rusted chain-link fences, cracked sidewalks, paint chipped homes pressed close together like they were bracing against the weight of time.

And then they waited.

Thirty minutes passed.

Then forty.

Harper shifted on his heels, glancing at the horizon. The early morning sun was starting to climb, casting long shadows over the street. Drug dealers were rarely punctual, but this was starting to feel like a waste of time.

Warren muttered beside him, "Starting to feel like a bust."

Harper said nothing, but his jaw was tight. He hated wasting time. Hated false leads. And yet, something about the stillness of the morning didn't sit right.

Just as they were about to pack up, headlights appeared down the street, rolling toward them at an easy, unhurried pace.

Harper straightened, expecting their suspect, but as the vehicle drew closer, his stomach sank. It wasn't an unknown dealer.

It was one of their own.

A white pickup truck rolled to a stop near their stakeout point, and behind the wheel, off-duty and out of uniform, sat Sergeant Marcus Hale.

Hale was one of Harper's favorite patrol Sergeants. He always pushed Harper, Warren and the other newer deputies to be proactive, to go look for crime, not just wait for it to occur. He called them his "go-getters," and loved the amount of arrests they got on his shift. He never micromanaged, and in fact, told more senior deputies on their shift to be more like Harper and Warren.

Harper's stomach twisted. Warren, on the other hand, perked up like a dog seeing its owner. "Hey, what's he doing here?" he whispered.

Harper didn't like it. "We never told him about this op," he muttered, his eyes narrowing.

Hale pulled up near their stakeout point, rolling down his window. "Harper, Warren. Thought I'd come check in, make sure you boys didn't need anything."

Harper forced a neutral expression. "Didn't know you were tracking this case, Sarge."

Hale chuckled. "Word gets around. Just wanted to see how my two best go-getters were doing." He gave them a mock salute, then rolled up the window and pulled away, the rumble of the engine fading as the taillights disappeared down the block.

Harper stared after him, a chill settling in his chest that had nothing to do with the cold air. As soon as Hale drove off, he turned to Warren. "This isn't right."

Warren frowned. "What do you mean?"

Harper nodded toward the tail lights disappearing down the road. "How did he know about this? We never told him. Only the informants and the detective who passed us the lead. No one else."

Warren shrugged. "It's Hale. He's been around forever. Probably just caught wind of it at shift change. Wanted to look out for us. No big deal. It's nothing. Let it go, Harper."

But Harper didn't answer. His mind kept circling back to the truck.

The dealer was supposed to be driving a white pickup.

Harper wasn't convinced. And he couldn't let it go.

He went back to the detectives. Explained what happened, laid out the things that didn't fit. Detective Marks listened quietly, then gave a shrug and a practiced smile.

"We'll take a look," he said. "But Harper…not every lead pans out. Sometimes it's just noise."

Before Harper could press, Alvarez himself stepped into the hallway, catching the tail end of the conversation.

"You brought this up already, right?" Alvarez asked, his tone casual.

Harper nodded. "Yeah. It just doesn't sit right."

Alvarez clapped a hand on his shoulder. "Then leave it with us. You did your part. Sometimes it's best to let things run their course. Don't start kicking rocks you don't need to."

The words weren't overtly threatening. Not then. Just a senior officer giving advice. But they stayed with him. Because Harper didn't let it go. He asked around anyway.

A few days later, the case went cold. His informants, once eager to talk, suddenly clammed up. Calls went unanswered. Meetings got canceled. Every thread he tried to pull unraveled before it led anywhere.

No arrests. No intel. No explanation.

It was like someone had built a wall around the operation overnight, and made damn sure no one got through.

Warren became distant after that. So did the detectives. So did Alvarez.

The warmth that had once defined their working relationships, the impromptu coffee chats, the backslaps, the quiet nods of approval, faded. The weekend barbeques with Warren and their families, the meet ups at the range to practice shooting drills, Warren was suddenly always *too busy*. Too tired. Working extra hours. "We'll catch up soon," he'd say. But they never did.

Alvarez stopped inviting him to briefings. The cases routed through his desk changed too, no longer slam-dunks or clean wins, but vague, half-baked assignments with messy paper trails and political landmines. Cases where nothing added up. Where the suspects had connections. Where the answers, somehow, were always just out of reach. It felt like a test. Or worse, a setup.

Harper still tried to push through. Still followed leads. Still believed in the work.

But then came the shift change.

Suddenly, Harper found himself reassigned under Sergeant John Dunham, a hard-charging, no-nonsense supervisor with zero patience for ambition and even less for questions.

Dunham ran his squad like a boot camp. Reports came back with entire sections rewritten, language Harper hadn't used, conclusions he hadn't drawn. His caseload was stripped down to nothing but traffic enforcement and low-level calls. Leads he'd been following vanished from the system. Detectives stopped answering his texts.

Dunham made it clear. Harper wasn't there to investigate. He was there to follow orders.

"Just stick to patrol," Dunham had said one morning, kicking back a routine report for minor formatting issues. "Let the real investigators handle the heavy stuff."

A few days later, he called Harper into his office. Sat behind his desk like a judge, arms folded across his chest, expression unreadable.

"You've got hustle," Dunham said. "But maybe it's time to think about a different track. Traffic's steady. Predictable. No headaches. Ever thought about getting on a motor?"

Harper blinked. "A motorcycle unit?"

Dunham smirked. "You'd look good in boots. Quit chasing ghosts, Harper. Be a cop. Not a crusader."

That was the message. Let it go. Move on.

But Harper didn't. He couldn't. Not quietly. Not completely.

He kept asking questions. Subtle at first. Then direct. A contact here. A favor there. A follow-up with an informant who still owed him a call.

He didn't say what he was chasing. Didn't need to. Because the wall around that old case was still there, and someone had worked hard to build it.

Six months later, Harper was on solo patrol when a warrant call came out involving a known violent fugitive spotted near the entertainment district. Backup was miles out, tied up on another call. The suspect was reportedly intoxicated and badgering restaurant patrons. Dispatch asked if he could respond.

Of course he would.

As he rolled toward the location, Harper's radio crackled to life.

"330 from 304," came the voice. Harper recognized the number. 304 was the patrol lieutenant. Alvarez

"330, go ahead," Harper replied.

"Be advised, the suspect has a history of resisting. Known to fight with law enforcement."

"330, I copy," Harper said. Then: "Are you en route to cover?"

A pause.

"Negative, 330. Already headed home for the day."

Harper's jaw tightened, but he didn't reply.

He arrived to find the suspect in a parking lot behind a row of bars and restaurants. The late October sun cast a hard glare across the asphalt, forcing him to squint. The man wasn't alone. A woman stood beside him, glassy-eyed and unsteady on her feet.

Harper stepped out, hand resting on his belt. "You're under arrest. Put your hands behind your back."

The fugitive was cornered, panting, twitchy, scanning for a way out. The woman started shouting almost immediately.

"Leave us the fuck alone, *pig!*"

Harper drew his taser. "Don't do it," he warned, his voice steady.

"330," he called into his radio, "where's my backup? I've got two subjects, non-compliant."

"Ten minutes out," came the reply.

Then the man *lunged.* The woman surged forward behind him.

Harper fired. The taser crackled and struck the fugitive, dropping him hard to the pavement. The woman froze, still screaming. Harper moved in fast to cuff the suspect, but the man wasn't done. He twisted violently, thrashing beneath Harper's weight, clawing at his belt and trying to buck him off.

"Stop resisting!" Harper shouted, struggling to get the cuffs on as the woman hovered nearby, closing the distance again, yelling.

"*FUCK YOU!*" the suspect bellowed, jerking like a wild animal.

Harper had no choice. He cycled the taser again. The electric buzz filled the air, and the man finally went still long enough to get him cuffed.

Harper was double-locking the restraints when he heard boots pounding across the asphalt.

Warren.

He jogged into view, gun drawn but unused, scanning the scene. "Damn," he said, breathless. "You good bro?"

Harper gave a short nod, his heart still hammering. "Yeah. Took care of it."

Warren helped walk the suspect to the back of Harper's cruiser. He didn't say anything else.

• • • • •

The next morning, after shift briefing, Sergeant Dunham pulled Harper aside and told him to report to the lieutenant's office. Harper headed down the hall, expecting a rundown on an ongoing case, maybe even a nod of recognition for the arrest the day before.

Instead, the atmosphere was stiff. Tense. Controlled.

"Take a seat, Deputy," Alvarez said, his expression cold. A man used to control, and someone who enjoyed it.

Harper sat, his gut already tightening.

"We have concerns," Alvarez began, his tone clipped. He slid a folder across the desk. "About an excessive force incident during your arrest yesterday."

Harper blinked. "The fugitive?" he asked, confused. "He resisted. I followed use-of-force protocol to the letter. It's all in the report."

"I haven't read the report. I watched your BWC footage. And that's not all," Alvarez interrupted, his voice like ice. "Deputy Warren has accused you of falsifying a report in a DUI investigation a few months back."

The words slammed into Harper like a freight train.

"What?" he said, stunned. "That's—that's not possible. I followed protocol. Everything I wrote was accurate."

Dunham didn't blink. "Warren says you added details to justify a warrantless search. That you embellished the subject's behavior to strengthen probable cause."

Harper stared at him, stunned. "That's a lie. I even had backup on that stop—"

"Warren was your backup," Alvarez said flatly.

Harper's mouth opened, then closed again.

The trap had already sprung.

Dunham leaned in, slipping into interrogation mode.

"Deputy Harper, isn't it true that field sobriety tests are supposed to be conducted the same way every time?"

"Y-yes," Harper said, trying to steady his voice.

"But you didn't this time, did you?" Dunham snapped, cutting him off.

"I did, though. I—"

"Deputy Warren said the subject actually passed the tests. But you wrote that he appeared impaired, even though he wasn't."

"What? He blew a .24. Why would I lie about that?" Harper asked, incredulous.

"I don't know. Why would you?" Dunham shoved the report across the desk, a small typo highlighted and circled in red ink. "Warren says you embellished. And here's a clear discrepancy."

"That's a mistake in the report," Harper said, jaw clenched. "Not a lie."

The interrogation went on for twenty more minutes. Harper was treated like a suspect—pressured, cornered, attacked. Dunham and Alvarez took turns accusing him of dishonesty, twisting his words, cutting him off. They treated Warren's statement like gospel and dismissed Harper's as defensive lies.

Finally, Harper buried his face in his hands. "No matter what I say, you're not going to believe me."

Alvarez raised a hand. "We're placing you on administrative leave while we investigate these allegations. Hand over your badge and weapon. Effective immediately."

Harper felt the floor tilt beneath him, his grip tightening on the arms of the chair. "This is a setup. Let me take a polygraph. Let me prove—"

"We'll consider that request," Alvarez said, already done. "For now, turn in your badge and gun. Go home. Wait for our call."

The weight of betrayal settled into Harper's chest like concrete. Slowly, he unholstered his service weapon and set it on the desk. Then his badge.

They didn't even look at him.

As he walked out of that office, the career he had built— his future, his identity—crumbled beneath his feet.

• • • • •

CHAPTER 9: BURIED TRUTHS

Now.

The morning after the shooting, the cabin was alive with movement.

Yellow evidence markers dotted the gravel drive like breadcrumbs, each one a reminder of the chaos that had unfolded hours earlier. Shattered glass sparkled under the morning light, crunching beneath booted feet. Inside, a low murmur of voices echoed through the narrow hallways as the Stonehaven PD investigative team methodically worked the scene, combing through every drawer, cabinet, and corner.

Outside, Clackamas County deputies managed the secondary crime scene, the area where the shots had been fired. The shooter's perch. The path of retreat. The blood spatter on the ground where Harper's rounds had struck their assailant. Every footprint and casing cataloged, every tree and stone studied like it held a secret.

The air was sharp with the scent of pine, gunpowder, and damp earth. The forest around them stood still, as if watching.

Despite being tucked away in the forest, the cabin radiated wealth. Rustic on the outside, the interior decor was minimalist but expensive. Custom light fixtures, handcrafted furniture, and clean architectural lines spoke of deliberate design rather than rustic charm. Every detail, from the imported stone countertops to the gleaming hardwood floors, hinted at luxury.

Detective Hurst moved from room to room, taking it all in.

The master bedroom had clearly been the site of Michael Grant's private retreats. A massive bed dominated the space, dressed in high-thread-count sheets and a sleek, charcoal-gray duvet. Nightstands with touch-sensitive lighting sat beside it, and a walk-in closet revealed shelves stocked with designer clothes and, more conspicuously, an assortment of sex toys and bondage gear tucked into sleek black cases.

"Guess this place wasn't just for business meetings," Hurst murmured, exchanging a look with a forensics tech.

In the next room over, what had once been a spare bedroom had been converted into a private gym. High-end equipment filled the space: Peloton bike, rowing machine, weight rack, and a full-length mirror. Even the yoga mats were top-tier.

But it was the office that drew the most attention.

Clearly Grant's command center, the office featured a sleek desk facing a large window, state-of-the-art video conferencing equipment mounted to the walls, and a computer setup that would put most tech startups to shame. Dual monitors, encrypted drives, noise-canceling headphones, all pristine.

Hurst stepped further in, her gloved hands brushing lightly across furniture and fixtures. She paused at the door to what looked like a converted closet, eyes narrowing as she noticed a bulge beneath the rug.

She crouched, tugging the rug back. Wood creaked as the weight shifted.

"Sarge!" she called out. Detective Sergeant Foster appeared in the doorway a moment later.

Hurst pointed to a recessed square in the floor, a trap door. Foster knelt beside her, helping lift the panel. Beneath it was a floor safe, Built directly into the foundation.

"Bingo," Hurst said. "This has to be what Holly was talking about."

"Any clue what the combo is?"

"Not yet. I've tried the obvious stuff. Grant's birthday, company founding date, even the code to the door. No dice."

And biometric?"

She shook her head. "Manual dial. Old-school."

Foster studied it a moment. "Let's not force it. If we trash the lock and there's a kill switch or data wipe, we lose whatever's inside."

"So we wait for Harper?"

Foster nodded. "He gets in people's heads better than most. If anyone can figure out what code Grant would use, it's Jake."

"I could try a few more things…"

"We'll wait. Document it. Secure the room."

Hurst exhaled. "Roger that."

The safe sat silently between them, a promise of secrets not yet revealed.

With the trap door resealed for now, Hurst moved back to the desk, rifling through folders and drawers. Most of it was standard, travel documents, financial summaries, and project briefs. But one manila folder near the bottom of a filing drawer caught her attention, with a smudged label and the word "Red."

She flipped it open.

"Huh. That's weird."

Foster glanced over. "What is it?"

"Land deeds. Blackridge County."

"Blackridge?"

"Yeah. County maps, survey plats, zoning stuff. Looks like a large parcel—wooded, undeveloped."

Foster took the folder. Flipped through it.

"Doesn't make sense," he muttered. "Grant's a tech guy. What's he doing buying farmland?"

Foster took the papers from her, flipping through them. "Maybe it was a side investment. Or maybe it's something else."

They exchanged a look, one that said they'd both seen enough to know nothing about this case was simple.

Cho chimed in from across the room. He sat on the edge of the bed, laptop open. "I pulled the tax data. The land's zoned agricultural. No utilities, no improvements. Just woods."

"And owned by Grant?"

"Not directly. Shell corp. Name's Thornewood Holdings. Registered in Nevada, PO box, no real paper trail."

Hurst crossed her arms. "So we've got a luxury cabin, a hidden safe, and now mystery land out in Blackridge?"

Foster nodded slowly. "And all tied to a man who just got murdered."

"Great," Cho muttered. "Just once, I want a boring case."

Foster almost smiled. "Careful what you wish for."

• • • • •

Harper sat at home, the stillness of the house unsettling. Alyssa had already left for work, and their kids were at school. The only sounds were the occasional creaks of the old floorboards and the low hum of the refrigerator.

He'd just wrapped up a meeting with his union rep and the department's union attorney. Later that day, he'd have to sit down for an interview with a detective from the Clackamas County Major Crimes Team, the outside agency investigating his shooting. State law required that any officer-involved shooting be reviewed by a third-party agency. Harper understood it. Agreed with it, even. But that didn't make the waiting any easier.

His department-issued firearm had already been turned in, his badge temporarily surrendered. Officially, he was benched. Not suspended. Not in trouble. But benched.

And that meant he was home, alone, with nothing but time and a restless mind.

He paced the living room, coffee growing cold on the end table. He'd tried to distract himself, read the news, scrolled his phone, but his thoughts wouldn't let him rest. Every minute he was off the case was another minute someone else might destroy evidence, disappear, or cover their tracks.

His frustration simmered just beneath the surface. And then, as it often did, his mind wandered backward. Back to the last time he'd been placed on leave. Back to Blackridge.

● ● ● ● ●

Then.

Deputy Harper had sat at home, the blinds drawn, the house quiet but tense. Erin moved through the kitchen with a kind of nervous energy, setting a mug of coffee in front of him as she joined him at the table.

Erin had always stood a little taller than most women—though still shorter than Harper— with a striking figure that once turned heads effortlessly. There was a quiet elegance to the way she carried herself in those early days, her posture confident, her movements assured. Her features hinted at Greek ancestry, with high cheekbones, a sculpted jawline, and expressive hazel eyes that danced when she laughed. Back in college, her presence was magnetic—dark hair always styled to perfection, a voice that never wavered when she spoke her mind. She was passionate, opinionated, and fiercely funny. Their connection had sparked instantly, intensely, and physically. The kind of love that that burned hot and fast, built on the illusion that young love alone could conquer everything.

Now, that fire had cooled.

Her hair was more often twisted into a loose, practical bun. The makeup came less frequently, applied with the same disinterest she now showed in conversation. The sharp cheekbones and full lips were still there, but they no longer softened when she smiled, because she rarely did. Her hazel eyes, once warm and full of mischief, had grown colder and more brittle. Especially when she was angry, when they seemed to harden into stone. She had gained weight over the last few years. Not dramatically, but noticeably, her hourglass figure fading into a pear shape. Enough that she noticed it. And while Harper never said a word, she did. Constantly. She mocked his workouts, said he looked too thin now. Accused him of not eating. Of trying to impress someone else. But Harper knew it was never really about him. Her resentment wasn't about his weight. It was about hers. About how the stress and bitterness had settled into her like concrete. How she had stopped caring, stopped trying, and couldn't stand the fact that he hadn't.

At first, she had been supportive, telling him they'd fight this, that the truth would come out. But that support had begun to fray at the edges, thread by thread.

"You'll take that polygraph and be cleared," she had said the night he was placed on leave, her voice steady, clipped with determination. "You didn't do anything wrong, Jake. They'll see that."

She'd sounded so sure. Fierce. Protective.

But as the days turned into weeks, that conviction had started to waver. Her tone softened at first, doubt creeping in like a draft through a cracked window.

"Why would they say that if it wasn't true?" she'd asked one night, her voice quieter now, searching. "I mean… are you sure you didn't mess something up? Even a little?"

And later still, that searching voice became something sharper, accusatory, biting. "I just don't get it, Jake. Why is this still happening if you're so innocent? Why are they all saying the same thing?"

Harper never raised his voice, never fired back. He just sat there, jaw tight, swallowing his frustration. She hadn't been in the field with him. She hadn't seen how politics could twist truth, how fast loyalty vanished when things got messy.

But then he was alone. Not just on paper, but in the quiet corners of their home, where support had curdled into suspicion, and love had been replaced by something colder.

The radio silence from his fellow deputies was deafening. Calls went unanswered. Texts ignored. Brothers in uniform who once laughed with him over bad diner food now acted like he didn't exist.

Two weeks later, Lieutenant Alvarez called Harper into another meeting.

The Sheriff was away at some FBI leadership school out of state, leaving Tom Alvarez in charge as acting sheriff. That alone put Harper on edge. Alvarez wasn't the kind of man who waited for oversight to flex authority.

Sergeant John Dunham sat beside Alvarez in the conference room, wearing the same smug posture, the same unreadable stare. The last time Harper had faced them both across a table, his world had begun to unravel.

Now, he could feel the same cold pressure settling in his chest.

He stepped into the room, back straight, jaw tight.

"Deputy Harper," Alvarez said, motioning toward the chair across from them. "Have a seat."

Harper did.

Dunham slid a file folder across the table, just like before. The same smug smirk on his face.

They wasted no time.

"Jake," Alvarez began, his voice clinical. "We've reviewed the allegations. Deputy Warren maintains his statements, says you used excessive force and falsified your DUI report."

Dunham leaned in slightly, tone flat. "Deputy Smith has corroborated the DUI claim."

Harper blinked, caught off guard. "That's a lie. You know it is. I want that polygraph."

Dunham shrugged, unapologetic. "We weren't able to schedule one."

"You didn't even *try*," Harper snapped, anger edging into his voice. "You never had any intention of clearing this up."

Alvarez held up a hand. "Let's not get emotional, Jake. I'm not here to debate it with you. You've always been a bit emotional. As far as I'm concerned, your use of force was excessive. Our findings are based on statements from your fellow deputies and a review of your reports. That's the process."

Harper stared at him. "You haven't even asked for my side of the story."

"We don't need it," Alvarez said flatly. "Frankly, *I* don't need it. That man you tased, his mother has ties to county commissioners. She's made noise. Now the county's breathing down our necks. This department doesn't need that kind of heat."

"You mean the woman who *interfered* in his arrest?" Harper said, incredulous. "She was screaming in my face, rushing at me, while I was about to be attacked."

"Then you should have tased *her*, Jake," Alvarez said.

Harper's eyes raised incredulously. He was about to push back again when Dunham cut in.

"There's more, Harper. One of your former FTOs, Deputy Daniels, came forward. Says you mishandled evidence during training."

Harper's jaw dropped. "That was years ago. That's ridiculous."

"It's a pattern, Jake," Alvarez said. "Use of force. Evidence problems. We can't ignore it anymore."

"So you're hanging me out to dry for optics?"

"No. I'm protecting this agency. As acting Sheriff, that's my job. And I can't live with what you've done."

Harper straightened. "I want my union rep."

Dunham leaned back in his chair, his smirk growing to a smile, tugging at the corners of his mouth. "They're not coming. The union's not getting involved."

Harper felt the floor tilt beneath him. "So what happens now?"

Alvarez's tone turned casual, too casual. "I'm terminating your employment, effective immediately."

Harper stared at him in disbelief.

"You're firing me?"

"I am."

Dunham slid a form across the desk and a manila folder labeled with Harper's name. It may as well have been a death certificate.

Harper pulled out his wallet, his hands trembling as he removed his ID card. He set it down on the desk, watching as Dunham picked it up without a word. Harper's breath caught. The tears came fast, hot, uninvited.

Alvarez stood, walked around the desk, and clapped him on the shoulder like it was a farewell party. "It's gonna be okay, Jake. You'll land on your feet. You're young, smart, you'll get a great job in no time. Just not as a cop. Not everyone is meant to do this job."

Harper looked up at him, the words burning into his mind. The smirk. The hypocrisy. The betrayal. The tears stopped, the sadness burning away to anger. *Why the fuck would they do this to me?*

He wiped his face with the sleeve of his jacket. "I want a copy of the employee manual. I'm going to grieve this."

Alvarez's tone turned cold. "Good luck with that. Now get out of my office."

• • • • •

Now.

Harper blinked and rubbed his eyes. The present day came back into focus, coffee cold, the television muttering a rerun of *Law and Order* in the background. He hadn't heard a word of it.

The ghosts didn't leave. Not really. They just waited until the house was quiet.

After the divorce with Erin, Harper was barely holding it together. The insurance investigator job was tedious, a far cry from what he once believed he was called to do. He felt like a ghost in a suit. He drank too much. Showed up late, left early. Jordyn, his coworker—the affair—tried to talk to him, but she only reminded him of the man he didn't want to be. He avoided her as much as he could.

Slowly, though, Harper began to emerge from that dark hole. He poured himself into fitness, finding strength in a disciplined routine of running, weights, and competitive volleyball leagues. He reconnected with old college friends, embracing trivia nights and game days. Normal, easy activities with people whose lives weren't tangled up in the toxic web of betrayal he'd endured in Blackridge County. Little by little, he felt himself returning to the version of Jake Harper he'd once known: focused, grounded, and cautiously optimistic.

It was that summer his friends introduced him to Alyssa Bennett. Neither of them had been looking for love, both weary from false starts and disappointments. But on a warm July evening, at a mutual friend's backyard birthday party beneath strings of glowing lights, Harper and Alyssa fell into easy conversation. From the first words exchanged, something clicked. There was no awkwardness, no guarded hesitation, just effortless connection. Being around Alyssa felt like finally exhaling after holding his breath for far too long.

She was beautiful in a way that quieted the noise around her—unassuming, yet impossible to ignore. Petite and naturally poised, with long chestnut hair that caught the light when she laughed and a smile that reached all the way to her eyes. Her beauty wasn't just physical, it lingered in the mind, in the way her presence filled a room without trying. There was a gentle confidence to her, a kind of sensual composure in how she moved, spoke, and touched. Harper noticed all of it, and more. After all he'd endured, it made his heart flutter, but after everything he'd been through, he kept his guard up, uncertain if he could let it fall again.

He tried to keep it casual. Light conversations, short messages, and polite restraint. But Alyssa made it hard to keep his distance. She was warm without being cloying, clever without pretense. There was a quiet strength in the way she held herself, a resilience that felt earned. And for a man who had spent years bracing for betrayal, it felt dangerous to let someone like that get close again. Still, he found himself thinking about her after the party. Her voice. Her laugh. The way she listened. And despite every warning his past had taught him, Harper called her two days later.

The conversations became less casual, learning about each other's pasts. Their triumphs, their stumblings, their hopes and dreams. His divorce. Her ex-fiancé. Bonding over their false starts in love.

Then, one afternoon, Harper's phone buzzed with a call from his Coast Guard Reserve command. There was an opening for a year-long deployment with an MSRT—Maritime Security Response Team—one of the Coast Guard's most elite units, specializing in anti-terrorism missions and high-risk operations. This was a chance to escape the suffocating spiral of his civilian life, a chance to reclaim the purpose he thought he'd lost forever. Harper didn't hesitate. He applied, tried out, and was accepted.

When he told Alyssa, he braced himself for disappointment, or worse, goodbye. But Alyssa surprised him. She understood, without explanation, how much this meant to him. She held his gaze and said simply, "You need to do this, Jake. I'll be here when you get back."

And somehow, he knew she would be.

The deployment was brutal and transformative. The days were long, filled with relentless training, tactical drills, and live operations. But for the first time in years, Harper felt sharp again—focused, useful, alive.

• • • • •

Then.

It was there, on that deployment, that he reconnected with Boatswain's Mate Second Class Logan Cross.

He had known Cross from years earlier, back when Harper was serving as a reservist during college at a small boat station. Cross had always been driven by principle, the kind of guy who did what was right without hesitation. One scorching summer afternoon, during peak boating season, their station had received an urgent distress call. A boater was tangled in the reel on a fishing boat and was bleeding badly. Cross, with Harper alongside, launched their rescue boat immediately, not waiting for the chain-of-command approval. Though command initially bristled at the breach of protocol, both men had earned the respect of their peers, and Harper had seen firsthand Cross's uncompromising commitment to doing what was right, consequences be damned.

Earlier that year, Cross had transferred to the MSRT as a full-time operator. When a team member broke his leg during a botched fast-roping exercise from a helicopter, Cross immediately thought of Harper. He personally pulled strings, vouching for Harper's skill, integrity, and decisiveness. Harper hadn't known it at the time, but Cross's recommendation had been the key to securing his spot on the team.

On deployment, Cross was exactly as Harper remembered, lean, fast, and intense. The kind of man who could run ten miles before sunrise, lift twice his own body weight, and still dominate in combatives training later the same day. Yet beyond the physical prowess, Cross carried himself with a quiet authority that inspired those around him. Steady, sharp, principled.

Together, they forged an even deeper bond, built on brutal workouts, midnight watches, and quiet conversations in the fleeting moments between intense operations. Their friendship grew stronger, now anchored by shared experiences and the enduring belief that right was right, no matter the cost.

He remembered one night in particular. The darkness had stretched across the horizon like an old wound, the sea still and waiting. After a grueling ten-mile run, sweat clinging to his skin and lungs burning, he had collapsed onto a shipping crate at the edge of the training yard. Cross sat down next to him, a bottle of water in one hand and that easy, knowing grin on his face.

"You keep running like that, and you're gonna give the young guys a complex," Cross said, nudging him with his shoulder.

Harper had managed a breathless chuckle. "Not trying to impress anyone."

Cross's smile faded, replaced by a look Harper hadn't seen before, serious and steady. "You're not here just to sweat out your demons, Jake. You're chasing something."

Harper didn't answer.

"I've been watching you," Cross went on. "You're sharp. Tactical. You've still got something in the tank. But the way you look at the world? Like it already beat you."

"I mean I did kind of get my teeth kicked in back in Blackridge," Harper said.

"Bullshit," Cross said. "You know it. You let it beat you, it'll keep doing beating you. But you're still breathing, still running, still fighting. That counts."

He paused, letting the silence speak before continuing.

"What are you gonna do when this deployment ends? Go back to that desk job? Fade back into that version of yourself who hated looking in the mirror?"

Harper hadn't answered. Didn't need to. Cross saw through it.

"You need to figure out who you are now. Not who you were. Not who they said you were." Cross stood, tossing the empty water bottle into a nearby bin. "Fix yourself, Harper. Not for them. For you."

That conversation had stayed with him long after his deployment ended. It had been the first step back, the moment he realized he wasn't broken, just buried.

• • • • •

"To love someone is to see all their failures and stand beside them anyway." - Unknown

CHAPTER 10: THE PATRON SAINT OF LOST CAUSES

Now.

Over the next few days, Harper did his best to relax. His statement to the Major Crimes detective had gone as smoothly as he could have hoped. His union rep and department attorney had reassured him afterward that it was a clean shoot, by the book. Still, being sidelined didn't sit well with him.

But if there was one thing he had learned—painfully—it was how to wait.

Alyssa had been his anchor during the forced downtime. She didn't tiptoe around him or pepper him with anxious questions. She gave him space when he needed it, challenged him when he got too broody, and reminded him, through small gestures and quiet strength, why he had built this new life with her. Just over five feet tall, she carried herself with quiet authority. Her figure was soft yet strong, more confident than curated. Her auburn hair often framed her face in loose waves, and her piercing blue eyes could warm or wound with a single glance.

She was ambitious, brilliant, and wickedly funny, with a kind of quiet confidence that made people listen when she spoke. She worked in philanthropy, coordinating community outreach programs and large-scale fundraising campaigns for causes that actually made a difference. They often joked that while Harper wore the uniform, *she* was the one saving the world.

But it wasn't just what she did. It was who she was.

She had a way of making everyone around her feel seen. Known. And when she loved, she did it completely, without condition or fear. That was what undid Harper the most. She never flinched at his past, never looked at him like he was broken. Instead, she challenged him. Saw the man he could become and refused to let him settle for anything less.

Their house was warm, lived-in, and cluttered in the way that meant *full*. Mismatched throw pillows. Finger paintings held to the fridge with alphabet magnets. The faint scent of cinnamon from a candle Alyssa had lit that morning. It wasn't picture-perfect, but it was theirs.

Harper made breakfast every morning. Adelyn, *Addie*, their daughter—three going on thirteen—sat at the counter, swinging her legs and asking a dozen questions about his job, each more unanswerable than the last. She gripped her sippy cup in one hand and smeared syrup in her hair with the other, giggling with uncontainable joy.

Harper laughed and shook his head, gently wiping her sticky curls with a wet paper towel as she tried to wriggle away. Moments later, she launched into a story about a playground battle between a princess and a dragon, acting out each scene with wild gestures and full commitment.

He did the dishes, still chuckling at her antics and animated storytelling. As he dried his hands, she hugged his leg, took hold of his hand, and whispered, *"I love you, Daddy."*

That one sentence nearly undid him.

Harper scooped her up into his arms and kissed her cheek, the sticky sweetness of breakfast still clinging to the toddler's skin. As he put her down, he stood at the edge of the counter, watching as his daughter skipped happily into the next room.

It grounded him. Recharged him. Reminded him of what he was fighting for—not just justice for Michael Grant, or to clear his name again—but to protect this fragile, beautiful life he'd clawed back from the wreckage of the last one.

● ● ● ● ●

Then.

Everything began and ended with Alyssa.

After returning from deployment, Harper threw himself into his job as an insurance investigator with renewed purpose. Gone was the hollow-eyed man who had barely shown up; now he was sharp, both in presence and mindset, continuing the disciplined physical fitness regimen he'd begun before deployment and refined overseas. Early morning workouts at the gym, meticulous grooming, and ironed shirts became part of his daily routine. Within months, he'd earned a promotion to Senior Investigator, leading a small team of his own.

But more surprising than his professional turnaround was discovering Alyssa was still available, waiting for his return. They reconnected effortlessly, friendly texts quickly giving way to coffee dates that stretched into long dinners and late-night conversations. Harper found himself captivated by Alyssa's easy laughter, her unwavering strength, and the way her blue eyes saw straight through the armor he'd built over the years. Being with her wasn't complicated, it felt natural, inevitable, as if they'd simply picked up where they left off before he shipped out. And one night, after hours of talking on her apartment balcony, Harper realized he hadn't felt that kind of peace in years.

There was something about Alyssa that quieted the storm in his chest.

They sat side by side on a small patio loveseat, city lights twinkling in the distance, her bare feet tucked under her as she sipped from a wine glass and laughed at one of his Coast Guard stories. Her laughter came easy, bright and unfiltered. When the conversation slowed, they didn't feel the need to fill it, comfortable in the silence, the closeness, the way her fingers brushed his without pulling away.

When Harper leaned in for a kiss, it was meant to be gentle. A quiet, tentative thing. But it quickly deepened, turned hungry, then softened again as Alyssa pulled away slightly, her forehead resting against his.

"Take me on a real date," she whispered.

And he did.

Their first official date was the following weekend. Harper showed up at her apartment in a dark button-down and jeans, freshly shaved and ten minutes early. Alyssa opened the door in a simple black dress, nothing flashy, but devastating all the same. The fabric clung to her like a secret, framing the soft turns of her waist and the long, bare lines of her legs. Her hair fell loosely over one shoulder, lips tinted just enough to make him wonder what that color would taste like. There was a confidence in the way she leaned against the doorway, one heel casually kicked back, eyes locking with his like she already knew the effect she had. Harper opened his mouth to speak. Nothing came out.

Later, she confessed to having taken a shot of tequila before he arrived—just one—to calm her nerves.

They went to a stylish, upscale Mexican place on the edge of downtown. Warm lighting, soft music, the scent of cilantro and grilled meat filled the air. The food was good, but the conversation was better. They talked about everything, work, family, childhood, regrets, and dreams. Harper found himself laughing more than he had in years. Alyssa's stories were animated and self-deprecating in the most charming ways. Her wit was sharp, but never cruel. Her warmth disarmed him.

After dinner, they walked. No destination. Just city streets and stories, arms brushing. When he dropped her off at the end of the night, he didn't expect more. He'd already felt more in a few hours than he had in years.

But Alyssa surprised him again.

After unlocking her door, she walked inside without a word, leaving it open behind her. The invitation wasn't spoken, it didn't need to be. It was in the slow sway of her hips, in the deliberate way her fingers lingered on the doorknob, in the glance she tossed over her shoulder. Her eyes held his for just a second longer than necessary, the barest smirk at the corner of her mouth. Certain. Unapologetic. Expecting him to follow.

Inside, they kissed again, deeper this time. Slower. Harper's hands trembled as he touched her, nerves colliding with desire. It wasn't just want, it was the raw ache of someone starved for connection. He hadn't been with anyone since the divorce. Hadn't trusted himself to be seen like that again. Not fully. Not honestly.

Alyssa must have sensed it.

She didn't rush. She kissed him with quiet patience, her hands firm but gentle, anchoring him in the moment. As she slipped the straps of her dress from her shoulders, letting it fall in a whisper to the floor, it wasn't theatrical. It was intimate. Each movement was deliberate, reverent. As she stepped closer and began to unbutton his shirt, her fingers grazed his skin with the kind of care that made his pulse stutter. It didn't feel like seduction. It felt like grace.

Harper's breath caught. She was breathtaking, radiant. Small and delicate in frame, she was impossibly sensual. The lamplight spilled over her pale skin, casting a golden sheen across her bare shoulders and the soft swell of her breasts. Her curves were generous for her petite size, full and inviting, framed by the tumble of auburn hair that fell around her like fire and silk. His gaze drifted over the gentle slope of her stomach, the subtle tension in her thighs, the way she stood with confidence, poised and open. But it wasn't just the sight of her that unraveled him. It was the way she looked at him. No hesitation. No fear. Just calm, clear hunger. Like she saw every jagged part of him and still wanted him.

She took control with quiet confidence, easing him back onto the bed with a touch that was both tender and commanding. She climbed onto him slowly, knees pressing into the mattress, thighs framing his hips as she settled into his lap. The heat of her body against his made him shudder. Her eyes held his, unwavering, like she meant to strip him down not just physically, but completely.

She rolled her hips against him, slowly at first, testing the rhythm, drawing a sharp breath from his lips. Her hands ran over his chest, nails lightly dragging through his hair, then down his sides, leaving sparks in their wake. Every movement was deliberate, her body moving above his in a rhythm that built steadily, mercilessly, until he forgot how to think.

Her mouth found his again, hot and demanding now, their kisses deepening into something hungrier. She whispered his name against his skin as she moved, breathy and close, her lips brushing his jaw, his neck, his shoulder. And still her eyes stayed locked on his, even as pleasure rolled through them both in waves. Every kiss, every thrust, every tremble was a wordless promise. That he was seen. That he was wanted. That whatever came next, neither of them would face it alone.

For the first time in what felt like years, Harper let someone see him. *Really* see him. Not the broken man. Not the disgraced deputy. Just *Jake*.

As they moved together, their bodies finding a perfect rhythm, building the tension between them until it was unbearable, the world around them dissolved into a blur of breathless urgency and rising heat. His hands gripped her tighter, her nails raked lightly across his back, her legs tightening around him as they climbed toward the inevitable. When release finally tore through them, the edge overtaking them, shuddering, gasping, clinging, two bodies locked in the same, exquisite surrender, it wasn't just physical—it ripped through him, raw and electric, leaving him gasping against her skin. In her arms, he felt something he hadn't in years.

Hope.

That night wasn't about sex. It wasn't about forgetting the past.

It was about reclaiming something that had been taken from him.

Alyssa gave him that without needing to say a word.

• • • • •

Harper knew early on that this was different. This was real.

Within a year, Harper and Alyssa moved in together. They rented a quiet condo in one of Stonehaven's older neighborhoods, a place with creaky floors and too much light in the mornings, but they loved it. It became their sanctuary, a space that slowly shifted from two lives into one. Alyssa brought warmth to every corner. Framed photos filled the walls, potted plants in the windowsills, mismatched mugs she insisted gave the kitchen character.

She made it a home.

And Harper, who had spent too long living out of duffel bags, cheap apartments, and a suitcase of regrets, finally began to feel something he hadn't in a long time: peace. The specter of his past didn't vanish, but Alyssa's presence softened its edges. She never pushed him to talk about Blackridge, but when he did, she listened, really listened. Without judgment. Without pity. Just patience and strength.

That was Alyssa. Fierce and kind. Soft where he was hard. Steady where he was uncertain.

And while she was drop-dead gorgeous, with a body that tested his self-control on a daily basis and blue eyes that burned with equal parts fire and warmth, it was more than just the way she looked. It was the way she walked into every room like she owned her space, never shrinking, never pretending. It was how she challenged him, pushed him to think harder, feel deeper, and be better. How she believed in him when he couldn't even look himself in the mirror. She matched him, moment for moment. Every debate became a dance. Every late-night conversation turned into a tug-of-war laced with laughter, frustration, and quiet revelations. And when the lights went out, when it was just the two of them under the covers, her whispered jokes and playful jabs made him feel like he was home.

The sex was incredible, electric and raw, a storm that grounded him even as it set him on fire. She moved with confidence and instinct, as if their bodies had always known each other. But it wasn't just the chemistry that left him undone. It was the way she touched him when the urgency faded, when the storm passed and all that remained was skin, breath, and closeness. It was how she saw through the cracks and wanted him anyway. Not as the fractured man left behind after everything fell apart, but as the one who had chosen to rise again.

She didn't complete him. She reminded him he was already whole.

She was everything he never thought he'd find again, and everything he didn't know he needed until she showed up and refused to let go.

Another six months passed, and Harper proposed at the same restaurant where they'd had their first official date. He reserved the same table, wore the same shirt—she noticed, of course—and ordered the same bottle of wine. Halfway through dessert, he pulled out the ring. No speech, no fanfare. Just a quiet, "I don't want to do life without you."

Alyssa teared up. Then she laughed. "Took you long enough."

A year later, they were married.

A year after that, just when Harper thought his heart couldn't possibly stretch any further, their daughter was born. Addie came into the world screaming, with a tuft of deep red hair just like Alyssa's, and a grip on his finger that nearly broke him. By the time she hit toddlerhood, that red had faded to a soft golden blond, but the fire hadn't gone anywhere.

Alyssa would just shake her head and laugh, watching their daughter stomp barefoot through the backyard in mismatched pajamas, dragging her favorite stuffed unicorn behind her like a battle flag. She was the spitting image of Alyssa as a kid, attitude and all. Fiercely independent, stubborn as hell and sweet in ways that snuck up on you. She worshiped her daddy, shadowing his every step when he was home, and made no secret that she expected the world to bend when she pointed. Most days, Harper didn't mind one bit.

Their life wasn't perfect.

But it was theirs.

Somehow, Alyssa—this fierce, brilliant, beautiful woman—made it all look effortless.

She balanced everything: a demanding career, their home, the chaos of parenthood. She packed lunches and negotiated major donations in the same breath. She knew how to soothe their daughter when Harper's patience wore thin, how to hold space for him on his worst days, and when to give him a loving nudge back toward the man he promised he'd be.

She was the kind of mother who knew just when to kiss a scraped knee and when to push a child to get back up. The kind of wife who didn't need to be the loudest voice in the room, because she already had Harper's full attention with just a glance.

Watching her juggle it all didn't make Harper feel inadequate.

It made him want to be better.

Now.

Standing in the kitchen of the house they bought together, the morning sun warming the hardwood floors, Harper watched her sip her coffee while their daughter colored in a half-finished coloring book at the table. Alyssa caught his eye and smiled. Just a small one, soft and knowing.

And in that moment, he wasn't the same man who had once handed over his badge in shame.

Harper was ready to get back to work.

● ● ● ● ●

CHAPTER 11: SHELL GAMES

A week after the shooting, Harper's phone rang just after sunrise. He stepped out onto the back porch, coffee in hand, and answered to the gravelly voice of Detective Sergeant Foster on the other end.

"Jake Harper. Wanted to let you know, you're clear," Foster said. "Grand Jury came back this morning. They ruled it a justified shooting."

Harper closed his eyes for a beat, the words settling over him like a warm wind. It had only been a few days, but they'd felt like a lifetime.

"Internal review wrapped too," Foster continued. "They found you acted within policy, defending your life, protecting Holly and Cho."

Harper let out a quiet breath, the tension finally beginning to unwind. "Appreciate you calling," he said.

"You earned it, bud," Foster replied. "The case is waiting, and there've been some developments you'll want to hear about."

It was a moment Harper wouldn't soon forget. The quiet, early-morning call that marked the end of the doubt that had hung over him since the shooting.

But just as the dust was settling, as the team headed back out to Welches, they received devastating news:

The cabin had caught fire overnight.

When Harper arrived at the smoldering ruins later that morning, the devastation was near total.

What once had been a secluded, high-end retreat was now a skeleton of charred timbers and scorched earth. Only a portion of one wall remained upright, blackened, leaning like a survivor too stubborn to fall. The roof had caved in entirely, and thick layers of ash coated what used to be polished floors.

A Sergeant from Clackamas County briefed him at the scene, his tone sheepish. "The guy we had posted here…he left for thirty minutes. Some emergency call just outside Welches. A bunch of units were fighting a suspect, and our guy—a rookie—didn't want to miss the action."

You've got to be fucking kidding me. Harper's jaw tightened. "He left his post?"

"Yeah. Didn't notify anyone until after the fact. By the time he got back, the place was already engulfed."

Hurst and Cho stepped beside Harper, staring at the ashes.

The fire marshal approached, removing his helmet and wiping soot from his brow. "Looks like arson," he said. "Accelerant traces everywhere. And this—" He held up a blackened glass fragment in an evidence bag. "Molotov cocktail. Someone didn't just want to cover their tracks, they wanted no trace left."

Harper looked at the ruin in front of him, the remains of a key crime scene now reduced to little more than cinders.

"Someone's scared," he muttered.

Cho glanced sideways. "Yeah. Scared we're getting close."

The air reeked of smoke and damp soot. Harper returned to his vehicle, popped the trunk and pulled on a pair of steel-toed construction boots, heavy-duty gloves, and a breathing mask.

The fire marshal approached, eyebrows raised. "I wouldn't recommend going in there. It's not safe."

Harper's expression didn't change. "I'll be careful."

Without waiting for a response, he made his way through the rubble. He moved carefully but with purpose, stepping around sagging beams and crunching across broken glass. He headed for what used to be the office.

Cho and Hurst stood back as Harper dropped to one knee and began digging with gloved hands. Soot rose with every movement. It took minutes, but then, he found it.

The safe. Still embedded in the floor. Undisturbed.

Harper stared at the keypad, his breathing mask fogging slightly with each exhale as he knelt in front of the scorched safe. The metal casing was blistered with heat damage, but the lock appeared intact. Behind him, the team and the fire marshal watched in silence

The marshal leaned over to Hurst. "What's he doing?"

"Hold off," Hurst replied. "Let's see."

Harper turned his head slightly. "That paperwork we found in the cabinet," he said, voice muffled through the mask. "The one tied to Blackridge, what did it say about the location?"

Cho flipped through his notepad. "Parcel number was tied to some rural property east of Highway 211. Just south of Maple Ridge, maybe a fifteen-minute drive from the county complex."

Harper nodded, gaze narrowing. That was farther than most official county properties—out past the logging roads and old farms. He knew that stretch of highway. Knew how isolated it was. His pulse ticked up.

No. That's too far out to be coincidence. But if it's what I think...

He glanced back at the keypad. His fingers hovered over the keypad. Five digits. A long shot, but his gut wouldn't let it go. He entered the numbers from memory, one after the other.

Click.

A soft pop echoed as the lock released.

Harper froze for a moment, then slowly opened the door. Inside, untouched by flame or smoke, sat a sealed manila envelope and a small external hard drive, nestled against the fireproof lining.

He snapped a photo with his phone, careful not to disturb anything, then placed both items gently into an evidence bag. Rising to his feet, he brushed ash from his gloves and made his way back toward his vehicle, his thoughts already racing ahead.

At the trunk, he pulled off the breathing mask and stowed it. Hurst joined him a moment later.

"How the hell did you know the code?" she asked, her voice quiet but firm.

Harper looked at her, then at Cho, his answer barely above a whisper.

"It was the badge number of my old lieutenant in Blackridge."

Hurst frowned. "Why would Grant use that?"

Harper didn't answer right away. He looked back toward the house, where the smoke still curled upward in lazy gray ribbons.

"What was he trying to tell us?" Hurst asked.

• • • • •

Back at Stonehaven PD, the mood was taut with anticipation.

Detective Hurst stood in the forensics lab with the external hard drive in gloved hands, her eyes narrowed behind rectangular glasses. The hum of specialized digital extraction machines filled the room, low and methodical, like the start of something important grinding slowly to life.

"It's encrypted," she said, not looking up. "Pretty solid stuff too, multiple layers of protection. Could be standard corporate security, but something tells me this isn't your average NDA folder."

"How long?" Harper asked, leaning against the doorframe, coffee in hand.

"At least a day," Hurst said, finally glancing his way. "The forensics rig will extract the data and start brute-forcing the passcodes. If we're lucky, there's no self-wipe function."

Harper nodded, leaning against the doorframe with arms crossed. "Just do what you can. That drive might be the key to this whole thing."

"I'll run a full passcode crack and image the entire device. Once that's done, we can sort through the contents without risking the original." She pointed to a deep black forensics workstation, where the drive was already connected. "Go play detective. I'll call when I have something."

With Hurst at work on the drive, Harper returned to his desk and carefully opened the manila folder they had recovered alongside it, making sure to take photos as he went. The documents were printed in color, professionally laid out. Whoever compiled them wasn't just keeping secrets, they were preparing them.

Maps. Satellite images. Financial transfers.

Most of the folder focused on a piece of land in Blackridge County, the same plot registered under Eagle and Talon Co., the shell company tied to Michael Grant. Harper recognized the coordinates from the parcel research Cho had done. But what he hadn't seen until now were the updated satellite photos.

What was once forest had been cleared. In its place stood a massive warehouse, partially completed, but clearly in use. Vehicles were parked around it, SUVs, box trucks, and a few sedans that looked too high-end for construction workers. Harper zoomed in on one image. Guard towers. Or at least, elevated platforms with canopies, placed at strategic corners of the fence line. This wasn't a warehouse. It was a compound.

Harper exhaled through his nose, tapping a finger against the latest image. "What the hell were you into, Grant?"

He flipped to another sheet. Property records, showing ownership under Eagle and Talon Co., the same shell corporation tied to the parcel. The purchase had been made less than a year ago. Fast work for such a large-scale buildout. Too fast.

Tucked into the stack of paperwork were financial documents. A wire transfer from a company called Thornewood Holdings—another shell, Harper assumed— had funneled a large sum to Eagle and Talon Co. The routing slipped through multiple intermediary banks, but the origination account was from Stone River Financial.

Thornewood Holdings.

Harper jotted the name down. The transfer also included partial ownership rights to the Blackridge County property, assigned to Thornewood Holdings. Which meant whoever was behind that name had skin in the game, serious skin.

He grabbed his phone and walked into Foster's office.

He picked up the images and walked them down to Foster's office. "You're gonna want to see this," Harper said, spreading the satellite photos out across the sergeant's desk.

"I also found a wire transfer," Harper said. "Large amount from a shell called Thornewood Holdings into Eagle and Talon. It's tied to ownership of that property in Blackridge. Origination bank's Stone River Financial. Looks like the funds were moved a few days before Grant was killed. It could've been a payout, or payment for services. Either way, it's our next breadcrumb."

It always comes down to money, doesn't it.

Foster picked up the wire page and scanned the small print. "Think it's tied to Grant directly?"

"I'd bet on it," Harper said. "Even if his name doesn't show up on the paperwork, someone close to him set this up. We need to follow the money."

Foster raised an eyebrow. "What's your next move?"

"I'll draft a warrant for the Stone River account," Harper replied, already reaching for his laptop. "I've got some friends over in their financial crimes unit. If I get this signed quick, I can call it in and get the account activity expedited. Should have it by tomorrow. Might lead us straight to whoever's behind this."

"Do it," Foster said. "This whole thing stinks like a damn offshore scam hiding in our backyard."

Harper nodded. "Understood."

He gathered the wire documentation and returned to his desk, the usual bullpen noise fading as he focused. The account number, the transfer amount, the timing—all of it told a story. It just hadn't revealed the ending yet.

He opened a fresh warrant template and began to type:

*Affidavit for Search Warrant - Financial Records
Detective Jacob Harper, Stonehaven Police Department,
hereby submits the following affidavit in support of a
search warrant for financial account records held by Stone
River Financial, associated with account number 1178-
8288-5479, registered to Thornewood Holdings, a
limited liability company registered in the state of
Nevada...*

As he worked, Hurst passed behind him, glancing at the documents in his hand. "Hard drive's still processing. Couple more hours, minimum."

"Good," Harper said, without looking up. "We're getting close."

Foster reappeared in his doorway. "Let me know when you get that warrant filed."

"I will," Harper replied. "This whole thing, it's too clean. Thornewood Holdings doesn't exist on any of Grant's business paperwork. Which means he was going to great lengths to keep it off the books."

"Or someone else was," Foster said. "And if that's true... we need to know who."

•••••

Harper submitted the completed warrant to the judge for review, attaching the supporting documents and an affidavit detailing the trail that led them to Thornewood Holdings. It was a waiting game now, one he'd learned to tolerate, even if it always left him restless.

He leaned back in his chair, the quiet buzz of the bullpen lulling him into thought.

Things hadn't always felt like this, sharp, dangerous, like stepping across a minefield with every new lead. There had been a time, not long ago, when things were finally turning around. When it felt like life had stopped kicking him down and started letting him stand.

It was right after he had cleared his name.

He had just come back from his MSRT deployment with the Coast Guard. A year of high-stakes ops and brutal training had forged him into someone stronger, more focused. He returned home in shape, sober, and determined to stay on the right track. The insurance job had promoted him, recognizing the shift in his demeanor and drive. He had recently moved in with Alyssa, and they were building a life together filled with hope instead of regret.

Harper had started fighting to overturn his termination. He hired a lawyer, gathered what evidence he could, and filed a tort claim against Blackridge County. Through his attorney, he began naming names, detailing the harassment he endured, the corruption he'd witnessed, the backroom deals and cover-ups that had poisoned the department.

But it wasn't enough.

Rather than face the claims head-on, the County moved to dismiss the suit, citing a supposed procedural flaw in the filing. A minor technicality, they'd claimed.

His lawyer swore it wasn't an error.

Harper hadn't been surprised. *They bought off a judge,* he remembered thinking, the bitterness sharp but familiar. *Typical.*

Just like that, the case was dead in the water. His certification remained suspended. His badge still out of reach.

Then, the news broke.

The same Blackridge County sergeant Harper had once suspected of dealing drugs—back when he was just a patrol deputy—had finally been arrested by the DEA.

Sergeant Marcus Hale.

A man Harper had once looked up to. Respected. Modeled himself after, in the early days.

It made the truth all the more bitter.

Hale had been selling narcotics to an undercover federal agent. And in an almost unbelievable stroke of arrogance—or stupidity—he'd actually *texted* about the deal while sitting in morning shift briefing at the department. The screen lit up right there at the table. Other deputies saw it. Some even read the message over his shoulder.

Right after briefing ended, Hale left the building in uniform, got into his department-issued truck, and drove straight to the meet.

The DEA arrested him in a gas station parking lot less than ten minutes later.

It was all over the news for days. Flashing headlines. Cable talk shows. Public outrage. A senior sergeant, indicted for trafficking narcotics and betraying the very badge he wore.

And caught in the wreckage was Deputy Nolan Warren.

Harper could still remember the moment he saw Warren's name in the official release. The betrayal came back like a fresh wound.

Warren had flipped early, trying to save himself. He confessed that Hale had paid him to tip him off about internal investigations, and worse, had ordered him to fabricate allegations against Harper. To paint him as unstable. Dishonest. Dangerous.

It had never been about Harper's integrity.

It had never been about a use of force.

It had always been about protecting Hale and his operation.

And whoever was protecting him.

Harper's hands had shaken when he'd read the words. *Vindication.*

Three and a half years too late, but it was there. He hadn't been paranoid. He hadn't imagined it. They had framed him, and now the world knew it.

With those revelations, the Department of Public Safety Standards and Training—the state body that handled officer certifications—had officially cleared his name. His record was amended. His police certification reinstated.

And his attorney didn't stop there.

With the leverage of Warren's confession and the federal indictment against Sergeant Marcus Hale, Harper's legal team secured a substantial settlement from Blackridge County. Multiple six figures. Enough to cover every legal bill. Enough to finally exhale. To start over with something close to security, and later, for he and Alyssa to buy their first house outright.

But justice, as always, was uneven.

The leadership at Blackridge—the ones who'd made the call to hang him out to dry—walked away clean. Lieutenant Tom Alvarez and Sergeant John Dunham both denied any knowledge of the scheme. They claimed they'd simply acted on the information provided by Warren.

No consequences. No accountability.

Just a shrug and a redirect.

Harper had his name back. His future.

But not his trust.

● ● ● ● ●

Then.

Harper had been going through emails at his desk a few months later when his phone buzzed with an unknown number. He almost let it go to voicemail but swiped to answer instead.

"Harper," he said, voice clipped from habit.

A pause, then a familiar voice. "Jake? It's Austin Briggs. Don't know if you remember me…"

Harper almost laughed. *Of course I remember you.*

Austin Briggs had been one of the few bright spots during Harper's years in the Coast Guard Reserve. They'd met while drilling at the same unit, when Harper was still piecing himself back together.

Briggs had been sharp, disciplined, and the kind of guy who could handle the weight of both command and camaraderie. He had since gone on to OCS, earning his commission and landing a billet on the sector's boarding team, where he led high-profile inspections and enforcement ops. The guy had a knack for walking the line between tact and toughness.

Harper, on the other hand, had stayed enlisted, drilling at a small boat station on the Willamette River in Portland. One weekend a month, he threw on the uniform, handled SAR drills, conducted local boardings, and kept his sea legs under him. It wasn't glamorous, but it grounded him. Reminded him of the parts of himself that still worked.

They hadn't seen each other in over a year, but Harper still remembered the long runs after drill weekends, the shared stories over chow, and how Briggs never treated him like damaged goods, even when the stink of Blackridge still clung to his name.

What Harper hadn't realized at the time was that Briggs was also a tenured detective with the Stonehaven Police Department.

"Yeah," Harper said, standing up from his desk as the rush of recognition hit him. "Of course I remember you. What's going on?"

Briggs chuckled. "So listen, this might be a little out of the blue, but we're hiring. Stonehaven PD, I mean. Patrol spots. And with your name cleared and your DPSST certs still active for another year or two, you're eligible for a lateral hire."

Harper didn't say anything at first. His heart thudded once, hard.

"I've already talked to the chief," Briggs continued. "Put in a good word. They'll bring you on as a lateral hire, no academy needed. Pay's solid, probation's shortened because of your previous time on. And more than that, this is your shot, Jake. Your chance to get back to what you were meant to do."

Harper sat down slowly, the weight of the words hitting harder than he expected. For years, the idea of wearing a badge again had seemed like a dream locked behind a door he no longer had the key to. But now, that door had cracked open.

He looked over at the photo on his desk—he and Alyssa, hand in hand walking along a beach, smiling beneath a canopy of summer sunlight—and felt something stir deep in his chest.

Redemption.

He wasn't sure he deserved it. But maybe… maybe he could earn it.

Harper hadn't looked back since.

Now, years later, sitting at his detective desk in Stonehaven PD, a warrant on his screen and a conspiracy unfurling in front of him, Harper realized something else:

He had earned this badge twice. And he wasn't about to lose it again.

• • • • •

"Nothing is hidden that will not be made manifest; nor is anything secret that will not be known." - Luke 8:17

CHAPTER 12: RESURFACING

Now.

Harper's laptop chimed with a new notification. The search warrant for the Stone River Financial account had been electronically signed by Judge Morales. He allowed himself a short exhale of relief, tension bleeding from his shoulders. *Another step forward.*

Reaching for his phone, he scrolled to a familiar contact, Bryan Sloan.

Bryan was one of Harper's oldest contacts from his insurance investigator days. They'd worked more than a few fraud cases together back when Sloan had been a senior analyst with another bank. Sharp, steady, and always three moves ahead, Sloan had a reputation for sniffing out financial deception like it was instinct.

Now, he was a supervisor at Stone River Financial, on one of their financial crimes teams.

Harper knew if anyone could help him cut through the red tape, it was Bryan.

The call connected after a couple rings.

"Sloan," came the voice on the other end, brisk and familiar.

"Bryan. It's Jake Harper."

"Harper! Man, it's been a minute. You still hunting bad guys, or did they finally put you behind a desk for good?"

"Still out here pretending I know what I'm doing," Harper said with a smirk. "Listen, I've got a warrant signed, just came through. I'm looking into a wire from a shell called Thornewood Holdings that hit an account tied to Eagle and Talon Co. You'll get the formal paperwork in a few, but I figured I'd give you a heads-up."

"Yeah, sure, shoot it over and I'll put it in the fast lane," Sloan replied. There was a pause, then a shift in tone. "Off the record, though, you didn't hear this from me yet, since we haven't formally processed your warrant... but Thornewood Holdings? It's been on our radar."

Harper straightened. "Go on."

"It's tied to another entity: Redhaven Global. They're linked through a bunch of shared wire transfers, common intermediaries, and similar routing paths. We've filed several SARs—Suspicious Activity Reports—to the feds on both companies in the last few months. The volume and opacity of the movement triggered a lot of red flags."

Harper grabbed a pen and started scribbling. "Redhaven Global?"

"Yeah. That's the name. If you want full details, you'll probably have to go through Oregon DOJ or FinCEN to get the SARs, but if you expand your warrant to include Redhaven, you'll get a fuller picture. Might save you some time."

"I'll get started on that right away," Harper said.

Then Sloan added one more thing. "Hey... does the name Alan Whitaker mean anything to you?"

Harper froze.

"He's listed as the registered agent for Redhaven Global."

Harper stared at the name he'd already written in his notes. The Vice President of Grant Technologies.

"Yeah," Harper said quietly. "It means something."

He ended the call and stood slowly, mind already turning. The web was growing, and now one of Grant's closest associates was at the center of it.

Redhaven Global.

Whitaker wasn't just protecting corporate secrets. He was hiding something much bigger.

Harper sat back down at his desk, fingers already flying across the keyboard as he opened a new affidavit template. His mind raced, but his hands moved with calm precision. Another shell company, another thread in a web that was starting to look more like a noose.

He glanced up at the whiteboard, where a tangle of names, arrows, and dates was starting to resemble something almost organized. Almost.

He began typing:

> *Affidavit for Search Warrant — Financial Records Detective Jacob Harper, Stonehaven Police Department, hereby submits the following affidavit in support of a search warrant for financial account records held by Stone River Financial, associated with account number(s) connected to Redhaven Global, LLC, a limited liability corporation registered in the State of Delaware, and tied through financial transfers to Thornewood Holdings and Eagle and Talon Co…*

He kept going, detailing everything Sloan had hinted at, without directly citing the call with Bryan. He laid out the connections between the shell companies, the ownership of the Blackridge County property, and the wire transfers already under scrutiny.

He paused for a moment, tapping a finger against the spacebar, thinking.

Whitaker.

That smug smile. That immediate refusal to talk about Grant's projects. The legal firewall he threw up like he'd rehearsed it. Now Harper knew why. *Whitaker wasn't just the gatekeeper.* He was part of the machinery.

Harper added a section about Redhaven's registered agent, noting its overlap with Grant Technologies' executive team. It was thin, but it was a bridge, and in cases like this, sometimes a single connection was all a judge needed to greenlight a deeper look.

He scanned the affidavit twice for errors, added his digital signature, and encrypted it before sending it through the secure judicial portal. It would hit the judge's inbox within minutes.

He exhaled, leaned back in his chair, and rubbed his temple. *Another piece on the board,* he thought.

Behind him, the low hum of the forensics rig processing the hard drive still filled the room with steady noise. Hurst hadn't returned with any updates yet, but Harper could feel momentum building. The shell companies. The money. The hidden property in Blackridge. And now Whitaker, who was no longer just a footnote, but a suspect in his own right.

He pulled out his notebook and flipped back to the first day, his notes from the crime scene. The blood. The struggle. The precision. Harper had called it personal.

But now?

Now it was starting to feel like business.

And someone had turned business into murder.

• • • • •

Night had draped itself over Stonehaven like a velvet curtain, the city lights muted against the darkness of the high-end suburbs just north of the river.

Harper sat behind the wheel of his unmarked car, his coffee cooling in the center console. Detective Sergeant Foster was in the passenger seat, cradling his own cup and watching the quiet, well-lit house across the street through half-lidded eyes.

Alan Whitaker's house appeared exactly as Harper expected, pretentious and calculated. Sleek, modern lines, oversized front windows, expensive landscaping, and a driveway that displayed wealth the way some men wore cologne: loud, and hoping someone would notice.

A white Tesla and a bright red Maserati sat parked side-by-side, both gleaming under the security lights. The three-car garage behind them was closed, but Harper had no doubt it housed more of the same. Everything about the house screamed curated luxury. The kind that came from money that didn't want to be asked where it came from.

"This guy really needs to dial it back a notch," Foster said, taking a sip from his coffee.

Harper gave a quiet grunt of agreement, eyes still fixed on the house.

They sat in silence for a few minutes, the engine off, the occasional car rolling past in the distance. Mature trees lined the street and pristine sidewalks. No barking dogs. No kids with basketballs. Just doctors, engineers, CEOs, and now, an executive vice president tied to multiple shell companies and, possibly, a murder.

Harper glanced over at Foster, grateful the sergeant had decided to ride along.

Foster wasn't just a solid supervisor. He'd been a steady presence since Harper joined the department. A no-nonsense kind of leader who never coddled, never sugar coated. But when he spoke, it carried weight. His encouragement never felt forced, and his criticism was always earned.

More than that, Foster had become a mentor. He'd helped Harper navigate the unspoken rules of the job—the departmental politics that existed in every agency—and guided him through the early growing pains of detective work. With years of experience as a Portland detective under his belt, Foster knew how to chase cases to their natural conclusion, no matter how messy the trail got. And he expected the same from his team.

Harper had learned a lot from him.

Still was.

"Thanks for coming out," Harper said.

Foster shrugged. "I figured you'd try to do this alone. You've got that lone-wolf thing going on lately."

Harper smirked, but it faded fast.

Foster turned toward him, his voice quiet. "You're doing good work, Harper. Real good. But your head's not always here."

Harper exhaled, eyes drifting back to the lit windows of Whitaker's house. "It's Blackridge," he said simply. "Everything about this case…it's pulling me back there."

Foster didn't interrupt. Just let the silence stretch.

"It's not just the location," Harper continued. "The money laundering. The corruption. The secrecy. It's too familiar. Like the same playbook… just higher stakes."

Foster nodded slowly. "I figured as much. I also figured you wouldn't say anything unless I called it out."

"I'm not trying to make this about me. It's just… when you've been through something like that, it's hard to separate the past from present. The names change. The city changes. But the rot? That's the same."

Foster sipped his coffee, considering that. Then he turned, voice firm but not unkind.

"Listen to me, Jake. You're a damn good cop. And you're going to be a damn good detective, hell, you already are. But you've got to stop letting your past carry the badge for you."

Harper glanced over.

"You survived it. You fought back. But if you keep measuring every case by what happened in Blackridge, you're gonna miss what's right in front of you. Learn from it, yeah. Carry the wisdom. But don't carry the ghosts."

Harper looked back at the house. One of the lights upstairs had just gone off.

"I hear you," he said finally.

Foster grunted. "Good. Now drink your coffee before it turns to ice."

Harper allowed a small smile. He took another sip and let the warmth settle in his chest. Outside, the night deepened. The Whitaker house stood still, unknowingly under the watchful eyes of two cops who weren't going anywhere anytime soon.

• • • • •

"Do not go gentle into that good night….rage, rage against the dying of the light" - Dylan Thomas

CHAPTER 13: NIGHTFALL

Then.

It was the third graveyard shift of four. *One more night and I go home to Alyssa.*

Three a.m., and the city of Stonehaven slept. Officer Harper had driven quiet laps around the streets, crept slowly through neighborhoods, and checked business doors to make sure they were locked. It was one of those nights where crime seemed to have taken the night off.

"33 Baker from 31 Tom," his radio crackled to life, the graveyard sergeant calling.

"33 Baker, go ahead," Harper replied.

"Code 6 at the Walmart parking lot," Sgt. Foster said, using the radio code for a car-to-car meetup.

"Copy," Harper said, his response clipped as he shifted the patrol car into drive.

When he pulled into the mostly empty lot, he saw Sgt. Foster's black-and-white Explorer idling near the center. Harper parked driver's window to driver's window, giving them both a clear 360-degree view, a habit born from caution and experience.

"Hey, Sarge!" Harper greeted with a grin.

"Hey Jake. Wanted to fill you in on something," Foster replied.

"Sure, what's up?"

"Well, I got the Detective Sergeant spot," Foster said. "I start next month."

"Hell yeah. Comin' off graves for good, huh?" Harper said.

"Oh yeah. Karly's thrilled to finally be on the same schedule again. You'd think after twenty-five years of marriage, she'd be sick of me," Foster laughed.

"That's awesome, Sarge. I'm really happy for you," Harper said. "Though I'm gonna miss these 3 a.m. chats. Helps keep me awake."

"That's part of why I wanted to talk. Wasn't just to brag on the promotion."

Harper quieted. He could tell by Foster's tone there was more coming.

"Briggs gave his notice too."

"What?!" Harper said, eyebrows shooting up. Austin Briggs was a hard charger. Hearing it secondhand caught him off guard.

"Yeah. He got picked up by HSI. He's going over as a Special Agent in their Portland office next month. He'll still be around, but that means there's going to be a detective slot opening."

Harper stared at him.

"I think you should put in, Jake," Foster continued. "I've seen your investigations. You're smart, thorough, and driven. You write search warrants, document everything, and talk to people in a way that gets them to open up…victims, witnesses, suspects, doesn't matter. You work cases like no patrol cop I've seen."

Harper's jaw dropped.

"I'm serious. You'll have to interview, sure, but you'll have my recommendation. No one else is even close to ready. You've put in the work."

• • • • •

Now.

Hours had passed in Whitaker's neighborhood. The occasional car broke the quiet rhythm of nighttime suburbia, the rustling of wind through manicured trees, and the quiet sip of coffee. Harper sat forward, one hand resting on the steering wheel, the other tapping lightly against his thigh.

Then—a car.

A silver sedan pulled up slowly to Whitaker's house, passed it, and parked in front of the house two doors down. It wasn't flashy. Not beat-up, either. The kind of car you didn't look twice at. It idled at the curb, headlights off, the silhouette of the driver barely visible inside.

Harper leaned forward slightly and squinted through the darkness.

He flipped open his notebook, pulled a pen from his pocket, and jotted the plate number in quick, neat handwriting.

Oregon plate. LHX 274.

"We've got movement."

Foster straightened. "That him?"

A moment later, the front door of the house opened. Alan Whitaker stepped out, pulling a coat around him, glancing both ways down the street before padding down the street to the waiting sedan. He opened the passenger door, slipped inside, and the vehicle pulled away.

Harper put the Durango in gear. "Showtime."

They pulled out slowly, headlights still off as they eased around the corner and trailed the car from a distance. Harper stayed back, two full blocks behind. He'd done this before, more times than he could count. His time as an insurance investigator had taught him to tail without being seen, to become just another vehicle in the stream. He hung back, kept the angles right, let the taillights be his guide.

But as the sedan continued east, away from the well-lit neighborhoods and toward the edge of Stonehaven, Harper tapped the steering wheel with his fingers as he felt that familiar tension crawl into his chest. The road was thinning out, the hour growing late. Fewer cars. Fewer excuses.

"This is getting trickier," he said.

"Just keep him in sight."

They crossed the city limit. Streetlights grew sparse. Trees crept in from the shoulder. Then, without warning, the sedan ahead accelerated, fast.

Tires screamed as it tore down a narrow country road, disappearing around a curve in a blur of red taillights.

"Shit," Harper said. He hit the gas, engine roaring.

"That's a dead end," Foster said, sitting forward. "No outlet for another two miles."

Harper killed the headlights and slowed at the mouth of the road. The Durango coasted in darkness as he rolled the window down, listening.

Silence.

Then, voices. Muffled. Male. Sharp and tense.

A shout. Then a plea.

Pop pop pop pop. Four rapid gunshots cracked through the trees.

Harper snapped the headlights on and floored it.

The Durango roared down the country road, gravel and dust kicking up behind it. As they rounded the bend, a silhouette came into view, a body slumped at the side of the road, lit up by the red and blue lights of Harper's SUV.

The sedan's lights flared. It peeled away from the edge of the forest, tires spinning as it raced back toward them.

"Fuck!" Harper yanked the wheel hard. The Durango veered onto the shoulder as the sedan tore past, a blur of dark metal and adrenaline. Harper's hand shot to the gearshift, but Foster's voice stopped him.

"Jake! Look!"

Harper's eyes locked on the figure crumpled in the grass.

Whitaker.

He was on his back, mouth open, gasping like a fish out of water, blood soaking through his shirt in spreading, pulsing blooms.

"Go!" Harper threw the car in park and jumped out.

They rushed to him. Harper dropped to his knees, trauma kit in his hand.

"Alan, hey, hey, stay with me," Harper said, voice firm but low. "Who did this?"

Whitaker's eyes fluttered, unfocused. His lips moved.

"Who did this, Alan?" Harper repeated. "Give me something. Anything."

Whitaker's gaze settled on him, panic widening his eyes. His lips parted. A breath, wet and shallow.

Then one word, choked through blood-flecked teeth: "Dunham."

Foster's head snapped up. Harper froze. The name hit like a hammer to the chest. Whitaker's breathing stuttered, wheezing turned agonal. Harper grabbed gauze, pressing hard against the wounds. "Stay with me! Dammit, stay with me!"

Foster was already on the radio, calling it in.

"Subject down, multiple GSWs to the chest…suspect vehicle fled westbound…send medical, send everyone!"

Harper kept working to seal the wounds, then starting chest compressions. Pressing. Desperate.

But it was too late. Whitaker gave one last breath, shallow and hollow. Then he went still.

As EMTs arrived and took over CPR, Harper stared down at the lifeless face, the blood on his gloves. His jaw clenched. *Goddammit.*

"Dunham," he whispered.

Sergeant John Dunham.

Blackridge County's golden boy. Alvarez's right hand. The former sergeant who'd helped railroad him out of law enforcement. And now, the current undersheriff of Blackridge County.

The pieces clicked. The shell companies. The warehouse. The betrayal.

Harper stood slowly, blood still on his hands, heart pounding in his ears. The ghosts weren't just echoes anymore.

They were back, and they were drawing blood.

• • • • •

The flashing red and blue lights lit up the narrow country road, casting long shadows across the dirt and gravel. The scene was tense, raw, uncontained. The EMTs had worked quickly, but there wasn't much they could do. Whitaker was still, his final breath already gone by the time they arrived, his body cooling under the cold wash of floodlights and fresh night air. As other officers and detectives arrived, not a single member of the responding units moved to touch the body.

Whitaker lay sprawled on the edge of the road, his torso soaked in blood, one hand curled near his chest, the other limp in the gravel. The shell casings that ended his life glinted faintly near his shoe.

Foster stood next to Harper, both men quiet under the weight of what had just happened.

"CSI's en route," Foster said, checking his phone. "Cho and Hurst too. We hold the scene. Nothing moves."

Harper nodded, still staring down at the man who had tried to run, who had secrets he might've spilled. If he'd only had five more minutes. The name *Dunham* echoed in Harper's mind like a war drum.

"County's already been in touch," Foster added. "They've officially turned this over to us. Given the connection to Grant, the property, the holding companies, it's ours."

Harper gave a shallow nod. "Good. We'll need their resources, but we need to stay lead."

He crouched near Whitaker's body, careful not to disturb anything. The man's lips were parted, eyes wide in a final expression of disbelief and pain. His chest was still now, no more ragged breaths, no more blood bubbling between clenched teeth.

Harper stood and peeled off his gloves. "He gave me a name."

Foster looked up. "Who?"

"Dunham," he said finally, voice low.

Foster turned. "You sure?"

Harper gave a stiff nod. "Whitaker said it with his last breath."

Foster frowned. "That name means something to you."

"More than I'd like it to." Harper peeled off his gloves, voice tightening. "John Dunham. He was the defensive tactics instructor at Blackridge County when I was there. Firearms too. Used to brag about being a former Marine and a failed MMA fighter, like the failure gave him extra grit."

"Charming," Foster muttered.

"He was a hammer looking for nails," Harper said. "Didn't believe in de-escalation. Hell, I'm not even sure he knew what the word meant. When he was a patrol sergeant, he'd go out of his way to provoke suspects, taunt them, crowd them, get them to take a swing just so he could say it was justified." Harper shook his head, his jaw muscles clenching. "I saw him do it once. Suspect ran his mouth during a tense stop with a wanted suspect. Nothing physical, just mouthing off. Telling Dunham he wasn't so tough without that gun and badge. Dunham didn't flinch, just took off his belt, set his gun and badge on the hood, and said 'Let's settle it.' Then he started circling the guy, fists up like it was a backyard fight."

Harper's voice dropped.

"They boxed. Right there in the street. When it was over, the guy was face-down on the pavement, bloodied and dazed. Dunham just stood over him, tossed him the cuffs, and said 'You lost. Put 'em on yourself.'"

He paused again, working his jaw.

"Afterward, I mentioned it to my FTO. Thought maybe we should write it up. He just laughed, like it was a joke. Said, 'That's what happens when you fuck with Sergeant Dunham.'"

Foster's eyes widened. "And your rookies?"

"He'd push them into confrontations, force adrenaline-fueled situations, then critique how they handled it. Made it a test of manhood. You failed, you were weak. You passed, he respected you...maybe."

Foster glanced toward the dark road. "Sounds like a ticking time bomb."

Harper nodded. "I think he was Alvarez's fixer. When I started asking the wrong questions about the drug case, Dunham started showing up everywhere. Reports I filed got changed. Calls got reassigned. He was always around, always watching. I'm telling you—he was part of it."

"And now he's the undersheriff."

"Yeah," Harper said. "Alvarez made commissioner, and Dunham took his place. Still carrying the same chip on his shoulder, probably still carrying the same Kabar. He carried that knife everywhere. Told everyone it was from his time in the Corps. I remember the way he looked at it. Like it was an extension of him. He never went anywhere without it."

Foster gave a low whistle, glancing toward the body again. "Then he's not just a memory. He's a suspect."

"We need to move on this," Harper said. "Before he disappears behind a badge and a lawyer."

Foster nodded, his jaw tight. "We'll get it done. But we do this smart. Paperwork, warrants, the works. You and me, we do not screw this up."

The night air pressed in again, colder now, heavier. Harper gave a nod, his gaze lingering on Whitaker's body. "He didn't have to die like this."

Foster looked over, expression unreadable. "You alright?"

Harper was quiet for a moment, jaw tight, shoulders tense beneath his jacket.

"No," he said finally. "But I will be."

He took one last look at the bloodstained gravel before turning toward the swell of flashing lights and uniforms gathering behind them.

"Justice isn't a job," Harper said, more to himself than to Foster. "It's a promise."

Foster looked at him for a beat, then nodded once. "Let's keep it."

Now Harper had something he hadn't had yet in this whole damn case.

A suspect.

A target.

•••••

Then.

He was a hammer looking for nails.

It was a quarterly weapons qualification at the Blackridge range, routine on paper, miserable in practice. The August sun beat down like a punishment, baking the packed dirt beneath their boots. Heat shimmered off the hoods of parked cruisers and stung the air with the faint scent of motor oil and dust. Deputies sweated through their tan uniforms, backs damp, polyester clinging to their skin like plastic wrap.

Harper stood at the line, shades low on his nose, watching the rookie two lanes down.

Sworn in that morning. Academy-bound next week. Couldn't have been more than twenty-two. His grip was too tight, his stance off, his hands twitching with every distant echo of gunfire from the other bays.

"Take a breath," Harper had said, his voice calm, patient. "Line up the sights. Let the target blur a little. Just feel the break of the trigger…squeeze, don't jerk the—"

"Deputy Harper," Sergeant Dunham's voice sliced through the air, sharp and uninvited. "Back to your lane."

Harper paused, turned halfway toward him.

Dunham was already striding over, boots kicking dust, mirrored sunglasses reflecting sky. "What's the matter, rookie?" he barked, voice loud enough to carry down the entire line. "You need a juice box before you piss yourself?"

The kid flinched visibly, face flushed beneath his earmuffs. He tried to reset his stance, but his arms shook slightly. His trigger finger hovered just above the frame, unsure.

Harper opened his mouth to step in again, but Dunham was already reaching into his truck.

From behind the seat, he pulled out the short-barreled carbine, matte black, tricked out, still wearing the SWAT emblem he wasn't technically allowed to wear anymore. The weapon gleamed under the sun, a slab of authority no one had the guts to question.

"Let me help you out," Dunham said with a smirk, stepping behind the rookie, just off his left shoulder, slightly behind. Too close. Way too close.

Harper's stomach turned. He started to step forward, but froze when Dunham raised the carbine.

The rookie exhaled, lined up his shot. His finger squeezed.

Dunham pulled the trigger.

A burst of automatic fire tore through the air, loud and jarring, echoing off the berm and bouncing back across the range in thunderous waves. The rookie jolted like he'd been shocked. His rounds went wild—high, left, low—punching erratic holes in the silhouette.

He lowered the weapon, eyes wide, chest heaving.

Harper stood frozen two lanes over, fists clenched, jaw grinding. The instructors said nothing. The others just looked away.

Dunham laughed. Full belly, like it was the best joke he'd heard all week.

"Well shit," he said, sauntering off like a cowboy holstering his iron. "Guess it's back to desk duty, huh? Better luck next time."

The rookie just stood there, still holding the pistol, still breathing too fast.

Harper didn't speak. Didn't need to.

Even then, he'd known what Dunham was.

●●●●●

"The universe is change; our life is what our thoughts make it."
- Marcus Aurelius

CHAPTER 14: THE TIES THAT BIND

Now.

The scent of blood and gunpowder still clung to Harper's jacket as he approached Whitaker's residence that morning to execute the search warrant. The DA's office and judge fast tracked Harper's affidavit, with Whitaker now lying in a morgue, the second body to hit Stonehaven in as many weeks. Harper's thoughts swirled, unfocused, the edges fraying with exhaustion. His jaw clenched as his phone buzzed during the drive. Cho. The house was still quiet. No movement in the hours since Whitaker's murder.

Harper stepped from his SUV, eyes taking in the sprawling house set against a backdrop of well-manicured lawns and carefully pruned hedges, a portrait of suburban opulence. Cho leaned against his vehicle near the driveway, offering Harper a nod as he approached.

"All quiet?" Harper asked.

"Not even a curtain moved," Cho replied. "Place has been dark since you left."

"Let's wake 'em up," Harper said, motioning to the team assembled behind him. *I hate this part*, he thought. The intrusion into the grief that would follow would be emotionally heavy, but he knew it was necessary. Necessary, and potentially life-saving, given how quickly the bodies were piling up.

The team moved quietly behind him, their footsteps muffled by the perfectly maintained stone walkway. Harper paused briefly at the elegant ironwood door, took a breath, and knocked firmly. Inside, the house remained still for several moments before faint noises stirred, lights flicking on behind frosted glass, footsteps shuffling toward the entrance.

The door cracked open, revealing a woman in an expensive white bathrobe. She was clearly just pulled from sleep, eyes heavy, face puffy but unmistakably maintained through money and modern medicine. Mid-forties, red hair artfully dyed, green eyes cautiously surveying Harper and his team. Her face held an annoyed expression, irritation thinly veiled behind polite curiosity.

"Mrs. Whitaker?" Harper asked gently.

"Yes, I'm Vanessa Whitaker. Can I help you?" Her tone carried mild annoyance beneath the veneer of politeness.

"Are you Alan Whitaker's wife?" Harper continued, his voice calm but firm.

Vanessa's expression shifted subtly, suspicion edging into her features. "Yes. What's this about?"

Harper displayed his badge clearly, meeting her eyes. "I'm Detective Harper, Stonehaven PD. We need to speak with you about your husband. May we come inside?"

She hesitated, eyes flicking between Harper and Hurst behind him, then stepped aside. "Yes, please, come in."

Inside, the home's luxury continued to impress. Polished hardwood floors, modern furniture, artwork likely chosen by a decorator rather than by sentiment. Vanessa guided them to a spacious living room, sinking onto a cream-colored leather sofa Harper imagined cost more than several mortgage payments. He and Hurst remained standing, respectful but authoritative.

"Are you investigating Grant's murder?" Vanessa asked, her gaze shifting between Harper and Hurst.

Harper nodded slowly. "Yes. Mrs. Whitaker, there's no easy way to say this, so I'll be direct. There was an incident last night, and your husband Alan was killed." He'd learned through experience that directness, though painful, was the most compassionate way to handle notifications. No room for false hope, no ambiguity.

Vanessa's eyes widened in horror, a trembling hand covering her mouth. "What? No… that…that's not possible. Alan said he was going for a walk…" she said, tears forming at the corners of her eyes.

"I'm deeply sorry," Harper continued gently but clearly. "Alan was found shot to death."

Vanessa crumpled forward, sobbing uncontrollably. Her carefully constructed façade shattered into raw grief as the reality set in. Harper let her take a moment, exchanging a brief, sympathetic look with Foster.

Finally, she composed herself enough to speak, voice shaking. "How? What happened?"

"We believe Alan met with someone shortly after leaving your home. They drove out of town. We think there was some kind of argument, and that individual shot your husband. He died at the scene."

Her tears flowed again, but softer now, grief shifting into confusion. "He didn't mention meeting anyone. He just said he needed some air."

Harper gave her space, allowing her emotions to settle before speaking again. "I know this is incredibly difficult, Mrs. Whitaker, but we need your help. Do you have any idea who Alan might have met? Any recent threats or arguments?"

She shook her head, clearly overwhelmed. "I don't know. Alan… he didn't involve me much in his work. We kept things separate. I run my own business. I'm a realtor."

Recognition clicked in Harper's mind; he'd seen her face before, plastered on park benches around town. "I understand," he said softly. "Do you recognize the name Redhaven Global?"

"No. Why, should I?"

"Just following leads. What about the name Dunham? John Dunham?"

Her eyes widened involuntarily, and she quickly masked her reaction. "He's called a few times. Alan told me he was an old friend from college. They talked business occasionally."

Harper made a mental note of her reaction. Dunham was definitely on her radar, whether she knew it or not. "Do you have somewhere you can stay, Mrs. Whitaker? Family or friends close by?"

"Yes," Vanessa nodded slowly. "My sister lives in Tualatin."

Harper offered a reassuring nod. "Good. That's ideal. We've obtained a search warrant for your home as part of our investigation. We need to examine Alan's personal effects, his office, really anywhere that might help us understand what happened."

He handed her a copy of the warrant, watching her reaction closely. She merely nodded, numbness overtaking her earlier grief. "He has an office just off the foyer."

"Could you show us, please?"

She led them to a small room just inside the entrance, impeccably organized but impersonal, more office space than sanctuary.

Harper pulled on blue neoprene gloves. "We'll begin here. Detective Hurst can help you gather personal items if you need to leave. Unfortunately, nothing of evidentiary value can leave with you tonight."

She hesitated, then shook her head. "I'll wait."

The team moved in behind Harper, methodically beginning their search. They were careful, respectful, but thorough. As he sifted through files and papers, Harper hoped somewhere in these meticulously kept secrets lay answers, answers that would unravel a tangled web, where money, power, and corruption blurred lines between friend and foe.

•   •   •   •   •

Later, Harper leaned against the briefing room wall, a paper coffee cup cooling in his hand. It was just past noon and the Stonehaven detective bullpen was packed tighter than usual. Sleep-deprived eyes scanned the case board, which had grown increasingly crowded with each passing day.

Foster went over what they had from forensics.

"Whitaker was killed by 9mm handgun, four rounds, hollow-points. The shooter at the cabin used a .308 rifle."

Harper stood at the head of the room, dry erase marker in hand, drawing a red line between Michael Grant and the new face now pinned to the board: Alan Whitaker.

"Same shooter," he said simply.

A murmur passed through the room. Harper stepped forward, holding up a report. "Crime scene techs finished processing the area around Whitaker's body late last night. Boot impressions. Danner Acadia, size 10.5."

Cho glanced up from his notebook. "That's what we found at Grant's scene, right?"

Foster nodded. "And Clackamas County just sent over their preliminary on the cabin shooting. Boot prints outside the cabin? Same size, same model. Danner Acadia."

Hurst raised an eyebrow. "That model's popular, standard issue for a lot of tactical teams and law enforcement." She looked at Harper. "Didn't you say something about that?"

Harper nodded slowly, jaw tight. "Yeah. Blackridge County issued Danners as standard when I worked there. And Dunham? He wore them religiously. Swore by 'em. Said they were the only boot worth a damn."

Foster scratched his beard. "That enough to tie him to the scenes?"

"Not on its own," Harper said, "but it's not just the boots. Dunham's got a slight limp. Took shrapnel in Iraq. He was a Marine, pre-law enforcement. I watched him drag that leg across gravel for two and a half years."

"Not to mention the Kabar," Harper added after a beat, voice sharpening. "He always had it on him. Used to say it was part of the uniform. Even kept it clipped inside his waistband after he made detective. Told everyone it was a 'tool of the trade.'"

Hurst glanced up. "We're thinking that's what was used on Grant?"

Harper nodded. "Based on the autopsy report—blade length, edge geometry, angle of attack—it's a textbook Kabar. Seven-inch fixed blade, 20-degree grind. That's not just close. That's exact."

Cho frowned, tapping his pen against his notebook. "He really carried that thing everywhere?"

"Everywhere," Harper said. "I watched him train rookies how to use it, told them it was the best backup weapon you could have. He even gave one as a gift to Alvarez when he got promoted to Lieutenant. The guy treated it like a badge."

Cho flipped through his notes. "All three scenes, Grant's condo, the cabin, Whitaker's dump site, all have print patterns consistent with a limp. The techs flagged the stride inconsistencies."

"It's Dunham," Harper said. "We're not going to get fingerprints or DNA unless he screws up, but the pattern is there."

Foster let out a low breath and looked back at the board. "A limp. The boots. The knife. And now he's tied to a dead man who named him with his last breath."

"Yeah," Harper said, jaw flexing. "Dunham's not a memory. He's in this."

Cho looked over his laptop. "I can reach out to some folks at OSP, see if we can get a full list of current and former law enforcement with that boot size and known injuries. Might give us more to cross-reference."

"I've got a guy at CGIS," Harper added. "I'll ask for a quiet pull on Dunham's military jacket. See what's in there besides the limp."

"Good," Foster said. He stepped back, tapping Whitaker's picture. "Someone's tying off loose ends. Fast."

Hurst crossed her arms. "What about Holly?"

"Still secure," Foster replied. "She's in a safe house."

Harper gave him a look.

Foster smirked. "And by that, I mean one of Hurst's vacant rentals."

Cho raised a brow. "Does she know that?"

"She's got a Netflix password and a fridge full of groceries," Hurst said. "That's as good as witness protection gets around here."

The room chuckled, but the tension didn't lift.

"Is she holding up okay?" Harper asked.

Hurst gave a small shrug. "As well as you'd expect. Could be worse."

Foster's smile faded. "We had a neighbor report someone idling outside Holly's place late last night. Uniform responded and found the back door glass shattered. She wasn't home, thank God."

Harper's jaw tightened. "They're hunting."

"Yeah," Foster said quietly. "And they're getting closer."

Harper stared at the board, his gaze bouncing between the three victims and the now undeniable thread connecting them. The same man. The same boots. The same violent precision.

The past had a way of circling back when you least wanted it to.

Foster looked to Harper. "What did you find at the residence?"

"Not much in plain sight," Harper said, rubbing his jaw. "Whitaker's house was too clean. Like someone scrubbed it, but not professionally. More like a panicked once-over."

"Wife?" Foster asked.

"Vanessa," Harper said. "She was… cooperative, but shaken. Claimed to know nothing about his business dealings, especially anything off-books. Either she's a hell of a liar, or he really did keep her in the dark. We'll reinterview her, but I don't expect much."

Hurst flipped open her laptop. "We did recover a burner phone hidden behind some books in his home office. SIM card's locked, but we've already requested the metadata from the carrier, calls, texts, tower pings. Shouldn't take long."

Foster nodded. "Could be something."

Harper glanced down at his notepad. "There was one more thing. In the garage—back corner, behind a stack of holiday boxes—we found a duffel bag with about a hundred grand in cash. His and the wife's passports. A couple changes of clothing."

The room stilled.

"Maps, too," he added. "Topographical. Printed from USGS datasets, high resolution, laminated. One of them was folded open, marked up in red Sharpie. A grid pattern overlaid on forested terrain. And dead center, circled twice, was a single word: *Redhaven.*"

Foster straightened, his brow furrowed. "Redhaven?"

"Yeah," Harper said. "We cross-referenced the terrain with satellite data. It's almost a perfect overlay for the area around that compound in Blackridge County. Elevation lines match. Tree density. Even the service road that cuts in from the south. Whitaker had a map of it. He knew exactly where it was, and how to get in."

"Redhaven isn't just a shell Corp," Harper said. "It's *the* place. The name. The compound."

He let the weight of it hang in the air a beat before continuing.

"And if that duffel's any indication, Whitaker wasn't just aware of it, he was gearing up for something. Could've been a visit. Could've been an escape plan."

Hurst glanced up from her screen. "Could explain why he was killed. He got cold feet. Or maybe someone thought he'd flip."

"Or maybe he was getting ready to talk," Harper said quietly. "And someone made sure he couldn't."

Foster glanced back at the board, at the pinned photos of Grant and Whitaker now connected by red thread. "That kind of money… a passport…. He was getting ready for something big. The kind of move you don't come back from."

Harper nodded. "And he ran out of time."

"Which means we need to move fast," Hurst added. "I've been combing through Grant's personal accounts. Outside the shell companies, everything's clean. Legit salary, no unreported income, no strange transfers. The man was meticulous. He used the companies as buffers, nothing shady touched his name directly."

Cho looked up from his notes. "I've been digging into personal connections. Grant didn't have many. Parents are retired, living in Florida. He set them up financially, and they keep to themselves. No siblings. The only person he regularly interacted with outside work was Holly."

Cho continued. "I talked to a couple of Grant's old classmates from Stanford. Said he always kept people at arm's length. Liked control, hated unpredictability. Had a tight circle in the Valley, but mostly transactional. Networking. Business. If there was anything deeper, like blackmail, coercion, or emotional leverage, I haven't found it yet."

"Keep digging," Foster said. "Someone had to know what he was really up to. And they either killed him for it, or tried to stop it from coming out."

Harper pulled out his notebook. "I ran the plate from the car our killer used last night. It was a rental, registered to a Caroline Winder out of Tigard."

"Give her a call. Let's see what she has to say about it," Foster said.

"Already done," Harper said. "She rented it yesterday. Said she got a text message with instructions: Rent the car, drop it off at the Walmart near her house. Two grand was wired to her as payment."

Cho raised an eyebrow. "What about cameras at Walmart?"

Harper shook his head. "It was parked too far from the entrance. No usable footage."

He paused, flipping to a fresh page in his notebook.

"We need to hit Grant Technologies," he said. "Both Grant and Whitaker's offices. Servers, internal emails, file archives, personal desks, the whole thing."

"You'll need a warrant," Foster said.

"Already on it," Harper replied. "I should have the affidavit ready in a few hours."

"Great. Let me know when you've got it. We'll split up the work."

Harper walked out to the hallway outside the bullpen, a fresh cup of coffee warming his hand, eyes locked on the whiteboard filled with faces and red-threaded connections. Dunham. The name felt like a poison slowly spreading back through his life.

No matter how far he'd come, how much he'd rebuilt, it felt like Blackridge kept dragging him back.

A ghost from his past was moving in the dark, and people were dying.

And now, that ghost had a name.

• • • • •

CHAPTER 15: ECHOES OF THE OATH

Then.

The conversation had been short, direct, and full of opportunity.

"I'm serious, Jake," Briggs said. "Stonehaven PD's hiring laterals. You've still got a valid certification for another year, and I've already talked to the chief. He wants to meet you."

Harper almost laughed. "You serious?"

"Dead serious. You've put in the work, man. You've earned this shot."

Briggs went on to explain that the chief was no stranger to what had happened in Blackridge. "He knows the score. And he doesn't hold it against you. Said something about how we don't leave good cops out in the cold just because someone else dropped the ball."

The words lit a fire in Harper's chest. He hung up and paced the room, palms sweating, heart pounding with something dangerously close to hope.

But before he could let himself believe it, he had to do one thing.

He had to talk to Alyssa.

That night, he and Alyssa sat down to talk, and he filled her in on the conversation with Briggs.

"The Chief wants to meet me tomorrow. Sounds promising," Harper said.

Alyssa had been quiet for a moment on the other end of the line.

"Jake," she said carefully, "this isn't small."

"I know. That's why I need you on board with it. If this works, if Stonehaven really is different, I could get my life back. The life I was meant to have. But if it costs us what we've built..." His voice faltered. "Then it's not worth it."

"I need to think about it," she had said. "But I'm glad you told me."

The next day, Alyssa told Harper to put his application in and meet with the Chief.

"I'm not saying yes," she had told him. "I'm saying, let's see where this conversation goes."

•••••

Harper arrived at Stonehaven PD early the next morning, dressed in a charcoal-gray suit and polished shoes, his best attempt at making a good impression without overplaying it. His tie felt tight around the collar, but he didn't loosen it. He wanted to look serious. Sharp. Ready. The station was modest, older brick exterior, tidy landscaping out front, a flag rippling in the wind. It didn't look like a department hiding rot in the walls. It looked functional. Solid.

The Chief's office was just off the main lobby, and he was shown in by a cheerful community service officer who couldn't have been older than twenty-two. Chief Merrick stood as Harper entered. Early fifties, barrel-chested with a trim salt-and-pepper beard, Merrick exuded quiet authority. He offered a firm handshake and gestured toward the seat across from his desk.

"Jacob Harper," he said. "Glad you came in. Detective Briggs's been singing your praises for weeks."

Harper smiled faintly. "Yeah, he's persistent."

Merrick chuckled. "And not wrong. Have a seat. You want coffee?"

"I'm good, thank you."

The Chief eased back into his chair, folding his hands on the desk. "Let's talk about the elephant in the room. Blackridge County."

Harper's posture stiffened slightly, but he gave a quiet nod.

"I've reviewed the reports, what's public, what's internal. I've talked to people at DPSST, and I've talked to people who worked with you *after* all that happened." He leaned forward slightly. "Let me say something plainly, so there's no guesswork: I know you got screwed."

Harper blinked.

"I don't know all the politics of Blackridge, and frankly, I don't want to. But I know what happens when the wrong people get a badge and a title. I also know what it looks like when a good cop gets caught in the gears. And Harper, it looks a lot like your story."

The Chief let that hang in the air for a moment, then leaned back in his chair again.

"Stonehaven isn't Blackridge. We're not perfect, but we take pride in what we do. We serve this community with integrity, not intimidation. Our officers are expected to be firm but fair. Smart, not just tough. And we've got each other's backs, as long as you're doing the job the right way."

Harper nodded slowly, unsure if the warmth in his chest was relief or disbelief.

"We've got a spot open," Merrick continued. "Lateral hire. You'd be on a shortened probation, but with your certification still valid, we can get you through field training quickly. Get you back in a cruiser where you belong."

Harper exhaled through his nose. "It sounds good. Better than I ever expected, honestly."

Merrick tilted his head. "But?"

Harper looked him in the eye. "But I need to talk to Alyssa. I already lost one relationship after all of this fell apart the first time. If I'm going back into law enforcement, I need her with me. All the way."

Merrick gave a knowing nod. "Smart man."

He reached for a notepad, scribbled something down, and tore off the sheet.

"Here's my direct number. If you want, I'll call the both of you tonight. Answer any questions she's got. Hell, she can grill me for an hour if that helps."

Harper cracked a smile. "You might regret that offer."

"I've been married thirty years. I've been grilled by the best," Merrick said with a wink.

Harper stood and shook the Chief's hand again, this time with a bit more confidence.

"I'll talk to her tonight."

"Good," Merrick said. "We don't eat our own here, Harper. If you're ready, we'd be lucky to have you."

•••••

That evening, Harper and Alyssa sat on the couch, her legs tucked beneath her, his nerves bundled tight in his chest. Their kids were down early for once, and the condo was unusually quiet. When the call came, Harper put it on speaker and set the phone on the coffee table between them.

Chief Merrick's voice came through steady, easy. Not polished like a politician, but clear and honest. He greeted them both warmly, thanked Alyssa for taking the time to talk, and jumped straight into what mattered.

He told her about the culture at Stonehaven PD, that their mission was to serve with compassion, not bravado. That they valued trust and teamwork, not ego and intimidation. He said the badge still meant something there, and they didn't throw their people under the bus to cover for poor leadership or politics.

"We don't chew up our own and spit them out," he said. "That's not who we are."

Alyssa had listened quietly at first, arms crossed, her face unreadable. But as Merrick continued talking about the kind of cop Jake was said to be, the kind of heart he brought to the job, something in her softened.

"I've heard what happened in Blackridge," Merrick said. "And from where I'm sitting, Jake didn't fail. He got failed. And I believe in second chances when someone's earned it."

Alyssa met Harper's eyes. Her hand found his, fingers weaving together.

When Merrick wrapped up—promising transparency, mentorship, and a fair shot—Alyssa thanked him. And then, once the call ended, she turned fully to Harper.

"I'm in," she said. "Let's do it. We give it a year. If it doesn't feel right, we walk away. But at least then, you'll know. You won't spend the rest of your life wondering."

Harper nodded, heart pounding, but lighter than it had felt in years. "Yeah," he said. "A year."

• • • • •

What followed felt like something out of a dream, one Harper hadn't dared allow himself for years.

The day he was sworn in at Stonehaven PD was overcast, but the light inside the department was warm. Jake Harper stood in front, dressed in a sharp navy-blue uniform and freshly shined dress shoes. His tie felt snug, his palms damp with nerves he hadn't felt since his first day at the academy. But this was different. This wasn't the start of something new.

It was a return.

Chief Merrick stood beside him, flanked by several command staff and officers in uniform. Rows of uniformed officers sat in folding chairs facing them, along with a scattering of family members and city officials.

Harper's heart thudded as his name was called.

"Officer Jacob Harper," Merrick said, loud enough to carry to the back of the room. "Please step forward."

Harper did, shoulders squared.

Merrick smiled and offered him a small nod as he raised his right hand and took the oath.

"To protect and serve the people of Stonehaven, to uphold the law with integrity and fairness…"

Harper repeated each line, voice steady.

When the oath was finished, Merrick turned to the crowd. "Officer Harper is coming to us as a lateral hire. After a few short weeks with his FTOs to knock the rust off, he'll be hitting the streets. For now, let's welcome the newest official member of the Stonehaven Police Department!"

There was applause as Alyssa stood from the front row, a small box in her hand.

With pride in her eyes and a knowing smile, she stepped forward, pinned the silver badge to his uniformed chest, and whispered, "I'm proud of you."

That moment—the badge, the applause, Alyssa's smile—marked the beginning of something Harper had nearly given up on.

• • • • •

The next ten weeks came fast.

Harper was paired with three different Field Training Officers, each with their own style, quirks, and expectations. The first, Officer Baird, was all by-the-book and stone-faced. The second, Officer Nguyen, had a dry sense of humor and sharp instincts. The last, Officer Thompson, had a relaxed demeanor but didn't let anything slide.

Harper kept his head down. Said little. He wasn't there to prove anything. Just to earn trust. To show he belonged again.

He ran traffic stops, responded to domestic calls, cleared buildings in alarm responses. It all came back quickly. The radio chatter, the mental calculus, the unspoken rhythm of the street. His FTOs wrote glowing evaluations: sharp instincts, great communication, solid officer presence.

They released him early from training. Solo patrol. A marked car, a call sign, and the beat.

It wasn't glamorous. But it felt right.

•••••

Harper worked swing shifts and graveyards, weekends and holidays. He didn't complain. He made arrests, broke up bar fights, calmed crying kids in the back of squad cars. He wrote good reports, backed up his partners, and made friends fast.

He began to enjoy it again. The unpredictability. The small wins, helping someone, solving something, being useful.

Then came the break that would define his early years.

A string of vehicle thefts hit the city. Nothing new, until one night, a Stonehaven police captain's personal truck vanished from his driveway.

The department was suddenly paying attention.

Harper poured over similar theft reports, digging through CAD logs and surveillance footage. He noticed a pattern: out-of-town plates, one particular neighborhood used as a staging area, and security footage of one suspect checking door handles.

He brought it to his sergeant, then to detectives.

He worked with officers in Vancouver, Washington, and helped connect the thefts to a car-theft ring with white supremacist ties. His name ended up on joint reports with multiple jurisdictions.

Weeks later, the suspects were in custody.

The officers found the captain's truck with only minor damage.

And Harper, standing before the whole department at the annual awards banquet, was awarded a meritorious service commendation by Chief Merrick.

• • • • •

CHAPTER 16: CROSSED WIRES

Now.

Harper and the team arrived at Grant Technologies just before 3pm. As they exited their vehicles, they moved briskly toward the main entrance, four uniformed patrol officers trailing behind the detectives in a tight wedge.

Inside the sleek glass lobby, several burly security guards moved to intercept them. Military tattoos. Muscle-first posture. The type who didn't ask a lot of questions.

"Stonehaven PD. We have a search warrant," Harper said, holding it up.

"Private property," one of the guards replied, stepping into Harper's path. "Mister Whitaker told us not to let any cops in anymore."

"Whitaker is dead," Harper said flatly, slapping the copy of the warrant into the man's chest and sidestepping him.

The guard moved again, blocking his path, this time grabbing Harper's left arm, tight and forceful.

"Still can't let you in, hoss—"

He didn't finish the sentence.

Instead of pulling away, like the guard clearly expected, Harper surged forward, shifting his weight into the man's center mass. He ducked low, driving his shoulder into the guard's beltline while sweeping behind his knees in one clean, practiced motion. The man's grip faltered as he stumbled backward and slammed onto the polished stone floor with a dull *thud*.

Harper came up quick, gun drawn.

The other guards reached for their sidearms, until they saw the rest of the room.

Hurst. Cho. Foster. And four patrol officers, weapons already drawn and steady.

"I'd suggest a different course of action," Harper said, voice calm but firm. "Unless you want to join your buddy in lockup for obstruction."

The guards froze, then slowly raised their hands.

"Cuff him," Harper said, nodding to the downed man.

Officer Garcia stepped forward, secured the guard in cuffs, and escorted him out. The remaining guards were quickly disarmed and led outside without further incident.

The detectives moved down the executive hallway, past Holly Blanchard's empty desk. The space was sterile and sleek, quiet in a way that felt loaded, like the calm before a storm.

As they neared the executive suites, Harper stopped.

"Sarge, take Whitaker's office. I'll handle Grant's. Hurst, get into their servers. I want everything. Emails, archived files, project folders, start pulling it all."

He turned to the patrol officers behind them.

"Clear the floor. Make sure no one's touching their computers. No phones. No one calling in a remote wipe. Get every employee into a conference room and keep them there."

Then, to Cho: "Start taking statements. Full names, phone numbers, personal emails. Anyone acting nervous, I want flagged."

Assignments given, the team nodded and split off, each moving with purpose.

The search was on.

●●●●●

Harper moved through Grant's office with practiced precision.

It was a lesson in luxury, every detail curated to convey power. A broad mahogany desk anchored the room, paired with a plush leather chair built for long hours and absolute comfort. In the center of the office sat a polished hardwood conference table surrounded by deep, upholstered chairs that probably cost more than his first patrol car. On a sideboard, a crystal decanter and matching glasses glinted beside a half-empty bottle of Pappy Van Winkle.

Just like the command center at the cabin, this office was made for a man used to control. Used to being the one in the room who made the decisions.

Above the desk, multiple high-resolution monitors were mounted in a sleek vertical array. A printed appointment calendar lay open on the corner, paper-thin and color-coded. Harper's eyes landed on a date circled in red ink: *April 14th.* Next week.

He flipped through drawers, checked the bookshelf, ran his fingers along the molding. Nothing obvious. No documents, no hidden compartments, no encrypted drives taped to the underside of furniture. Just the calendar. He made a note and moved on.

Whitaker's office was a different beast.

The moment Harper stepped inside, he was struck by the flash. Where Grant's space spoke of influence, Whitaker's screamed wealth. Shiny surfaces. Statement furniture. The floor was padded with an imported rug so thick it muffled his steps. A scale model of a Maserati gleamed atop a floating shelf, lit by a subtle LED glow.

Foster was crouched at the desk, working the lock on a drawer with his folding knife. The tumblers of a cheap desk lock gave way with a soft *pop.*

The Sergeant didn't hesitate. He pulled the drawer open and began sorting through its contents with methodical efficiency. A bottle of high-end scotch. A couple of glass tumblers. Harper watched him set them aside, then rap his knuckles against the drawer's base.

Thunk.

Foster paused and looked up, raising an eyebrow.

Harper smirked. "How cliché."

With a quick twist of the blade, Foster pried loose the false bottom. Beneath it sat a slim thumb drive, a neat stack of hundred-dollar bills, and a snub-nosed .38 revolver.

Harper let out a slow breath. "Well. That's not nothing."

• • • • •

A few hours later, the team was back at headquarters, gathered in the briefing room as they compared notes.

Cho went first. "I interviewed everyone I could. Most of the employees still in the building were programmers, IT, and sales staff. Not exactly high-level access. There was one exec from HR, a mid-level guy. Said he didn't know anything either. Claimed the private security showed up a few days ago, right after Harper came in to interview Whitaker. Whitaker told them it was a precaution after Grant's murder. Tensions have been high ever since."

Hurst picked up next. "I got into their internal servers. It'll take time to comb through everything, but I'm running keyword filters now. So far, it lines up with what Cho got from the staff. Most of the people at Grant Tech were in the dark. It's looking like this was a top-down operation between Grant and Whitaker."

Harper leaned forward. "What about their emails? Files? Anything beyond what we already found?"

Hurst shook her head. "So far, everything looks scrubbed. No smoking guns in the inbox. But I did find a draft press release, it teased some kind of announcement, big shift coming. The usual PR fluff. Said the company was on the verge of a 'new era' that would redefine their legacy. But no details."

"Speaking of legacy, where are we on the hard drive?" Harper asked.

Hurst leaned back, rubbing at her temples. "Still locked out," she muttered. "Grant's encryption is no joke. I've got another brute-force cycle running, but we're easily looking at another day. Maybe more."

Harper exhaled, frustration tugging at the edge of his voice. "Keep at it. That drive holds secrets someone was willing to kill for."

Hurst gave a slow nod, then added, "I did hear back from OSP about the boots. Turns out they don't exactly keep a database of officer shoe sizes. Big surprise. So unless your contact came through…"

"They did," Harper said. "My guy at CGIS pulled Dunham's military jacket. He left the Marine Corps as a sergeant, medical discharge after combat in Iraq. Not a lot of detail, but there was an NJP in his record. Something about beating a detainee half to death during an interrogation. Other than that, clean file."

Foster raised an eyebrow. "Sounds about right."

Harper continued, "He confirmed Dunham's boot size, ten and a half. Same as the impressions from all three scenes."

They let the weight of that settle before shifting gears.

Harper and Foster laid out what they'd found in Whitaker's office.

"The gun came back clean," Foster said. "But the thumb drive…that's where things got interesting."

He looked to Harper to finish.

"It had backup plans," Harper said. "New identities for Whitaker and his wife. A list of non-extradition countries. And contact info for private jet charter services. Our guy wasn't just thinking about running, he had the exit route mapped and ready."

"What about Whitaker's burner?"

"A lot of calls to and from a number with a Blackridge area code," Cho said. "Problem is, that number's also a burner. No subscriber data, no billing records. Could've been anyone."

"Any pattern to the calls?" Foster asked.

"Mostly short," Cho replied. "Some just a few seconds. Almost like check-ins."

Harper leaned forward, eyes narrowing. "Anyone call that number after Whitaker was killed?"

Cho flipped through his notes. "Nope. But there was one missed call, about fifteen minutes before he was shot."

The room went still.

Harper processed it quickly. "So, five minutes before the rental car picked him up at the house."

He glanced at Foster, then back to Cho.

"That's not a coincidence," Harper said. "That's the setup. Dunham was arranging the meet before he pulled the trigger."

"Where are we on the financials?" Foster asked.

Harper opened his mouth to respond, but was interrupted by the soft *ping* of his inbox.

He glanced at the screen.

An unread email sat at the top. From Bryan Sloan at Stone River Financial. The subject line was short, direct:

Subject: *Requested Records (Secure Download Link)*

"Speaking of," Harper said, sitting down to read it.

Harper clicked into the email, quickly scanning Bryan's brief message:

Jake,

Got everything you requested. You were right— this one smells off. Secure link below. Let me know if you need anything else.

Stay safe,

Bryan

Harper opened the encrypted link, swiftly authenticating through the bank's secure portal. A compressed folder downloaded within seconds. His pulse quickened as he extracted the files, a cascade of documents flooding his desktop: financial records, wire transfer statements, and bank ledgers. A digital labyrinth of data demanding to be unraveled.

Patterns emerged swiftly.

Large, structured money transfers moved steadily from Grant's various shell corporations. Entities cloaked behind vague, meaningless names like Eagle and Talon, Thornewood Holdings, and Redhaven Global. Transactions bounced through multiple intermediary banks, weaving offshore to carefully conceal their origins. Yet beneath the web of obfuscation, Harper's practiced eye immediately recognized a familiar signature.

Money laundering. Textbook operations.

As he traced each transaction meticulously, Harper discovered unmistakable financial footprints leading directly to John Dunham. Withdrawals timed perfectly with deposits into accounts indirectly linked to the undersheriff. Dunham had been careful, but not careful enough. His involvement, hidden beneath layers of shell companies, offshore accounts, and falsified invoices, was now becoming clear.

Then there were the cash transactions, consistent deposits hovering just beneath the ten-thousand-dollar threshold, strategically placed to avoid triggering mandatory Currency Transaction Reports to federal authorities. Harper recognized the tactic immediately: structuring. Such a steady volume of structured cash deposits, laundered carefully through wire transfers and shell corporations, typically indicated serious organized crime. Narcotics, human trafficking, or sex trafficking.

The deeper puzzle remained Alvarez.

Harper scoured each file for even the faintest trace of Blackridge County's commissioner. Yet Alvarez's name never appeared. No direct deposits, no overt payoffs. If Alvarez was involved—and Harper was certain he was—the commissioner had insulated himself well, layering deception upon deception to stay beyond direct reach.

Frustration tightened Harper's muscles, his jaw clenching as he leaned back in his chair. Alvarez was smart. Methodical. Financial records alone wouldn't bring him down. Harper exhaled slowly, refocusing on what he could confirm without question.

His eyes returned to the compound in Blackridge County. Satellite images accompanying the files displayed significant activity: expensive vehicles, a heavily guarded perimeter, and a large, newly constructed facility whose purpose remained obscured. Harper zoomed in, unease churning in his gut. Whatever was happening out there carried Grant's fingerprints, and Dunham appeared to be the enforcer. But what exactly were they manufacturing—or hiding—within that secluded compound?

Hours later, his eyes stinging from poring over hundreds of transactions, Harper stood, stretching until his back cracked audibly.

Foster glanced over, silently awaiting an update.

"Money's flowing heavily through Thornewood and Eagle and Talon," Harper began, voice weary but firm. "Dunham's fingerprints are all over it."

Foster approached, eyes scanning highlighted sections of Harper's monitor. "So how does Grant fit into all of this?"

"Grant wasn't just financing whatever they're doing in Blackridge, he was actively involved. And whatever's happening out there is big enough that someone's willing to kill anyone who even starts sniffing around."

Foster folded his arms, jaw tightening. "Any idea what they're doing there?"

Harper exhaled slowly, shaking his head. "Not yet. But considering the volume of structured cash transactions being funneled through these shells, my guess is narcotics or human trafficking, or both. Dunham's role is clear. Alvarez, though...he's still insulated, untouchable. If he's pulling the strings, he's smart enough to do it through layers of proxies."

Cho, who had been quietly reviewing surveillance footage nearby, finally spoke. "So what's our next move?"

Harper tapped his pen against the desk thoughtfully. "We need eyes on that compound. We need solid, undeniable evidence linking Dunham directly to criminal activity."

Foster raised a skeptical eyebrow. "You thinking surveillance?"

"I've done plenty of covert surveillance at the insurance company," Harper replied.

Foster shook his head, caution evident. "This isn't catching someone faking a slip-and-fall for an insurance payout, Jake. It's a highly guarded compound in isolated territory."

Harper met Foster's gaze steadily. "Sergeant, I trained in SERE and counter-surveillance operations with MSRT. Sneaking into remote terrain to observe hostile targets isn't exactly new ground for me."

Foster rubbed the bridge of his nose, clearly weighing the risks. "We've already got two bodies, plus that shooting in Welches. Another incident, especially outside our jurisdiction, won't help. You got anyone out there you trust?"

"Not exactly," Harper admitted. Then a slight smile formed on his lips. "But we do have federal resources we can leverage. Homeland Security might be interested, especially once they hear about the money laundering and potential human trafficking angles." He thought immediately of Austin Briggs, his former colleague who had transitioned from Stonehaven PD to a Special Agent position with Homeland Security.

Foster's shoulders relaxed slightly. "Good. Loop him in, keep me informed." After a pause, he gave Harper an approving nod. "And Harper? Get some sleep. Good work."

Harper exhaled slowly, determination settling back into place. "Justice doesn't sleep. Neither do we."

Foster met his eyes, silent understanding passing between them. "Right is right."

Harper nodded, voice steady. "No matter the cost."

• • • • •

Harper drove home, exhausted. It had been a hell of a day.

He came in through the garage, kicked off his bloodstained Chucks, and headed straight to the laundry room. Without hesitation, he stripped down and threw everything into the wash. The hot shower that followed helped wash away the grime, and the memories.

Whitaker's murder.

Telling his widow he wasn't coming home.

Tomorrow's mission.

Afterward, he threw on an old T-shirt and sweatpants and walked into the living room, where Alyssa was playing with their daughter, Adelyn.

"Daddy!" Addie squealed, running toward him with her arms wide open.

Harper scooped her up and spun her around, holding her close. It was moments like these that reminded him why he did what he did, why it all mattered.

After putting Adelyn down, Alyssa was waiting.

"Hey, sexy," she said with a smile, then kissed him.

"Hey, beautiful," he whispered, giving her ass a quick squeeze.

Addie, oblivious, was already glued to a cartoon about a talking dog.

Harper and Alyssa moved into the kitchen and made dinner together. They sat down as a family, pasta and garlic bread for the grown-ups, mac and cheese for Adelyn. Laughter echoed through the house as their daughter got cheese sauce in her blond curls.

Later, after giving Addie a bath and putting her to bed, Harper and Alyssa curled up on the couch to catch up.

"How are you, stranger?" she asked.

"I know. It's been a lot lately," he said.

"I'm just teasing," she said gently. "But seriously…are you okay? I'm guessing today was a lot."

She always knew. She always saw through the armor.

Harper nodded. "It was."

He filled her in, broad strokes, skipping the bloodier parts. She already knew about the murder; he'd called earlier, a habit he'd kept from his patrol days to spare her from finding out on the news. But now, he shared the deeper threads. Whitaker's murder, the surveillance, the searches of the house and Grant Industries. The ties to Blackridge. To Dunham. And the plan to surveil the compound with Briggs in the morning.

"I don't like this," she said quietly. "He already tried to kill you… after getting you fired… and now you're going back there."

"I know," Harper said. "But I've got to see this through. I have to put this case to bed."

Alyssa sighed, the kind of sigh that came from love wrapped in worry. She knew her husband too well. Once he latched onto something, he didn't let go.

"Just… please be careful," she said. "I need you to come home to us. I don't know what we'd do without you."

She leaned over and rested her head on his shoulder. They stayed like that for a while, silent, simply enjoying each other's company, the silence saying everything words couldn't. Just holding each other, sharing the stillness before the storm.

A few short hours from now, Harper would be on the road again.
Back to Blackridge.

• • • • •

CHAPTER 17: WHAT LIES BENEATH

The following morning, Harper stood beside Special Agent Austin Briggs in front of a long table cluttered with surveillance equipment, maps, laptops, and tactical gear. Three other Homeland Security Special Agents gathered around them, listening carefully as Harper walked them through the latest developments.

Briggs and the special agents assembled before him were an eclectic crew. One agent leaned casually against the wall, arms crossed, eyes alert but relaxed. Another checked each piece of gear with practiced efficiency, her movements precise and unhurried. Harper recognized the quiet professionalism, reminiscent of his own team back in Stonehaven. Except here, federal funding showed in the sleek fleet of unmarked vehicles parked outside, the cutting-edge surveillance drones, and high-powered optics spread across the briefing room table. The team was clearly accustomed to difficult, complex operations.

After concluding the briefing, Briggs placed a reassuring hand on Harper's shoulder. "We'll take my ride, Jake. That car of yours screams 'cop' from a mile away. No offense"

"None taken," Harper said. "But you've gotta admit, the Durango is pretty slick."

Briggs chuckled and rolled his eyes. "Come on, get in the van," he said, giving Harper a playful shove toward the exit.

Outside, Harper took in the impressive sight of their convoy. At the center was a nondescript gray minivan, followed closely by a dark SUV brimming with equipment. As Harper climbed into the van, his fingers flexed unconsciously, adrenaline already beginning to buzz beneath his skin. He felt his pulse quicken slightly, breath deepening as muscle memory began to take over, his senses sharpening for the operation ahead.

The drive east to Blackridge County took nearly three hours, winding through the deepening shadows of Oregon's dense forests. During the ride, Harper spoke quietly, his gaze steady and distant as he recounted the twisted paths of the investigation. Occasionally, Briggs glanced over, eyebrows furrowing slightly, his jaw tightening as he absorbed the details. Connections between Grant, Dunham, Alvarez, and the dark, insidious threads that reached back to Blackridge County and the false allegations that had nearly destroyed his life.

When Harper finally finished recounting the tangled web, Briggs blew out a long breath. "Damn, Jake. This goes deeper than I thought."

Harper leaned back against the headrest, eyes sharp and focused. "Every time I think I've reached the bottom, there's another level. More bodies, more lies. We need eyes on whatever they're hiding in that compound. It's the only way we'll get ahead of this thing."

Nightfall had descended by the time they reached a secluded rock quarry, a natural staging point miles away from their target. The vehicles pulled into the gravelly clearing, headlights flickering briefly before shutting off, plunging them into darkness.

The team reassembled at the rear of the van, gearing up under the dim glow of red tactical lights. Harper donned camouflage fatigues—his personal set from his days at the Coast Guard MSRT—paired with a plate carrier marked with low profile federal patches provided by HSI. He moved with ease, fingers gliding along buckles and straps. The worn fabric settled around him, bringing with it memories of countless missions past. He secured his duty rifle, checking optics and magazines with steady hands, muscle memory guiding every motion. And lastly, a camera fitted with a long range lens.

"Back in your element, huh?" Briggs remarked quietly, watching Harper from the corner of his eye as he adjusted his own gear, a low-profile carrier over a dark tactical shirt, an FBI-style windbreaker packed neatly into his bag, just in case official identification was needed.

"Like riding a bike," Harper replied dryly, fastening his helmet and carefully mounting the night vision goggles Briggs had handed him. As he powered them up, the darkness became illuminated in green clarity, his vision sharpening in the monochromatic glow.

Nearby, other agents strapped on their own gear. Plate carriers, tactical helmets fitted with night vision, and compact rifles that gleamed matte black in the pale glow. Radio checks echoed softly in the dark, calm and professional. A sleek surveillance drone, black and silent as death itself, sat ready for deployment in its rugged transport case.

After final preparations, Briggs gathered them once more around a laminated topographical map illuminated by muted red penlights. His voice was low and steady, radiating confidence and control.

"Alright, listen closely. We leave the vehicles here and move in quietly on foot. We'll hike in a few miles through thick cover to this position," he indicated a marked spot at the edge of Bureau of Land Management property, barely outside the perimeter of the compound. "The terrain's uneven, so stay quiet and move slow. From here on out, we go fully dark. NVGs only, no flashlights. I don't want to give them any reason to think we're out there."

Harper nodded in agreement, familiar with the tactics from his military counter-drug operations. He breathed steadily, feeling that comforting shift deep within, instincts honed through years of training taking hold.

"Any questions?" Briggs asked, scanning the group.

When none came, he nodded decisively. "Let's move out."

They set off in disciplined silence, melting into the trees. Harper quickly found his rhythm. Quiet steps, deliberate movements, and instincts tuned to the sounds of the forest around him. Leaves rustled softly beneath cautious steps, the earthy scent of damp pine filling his nostrils as he navigated carefully through dense brush. His eyes swept the shadows, each movement measured and silent. The cool night air, tinged with the scent of pine and damp earth, brought memories rushing back: long nights spent waiting, watching, hunting unseen threats in darkness just like this.

Despite everything that had led him here—the twisted paths, betrayals, false accusations—Harper felt a familiar calm descend as he moved deeper into the forest. He was exactly where he belonged, back in his element, ready to uncover the hidden truth beneath layers of shadows and deceit.

●　●　●　●　●

Then.

The cool, pre-dawn air carried the tang of salt and fuel during the mission brief, delivered swiftly and concisely by Lieutenant Commander Kyle Hirsch, the cutter's XO, whose personality was as focused and no-nonsense as the orders he gave. The team was assembled quietly on the forecastle—pronounced "focsle"—of the USCGC *Active* (WMEC 618), a 210-foot medium endurance cutter whose fifty-year history was rich with missions exactly like this.

They felt the cutter rocking gently beneath their feet as it moved slowly through the seas. The *Active* had been holding station near the Strait of Malacca for nearly two weeks of a month-long patrol through Southeast Asian waters. The MSRT unit had arrived via helicopter from Indonesia the previous day after the hijacking situation aboard the Maersk *Texas*, a 350-foot oil tanker, had escalated dramatically. Pirates had seized the tanker in the early hours the previous morning, their original intention likely to steal its oil, blend it with legitimate cargo, and sell it illegally in Singapore.

"We believe the pirates are affiliated with an Indonesian criminal syndicate," Lieutenant Commander Hirsch said, his voice crisp in the pre-dawn quiet. "Initially, their goal was straightforward oil theft. Bunkering."

Maritime Enforcement Specialist Second Class Harper nodded to himself, recognizing the terminology from countless training exercises back stateside.

"The situation deteriorated overnight," Hirsch continued. "Intel confirms one crew member was killed after attempting resistance. This is now a hostage scenario, and we anticipate further escalation unless we intervene swiftly."

Hirsch paused, surveying the determined faces around him. "The small boat launches at 0330, aiming to reach the *Texas* no later than 0415." He turned toward Boatswain's Mate Second Class Cross and nodded for him to continue the brief.

Cross stepped forward confidently. As the small boat coxswain, he had operational control of the approach. "We'll run dark, no lights, approaching from astern to mask our approach behind the tanker's engines. Once alongside, there's a Jacob's ladder left hanging off the stern by the pirates. Harper, you're point. Get onboard first and secure the area, then we move silently."

Twenty minutes later, the small boat sliced swiftly and quietly across the waves. Cross was calm, steering expertly, glancing occasionally at Harper in silent communication. As they closed in on the massive hull of the Maersk Texas, Harper steadied himself, drawing on muscle memory from countless boarding drills and operations.

With precise timing, Cross maneuvered the small boat alongside the towering stern. Harper reached out for the Jacob's ladder, the rough fibers biting into his gloved hand. The ladder swung briefly as he grabbed it, muscles straining as he felt the boat fall away beneath him. Harper pulled himself upward, his breath coming quick but controlled, pulse hammering against his throat, the sea spray stinging his skin as he climbed swiftly over the tanker's railing.

Vaulting quietly onto the Maersk *Texas*, Harper brought his M4 smoothly up, eyes sharp behind his NVGs. He immediately pivoted aside, weapon raised, eyes scanning sharply across the deck's shadowed corners as GM2 Matthews and BM3 Cronkite surged silently over the rail, seamlessly forming their practiced tactical wedge. Harper signaled forward, the trio advancing with practiced precision, their NVGs painting the deck in shades of ghostly green as they advanced carefully toward the crew quarters.

Within moments, Harper's gaze landed on the pirate, a thin, weary-looking man, slumped unconscious in his chair with a battered AK-47 cradled carelessly. He sliced his hand downward sharply. Matthews lunged smoothly, seizing the pirate's weapon with one hand, pressing the man's head firmly backward with the other, his palm muffling the started man's mouth. Harper stepped forward simultaneously, pressing the cold muzzle of his carbine firmly against the pirate's forehead.

"Quiet," Harper growled, voice low and fierce. "Don't move." The pirate's eyes snapped open wide, startled terror clear even without a shared language. Matthews secured him quickly, muffling any potential outcry. Harper held up a single finger. *One down, four to go.*

He pointed to the door to the crew quarters. Matthews took position at the door handle, Harper prepared to breach, while BM3 Cronkite moved behind him, giving Harper's shoulder a reassuring squeeze to signal readiness.

He exchanged a quick, confirming nod with Matthews, muscles coiled in readiness. The door swung open suddenly, and Harper swept inside, heartbeat roaring in his ears as he swept right. Harper kept his finger tight along the trigger guard, vision sharp and clear through the night vision glow. Cronkite mirrored him, moving fluidly to the left.

Two pirates stared dumbly, one half-asleep, the other caught off guard. Rifles dropped immediately, clattering noisily to the metal floor as the crew hostages looked up, eyes wide with desperate hope. Harper exhaled sharply, quickly signaling the hostages to silence as they secured the pirates with crisp, practiced efficiency.

Too easy, Harper thought, briefly wary.

The relieved crew members eagerly helped secure their captors with flex cuffs. An officer wearing shoulder boards spoke urgently to Harper in heavily accented English, likely Spanish.

"The captain and XO, they're on the bridge," the officer said quickly. "Two more pirates there. Smarter, more dangerous."

Harper nodded, activated his helmet mic, and radioed Cross. "Cajun Actual, Cajun One. Crew quarters secure, three tangos down. Moving to bridge to secure remaining hostages, over."

"Roger, Cajun One," Cross's reply came sharply. "Proceed with caution. Out."

Cronkite remained behind, guarding the crew and prisoners, as Harper and Matthews pressed onward through the tanker's dark passageways, NVGs back down, carbines at the ready. Approaching the bridge, raised voices carried through the metal corridors. Harper paused at the staircase, listening carefully, then moved stealthily upward.

Moments later, at the staircase to the bridge, Harper paused, listening intently as raised voices pierced through the tanker's metallic hull. He breathed slowly, deliberately, centering himself. Adrenaline surged through him, sharpening senses to a razor's edge. Through the bridge door's window, Harper assessed the scene: the XO at the helm, watched closely by one pirate. The captain, standing tense and defiant, argued with a second pirate, clearly the leader.

"They won't give you anything more," the captain insisted desperately.

"Then you die!" the pirate leader shouted, raising his rifle aggressively.

"GO GO GO!"

Adrenaline surged through Harper's veins as he drove his boot into the bridge door. It burst inward with a metallic crash. "U.S. Coast Guard!" he shouted, rifle up, finger ready, Matthews close behind.

One pirate stood over the ship's captain, rifle raised, but the slamming door pulled his attention. He turned his head, just for a second.

In that second, the captain lunged and grabbed the pirate's AK47.

The two men grappled, twisting toward the bulkhead. Harper tracked the chaos, but there was no clear shot. He surged forward, closed the distance, and brought the barrel of his rifle into the pirate's nose with brutal force. Bone crunched and blood sprayed as the man collapsed.

Matthews barked commands to the second pirate, whose hands immediately shot upward, weapon clattering harmlessly to the deck.

Harper keyed his mic, voice calm despite the pounding in his chest. "Cajun Actual, Cajun One. All tangos secured, hostages safe. Ship secure, over."

Cross's voice came through clearly, pride evident beneath professional composure. "Good copy, Cajun One. Mission accomplished. Stand by for additional support. Out."

Harper exchanged a brief nod with Matthews, a sense of accomplishment passing silently between them. *Mission accomplished.*

• • • • •

CHAPTER 18: IN THE CROSSHAIRS

Now.

The two-mile hike was slow going, winding uphill through dense woods. Sweat soaked into Harper's combat shirt, sticking the fabric to his back and chest. Yet, despite the exertion, his breathing remained steady, controlled, and even, thanks to the rigorous daily regimen he maintained. Years of relentless running, weight training, and discipline had honed him into prime shape, fit and ready for duty.

As Harper, Briggs, and the Homeland Security agents arrived at their surveillance point—a densely wooded hillside overlooking the compound—the team moved swiftly and silently into prearranged positions. Most of the agents fanned out, blending seamlessly into the darkness to establish defensive perimeters against potential ambushes. Harper and Briggs took point, creeping forward to a concealed vantage point nestled between thick brush and low-hanging branches.

Through the soft green illumination of his NVGs, Harper's breath hitched at the clear sight of the compound unfolding below. Razor wire snaked along the perimeter fence, glittering faintly under infrared vision. Armed guards stood attentive at the only two entry gates, weapons slung casually but clearly ready. Even from this distance, Harper could discern their alert, practiced posture.

In the center of the clearing stood the building itself, a large, starkly utilitarian structure that radiated quiet menace. Expensive vehicles gleamed under moonlight, clearly visible even in monochrome night vision: a sleek Maserati, a flamboyant Lamborghini, and multiple high-end SUVs and pickups customized with costly upgrades.

"We're not going to be able to get any closer with those guards," Briggs said.

"My thoughts exactly. That's why I brought this." Harper carefully removed the NVGs, switching smoothly to the specialized long-range camera he'd personally selected during his insurance surveillance days. The familiar weight of the lens brought a quiet comfort. Adjusting his focus meticulously, Harper began methodically capturing every license plate, every vehicle angle, and every face visible in the compound's faint security lighting.

Hours ticked by, marked by the quiet rustle of wind through branches and the occasional distant engine rumble. Vehicles drifted in and out intermittently, always expensive, always discreet. Harper silently cataloged every arrival and departure. He didn't recognize the faces, but their wealth was unmistakable. Tailored suits, designer sunglasses even in darkness, confident postures of people accustomed to power. Harper felt the tension coil tighter within him with each new image, sensing they were close, dangerously close, to unraveling the thread connecting this place to something far darker.

Then, just as the first faint threads of dawn began threatening the eastern horizon, a sleek black Tahoe emerged from the shadows, rolling to a stop near the main entrance. Harper's pulse quickened, fingers tightening reflexively around the camera grip as he zoomed in.

A driver emerged first. He was clean-cut, wearing a crisp suit that whispered discreet professionalism. He circled the vehicle briskly, opening the back door with practiced courtesy. Harper's heart skipped as he snapped several rapid-fire images.

The passenger stepped out, revealing a heavyset Latino man whose imposing figure was obvious despite the distance. His dark hair, salt-and-pepper with a matching mustache and neatly trimmed goatee, glinted faintly beneath the compound lights. Glasses, an expensive tailored suit, and an unmistakable air of arrogant authority.

Harper's blood ran cold, recognition instant and visceral. His heart hammered in his chest. His fingers tightened instinctively on the camera, muscles locking rigidly for a brief, intense moment.

Alvarez.

He forced himself to remain steady, ignoring the adrenaline surging through him as he documented every detail. Alvarez's slow, swaggering stride toward the compound entrance, his expression casually self-important, suggested he felt invulnerable to consequence. Harper captured it all, ensuring there'd be no room for doubt. *Got you, fucker.*

"Alvarez is here," Harper whispered urgently to Briggs. "I've got clear visuals."

Beside him, Briggs stiffened, leaning closer. "You're sure?"

"One hundred percent," Harper replied, taking another careful series of shots as Alvarez disappeared inside. "We've got him."

They waited silently, muscles taut, nerves vibrating with anticipation, until Alvarez reappeared nearly an hour later. Alvarez walked casually back to the SUV, adjusting his suit jacket and leisurely tucking in his shirt, the casual air of a man who believed himself untouchable.

Harper photographed each movement, capturing Alvarez's smug confidence in crisp digital images. He zoomed in carefully on Alvarez's face, memorizing the satisfied arrogance there, and made sure to document both front and rear license plates as the SUV pulled away smoothly from the compound gates.

As the Tahoe vanished down the darkened road, Harper lowered his camera, releasing a slow, measured breath.

"That's a wrap," Harper said softly, breaking the tense silence.

"You got what you need?" Briggs asked quietly.

Harper nodded, slipping the camera securely back into its protective case. "For now. Let's get out of here before dawn lights us up."

The team withdrew as silently as they'd arrived, melting back into the dense tree cover and returning to the unmarked vehicles parked miles away. Throughout the long drive back to Stonehaven, Harper's mind raced, analyzing what he'd seen. His pulse hadn't slowed; he could still feel it hammering insistently, matching the rhythm of tires against pavement. He finally had something tangible, a direct, undeniable connection linking Alvarez to the heart of the conspiracy. Now all that remained was unraveling precisely what they were hiding inside that fortified compound.

Back at the Homeland Security office, Harper turned to Briggs, gratitude clear in his eyes.

"I'll keep you looped in on the hard drive once Hurst breaks it," Harper promised.

Briggs clasped his shoulder firmly, eyes intense. "You need anything, just call. Especially if there's clear evidence of trafficking. We'll get you whatever resources you need to tear this thing apart. If you give us enough, we'll prosecute federally while you nail them on state charges."

Harper nodded, feeling a new surge of determination. "Count on it."

As Harper climbed back into his Durango, driving the familiar roads toward home, he found himself lost in thought. Memories rose like specters from the shadows—old betrayals merging seamlessly with the fresh, sharp-edged truths he now held; the shadows of his past intertwined now with the shadows of the present. He had a clear target, concrete evidence, and support from people he trusted. Yet he couldn't shake the lingering chill at seeing Alvarez's face again—the embodiment of corruption he'd once tried and failed to expose.

This time, though, would be different.

•••••

Harper arrived home around eight in the morning, parked the unmarked car in the driveway, and entered quietly through the garage. In the downstairs laundry room, he stripped off his sweat-soaked fatigues and tossed them directly into the washer. He sent a quick text to Foster, updating him on the success of the operation, and letting him know he'd check in again after he'd slept for a few hours. Foster's reply came almost immediately, telling Harper the hard drive still hadn't been cracked, and instructing him to take the day off and rest.

Ascending the stairs to the bedroom, Harper paused briefly and smiled softly at the framed photos lining the walls, snapshots of their family frozen in time. Alyssa laughing in the kitchen, their daughter bundled in a winter coat, playing in the snow. Little moments, ordinary and sacred. Reminders of why he did what he did. Why he fought so damn hard to make the world better, for them.

In the bathroom, Harper stepped into the shower, sighing as hot water washed away the grime, tension, and fatigue from the overnight surveillance operation. The steam enveloped him, relaxing muscles he hadn't realized were tight until now. After several minutes under the stream, he stepped out and wrapped himself in a towel, brushing his teeth slowly, savoring the mundane routine.

The bathroom door opened quietly behind him, and he felt Alyssa's familiar arms slip around his waist, pressing against his back.

"I missed you," she whispered, her voice soft and inviting.

He turned to face her, feeling a rush of warmth at the sight of her smile. Alyssa stood on tiptoe, her mouth meeting his in a deep, passionate kiss that sent electricity through his veins.

When she finally pulled away, Alyssa raised an eyebrow, her voice teasing and husky. "Addie's at daycare. And I took the morning off."

Harper felt his body respond immediately, matching her playful expression with one of his own. "Then let's not waste any time."

Alyssa's breath whispered warmly against his skin, sending shivers along his spine. Harper's towel slipped unnoticed to the floor as he pulled her closer, feeling her heartbeat quicken against his chest. He lifted Alyssa into his arms and carried her swiftly to the bed, laying her down gently. Clothes came off quickly—her shirt and jeans tossed carelessly aside—replaced by hungry kisses trailing over goosebump laden skin. Moments later, he was on top of her, their bodies entwined and moving together in practiced rhythm. Alyssa's legs tightened around him, her moans deepening as they moved closer to release.

Together they found that familiar, powerful peak, with Alyssa's voice calling out his name, Harper's breath hitching as he let go. Afterwards, spent and content, Harper fell into a peaceful, dreamless sleep, Alyssa curled close against him.

● ● ● ● ●

CHAPTER 19: THE SHATTERED

The next day, Harper strode into Stonehaven PD rested, focused, and ready. After a good night's sleep—and a peaceful morning with Alyssa—he felt centered. Clear-headed. Eager to finally get his hands on what Grant had been hiding.

As he stepped into the detective bullpen, Harper paused mid-step. Cho, Foster, and Hurst sat at their desks, all three watching him with carefully neutral expressions.

"What?" Harper asked, his gaze narrowing slightly. He caught the twitch at the corner of Hurst's mouth, the effort to maintain a poker face faltered. She cracked first, laughing openly, and the rest followed.

"The hard drive's cracked, Jake," Hurst announced, her eyes bright with pride. "Finally broke through last night. The imaging finished up this morning." She lifted an external drive off her desk, marked neatly with a piece of tape labeled *SPD Evidence - Grant.* "Here's your searchable copy. Have fun."

Harper grinned broadly as he took the drive, adrenaline already spiking. "Outstanding work, Hurst."

He settled quickly at his desk, plugged the drive into his desktop, and began diving into the vast trove of data. Files opened before him, spreading out digitally like fragments of a puzzle waiting to be assembled. Within minutes, he was utterly lost in Grant's meticulously documented secrets.

It was staggering. Harper quickly located spreadsheets with comprehensive breakdowns of shell corporations including Redhaven Global, Thornewood Holdings, Eagle and Talon, each with clear ties to Grant Technologies. Carefully constructed financial records detailed wire transfers, cash exchanges, offshore accounts, and how it all flowed to the compound in Blackridge County.

But the files went deeper than financial crimes.

Harper's pulse quickened as he clicked open a document titled simply: *Redhaven Plan.*

What he read froze his blood.

In precise, chilling detail, Grant had outlined the true nature of the compound.

A trafficking hub.

Women. Teens. Children. All held captive, their innocence commodified, sold to feed the darkest appetites of powerful men.

Harper's hands trembled with rage as he read the document. Nauseating descriptions were coldly laid out in neat columns. Ages, "attributes," and price lists. The raw transactional cruelty of it made his stomach clench painfully. Harper had witnessed horrific things in his career, but this, this hit him differently. The predatory precision. The callousness. The absolute disregard for human life.

The operation was horrifyingly systematic. Clients paid exorbitantly for secrecy, indulgence, and silence. In return, beyond monetary compensation, these powerful visitors offered influence, favors, and connections.

Grant had carefully detailed his own involvement. Through multiple shell corporations, he funneled substantial investments directly to Eagle and Talon. In exchange, Grant received promises of political influence, streamlining his company's ability to land lucrative government and defense contracts. Grant Technologies was expanding aggressively into drones and advanced AI. Military contracts would elevate Grant from influential CEO to national power player, wrapped publicly in the deceptive sheen of patriotism.

Harper leaned back, dragging both hands over his face as he tried to regain composure. He could hear the hum of voices around him, conversations between his colleagues fading into white noise. He was frozen, overwhelmed by the calculated depravity on the screen before him.

He scrolled further.

A ledger appeared. Codenames. Clients. Visitors. Handlers. The identities were obscured, but two stood out like rot beneath the surface:

Kingpin. Hammer.

Harper's gut twisted sharply. Alvarez. Dunham. It had to be. One pulling the strings, the other enforcing them with violence.

Harper felt Foster's presence before he saw him, looming silently over his shoulder, absorbing the details with quiet fury.

"Jesus Christ," Foster breathed. "This is worse than we thought."

Cho leaned forward, face pale, fingers steepled. "He had all of it, transfers, shell companies, even travel manifests. Why keep records like this?"

"Insurance," Hurst said quietly. "If it went south, he'd bury someone else instead of himself."

"Or blackmail," Foster added. "Grant wasn't just a player. He thought he was untouchable."

Cho looked up. "What if someone found out he kept records? That's motive for murder right there."

Harper nodded, throat tight with rage. "There's mention of a full client list, but it's not here. He says it's stored *on-site* at the compound in Blackridge."

"Of course it is," Foster muttered darkly. "Insurance for whoever's running security. You keep your evidence close to the chest."

Harper's jaw set. "Then we get inside. We corroborate this. And we bury Alvarez, Dunham, and every bastard tied to it."

Foster straightened. "You've got enough to loop in Briggs now. HSI can bring federal weight. Warrants. Teams. Full resources."

Harper stared at the screen one more time. "If this checks out, they'll bring everything."

"They better," Foster said. "God knows how many lives are on the line."

A long, heavy silence settled in.

Then Foster placed a hand on Harper's shoulder, brief, but solid. "Good work, Jake. I'm glad it's you on this. Justice deserves nothing less."

Harper nodded. "We owe it to every victim in that place. Justice isn't optional."

Foster turned and walked off, already reaching for his phone.

Harper sat still for another moment, eyes fixed on the screen. His fists clenched.

He had proof.

He had names.

He had a mission.

They were going to get inside that compound.

• • • • •

Harper dialed Special Agent Briggs, eager to loop him into the developing storm. He laid out every angle of the financial documents, Grant's twisted business plan, and the coded ledger. He made his case swiftly, clearly, frustration evident as Briggs responded with cautious reserve.

"Jake, I'm going to need more than this," Briggs finally said. "For a federal warrant, we need something concrete tying the compound directly to trafficking. Otherwise, Grant's 'business plan' reads like the plot to a bad movie to any AUSA or federal judge."

"C'mon, Austin," Harper shot back sharply. "We both know this isn't fiction. Grant detailed everything. He left nothing to the imagination."

"Yeah, we both know it," Briggs countered evenly. "But what did I teach you at Stonehaven? Knowing something and proving something—"

"—are two different things," Harper finished, sighing heavily. He knew Briggs was right, but that didn't make it easier. "Fine. I'll get corroboration. But when I do, I need you ready to move."

"You bring me proof, and we'll hit that compound hard," Briggs promised.

Harper ended the call, tension coiled tight between his shoulders. *We are so close*, he thought bitterly. Each step forward seemed to slam him straight into another wall.

But Harper was nothing if not relentless. He took a breath and steadied himself, repeating the mantra drilled into him during his early patrol days: *Start at the beginning. Work the problem. Solve the case.*

Michael Grant had been murdered in his home by someone using a Kabar knife. *Dunham practically slept with his.*

Grant was sleeping with Holly Caldwell, which led to the cabin in Welches, where a shooter armed with a .308 rifle had ambushed them. Harper had returned fire, wounding the shooter, whose blood had been collected at the scene. The shooter had worn size 10.5 Danner Acadia boots, worn unevenly, consistent with Dunham's characteristic limp.

The hard drive recovered from the cabin had provided direct links between Grant's shell companies—Redhaven Global, Thornewood Holdings, Eagle and Talon—and the compound in Blackridge. It also connected Alan Whitaker, the second victim in this bloody web. *Whitaker.* The second body in this case. Harper shook his head remembering how Whitaker had died. Whitaker had been gunned down execution-style by someone wearing identical boots: *Dunham, again.*

Even caught up in all of this, no one deserved to be gunned down in cold blood.

Then there was the compound itself, where Harper and the Homeland Security team had photographed Alvarez arriving, the self-assured commissioner clearly in bed with Eagle and Talon. But there was more there. Harper felt it, an elusive thread waiting to be pulled.

It all leads back to that compound. Grant's business blueprint clearly laid out the plans for sex trafficking in exchange for political favors for his company, to get military contracts and propel Grant Technologies to the next level.

The cars. The vehicles he'd photographed outside the compound, their license plates clearly visible. Harper snapped into action, pulling up each plate number, running them meticulously through LEDS/NCIC and the DMV. Connections emerged swiftly: city councilors, state senators, county commissioners, federal and local judges, even a U.S. congressman. A network of political protection, all of it centered on the compound. It explained Grant's bold confidence, his path to lucrative government contracts neatly paved through political blackmail.

Yet amid the luxury cars and powerful names, one outlier caught Harper's attention: Raul Estrada. No politician, no judge, just a middle-aged security guard living quietly in Blackridge. An unremarkable gray Toyota Camry registered in his name had sat discreetly amid luxury vehicles at the compound.

Harper kept digging. Another vehicle appeared in Estrada's DMV file: a white panel van.

A cold whisper stirred in Harper's memory, something from years before, a faint but persistent itch. Harper traced Estrada's address history. Before Blackridge, Estrada had lived in Cottage Grove for a year, and prior to that, in Neskatah County, near the tribal reservation, where he'd worked as a janitor and handyman for nearly a decade.

The Confederated Tribes of the Neskatah Reservation. Missing women.

The thought slammed into Harper, memories from patrol briefings and frustrated detectives flashing to the surface. Names they'd never forgotten. Faces from bulletins that never had updates. He pulled up old case files, sifting through dusty databases and archived bulletins. Hours slipped by unnoticed as his mind raced, fingers flying across the keyboard.

And there it was. A two-year-old bulletin from Cottage Grove PD. Two homeless women had vanished, witnesses recalling vague mentions of a job opportunity. The last sighting was of the women climbing into a white panel van.

His pulse quickened. Harper dove deeper, reaching further back, scanning tribal police bulletins from Neskatah. The pattern emerged like a slow-building horror: young Native women and girls reported missing over a ten-year span. Witnesses described a gray Toyota Camry or a white panel van. Sometimes both. The driver was always vaguely described. Hispanic, middle-aged, mustached. Never named.

Then the deeper patterns surfaced.

Grooming. Manipulation.

In several cases, family members reported their daughters or nieces had started acting strangely before disappearing. Becoming secretive. Defensive. Talking about a new boyfriend, someone no one had ever met. Some of the girls had been working retail, food service, or seasonal jobs, saving for something they wouldn't fully explain.

One mother said her daughter kept hiding her phone. Would smile quietly to herself when texting. Said she was in love. Said she was finally going to get out.

A few of them even talked about marriage. A new life. A fresh start across the state.

Just needed to follow this man to it.

Some of the families remembered a name.

Raul.

It showed up more than once. Never a full name. Always just that, *Raul.*

This is it.

He immediately called Cottage Grove PD, requesting case files on the missing women. Next, he dialed the Neskatah Tribal Police, reaching Detective Taylor Kalama. Harper explained the connection he suspected between their cold cases and his ongoing homicide investigation.

"You're telling me these disappearances could be connected to a trafficking ring?" Kalama's voice tightened over the phone, urgent and hopeful.

"Yes," Harper confirmed gravely. "Send me everything you've got. Let's see if we can finally put some ghosts to rest."

"Sending now," Kalama replied instantly. "Anything else you need, just ask."

Harper spent the next several hours poring through the emailed files, reading witness statements, missing person reports, and crime scene photos. The pattern became undeniable: women, vulnerable teenagers, even children, targeted, isolated, and systematically taken. Raul Estrada's presence was subtle but undeniable, moving quietly through communities overlooked by society, preying on those least likely to be missed.

Harper's stomach twisted painfully. He kept going, driven by instinct and mounting dread. Then, at last, a single, damning case stood out among the rest.

A witness from the reservation, years old, buried deep. Two teenage girls, last seen at a roadside store. The clerk watched them climb into a white panel van, laughing, excited. She remembered a partial plate: *H-498*. But one detail stood out even more.

She'd heard one of the girls call out the driver's name. Raul.

Harper clenched his fist in grim triumph. *Fucking bingo.*

His chest ached with anger and resolve. He was so close to the link he needed, the corroboration that would force Briggs and federal prosecutors to move on the compound.

They needed to tie Estrada to the compound. To the missing women. The missing girls.

He wasn't just a name in a ledger. He was a predator. A trafficker. He moved through the overlooked places, found vulnerable girls, offering them love. Offering them a future. And then disappeared them.

This wasn't just a homicide case anymore.

• • • • •

CHAPTER 20: THE FRACTURED

Early the next morning, Harper and Sgt. Foster were back on the road, heading toward the Neskatah Tribal Reservation. Three hours of highway stretched ahead of them, the rolling hills of western Oregon unfolding beneath an overcast sky. They were scheduled to meet Detective Kalama to go over the connections to Raul Estrada. Connections Harper hoped would finally break the case open.

The steady hum of tires on asphalt filled the comfortable silence inside the vehicle, both men absorbed in thought. Eventually, Foster glanced at Harper with a faint, amused smile.

"You know, Jake," Foster said casually, "your tenacity hasn't changed one bit."

Harper raised an eyebrow, curiosity piqued. "How so?"

"Remember that doctor you put away on that domestic violence case back when you first joined Stonehaven PD? What was his name, Jefferson?"

"Dr. Jackson," Harper nodded slowly, a brief smile pulling at his mouth. "Of course. Why?"

"Just remembering how relentless you were, even then. Your FTO didn't know what to make of you." Foster chuckled softly. "What rookie—lateral or not—goes out and gets a search warrant on a misdemeanor DV during field training?"

Harper laughed, shaking his head. "I couldn't let it go. That guy thought he was untouchable, hiding behind a fancy job and big house. You remember the victim? She'd been ignored for months, afraid to speak up because she didn't think anyone would believe her over some respected doctor."

"And then in comes Jake Harper," Foster added, "a beat cop barely out of field training, writing affidavits and knocking on judge's doors at midnight. You should've seen the captain's face when he found out what you'd done. The rest of the Sergeants couldn't stop talking about it. But you got the search warrant, got the evidence, and put Jackson behind bars. The look on that doctor's face when he realized he wasn't untouchable…damn."

Harper gave a short, quiet laugh, memories stirring. "Justice doesn't wait, Sarge. Neither do I."

Foster glanced over, nodding slowly, his expression thoughtful. "Yeah. That's exactly my point."

• • • • •

Then.

Officer Harper was in the final phase of his Field Training and Evaluation Program (FTEP), working alongside his third and final Field Training Officer, Brian Thompson. It was well after midnight when the police radio crackled to life, slicing through the calm silence in the cruiser.

"33 Baker, domestic disturbance in progress at 2555 SW River Road, Apartment 39," the dispatcher announced, her voice crisp and clear despite the early hour. "Multiple callers reporting a female screaming for help, sounds of a struggle, and a loud crash."

Harper keyed up his radio immediately. "33 Baker, en route code three." He hit the emergency lights, their flashing blue and red illuminating the night as the Ford Explorer surged forward, its siren splitting the stillness. Thompson quietly observed from the passenger seat, gripping the door handle as Harper navigated the SUV expertly through Stonehaven's quiet streets, his pulse steady even as adrenaline began to flow.

Minutes later, Harper killed the lights and sirens, pulling into the parking lot just short of the apartment building. He exited silently, Thompson close behind, both officers moving swiftly through shadows toward apartment 39. Harper listened carefully as they approached, quickly picking out the muffled sound of a woman crying. Assessing the scene, he moved cautiously but decisively toward the apartment door. Harper stood to the side of the door and knocked firmly four times, the sharp raps echoing with authority.

A woman opened the door a crack, wary eyes regarding Harper and Thompson with open suspicion. She wore a bathrobe hastily tied around her, blonde hair disheveled, mascara running in dark trails down her cheeks. Fresh bruises bloomed along her arm, redness circled her neck, and a fresh scratch marred her left cheek. Harper immediately noted the pinpoint redness in her eyes and around her throat. *Petechiae*, Harper thought, recognizing the tiny ruptures of blood vessels under the skin and in the eyes, knowing they were clear indicators of strangulation.

"What do you want?" she asked defensively, eyes darting nervously over her shoulder into the dark apartment behind her.

"We received a call about a disturbance here," Harper said gently. "Ma'am, are you okay?"

She regarded Harper with bitter skepticism. "Why do you care? You cops always take his side."

Harper softened his voice even further. "My name's Jake. I'm here to help you. Can you tell me your name?"

"Ashley," she replied cautiously.

"Ashley, is there anyone else inside?" Harper asked quietly, his voice firm but reassuring.

She hesitated, fear clearly tightening her expression. "No," she said finally, but the quick glance behind her betrayed the lie.

Harper met her gaze and softened his voice further. "Ashley, please step outside with my partners. You're safe now."

As Ashley stepped out, attempting to close the door behind her, Harper subtly placed his boot in the doorway, preventing the latch from fully engaging. He lowered his voice as she passed. "Ashley, the man who hurt you, he's still inside, isn't he?"

Ashley hesitated, then nodded quickly.

"His name?" Harper pressed gently.

"Jeff," she whispered shakily. "He choked me. Hit me. He…he wanted sex, and when I said no…" Her voice trailed off as fresh tears welled.

As another responding officer carefully guided Ashley away, Harper drew his Glock 9mm, its red dot optic and weapon-mounted flashlight illuminating the narrow hallway inside. Thompson drew his sidearm as well, following Harper's lead.

Harper called inside the door. "Stonehaven PD! Jeff, come out here so we can talk."

No reply.

"Stonehaven PD," Harper called clearly. "Jeff, make yourself known now."

Silence.

Stepping cautiously inside, Harper activated his flashlight, slicing the darkness apart. His training took over, his movements precise and deliberate as he carefully "sliced the pie", checking each corner methodically, minimizing exposure as he searched room by room.

In the darkened living room, Harper's flashlight fell upon a man seated on the sofa, casually holding an ice pack to his knuckles. He was tall and powerfully built, with a bald head, gray goatee, and muscle rippling beneath a tight shirt. He stared defiantly at Harper.

"Who the fuck are you?" the man demanded, voice low and dangerous.

"Stonehaven PD," Harper responded firmly. "Keep your hands where where we can see them."

Instead, Jeff launched himself off the couch, rage fueling his charge toward Harper. "Get the fuck out!" he roared as he charged towards Harper. Making a split-second decision, Harper swiftly holstered his weapon. He ducked sideways, narrowly avoiding the larger man's momentum, then pivoted smoothly, using Jeff's own strength against him. In one fluid motion, Harper took the larger man to the ground, twisting him onto his stomach and applying weight to pin him firmly.

Jeff roared in anger, struggling wildly against Harper's grip. Thompson quickly moved in, securing Jeff's legs while Harper skillfully manipulated the man's upper body, utilizing controlled pressure on his arm and shoulder to maintain control.

"Stop resisting! You're under arrest!" Harper commanded sharply.

Jeff continued to fight and curse, making wild threats as he struggled beneath the officers. Harper increased controlled pressure, carefully and intentionally, until a loud *pop* indicated Jeff's shoulder had dislocated. Instantly, the fight drained from Jeff's body, and Harper swiftly applied handcuffs.

Harper radioed for medics to evaluate Jeff's shoulder. He sat him back on the couch, reading him his Miranda rights clearly from a card he carried.

"What's your name?" Harper asked calmly once he finished.

"Dr. Jeff Jackson," he spat bitterly, wincing in pain.

"What happened tonight, Jeff? Why charge at us?"

Jeff scowled, jaw tightening. "Thought you were intruders."

"Come on," Harper said patiently, tapping the body camera on his chest. "We announced ourselves clearly. Is it because you hit Ashley and didn't want to go to jail?"

Jeff sneered. "Man, screw you. That bitch attacked me. I recorded the whole thing. Check my phone."

"Can I see it?" Harper asked smoothly.

"Fine. Phone's on the table. Code's 6237," Jeff snapped angrily.

Harper located the phone, opened it, and found the most recent video. Carefully staged, clearly mid video, it began with Ashley's screams and threats, conveniently omitting any of Jeff's actions prior. Harper narrowed his eyes.

"Where's the rest of the video, Jeff?"

Jeff hesitated, eyes flickering nervously. "I don't know what you mean. I want my lawyer."

Harper nodded coolly. "Fair enough. I'm seizing this phone and applying for a search warrant. We'll find the full recording."

"You can't do that!" Jeff shouted furiously.

"I just did," Harper replied calmly, walking away.

Outside, Harper interviewed Ashley thoroughly, hearing her account of Jeff's assault: forcing entry into her home, refusing to leave without sex, choking her viciously while mocking her weakness, recording her pain as some twisted power play. Harper felt cold fury, carefully hidden beneath professional composure. Ashley's story painted a chilling picture of systematic control and violence hidden behind Jeff's respectable veneer as a local family doctor.

True to his word, Harper swiftly obtained a warrant for Jeff's phone, quickly locating the full, damning video, confirming Ashley's account precisely. Harper meticulously documented every detail, ensuring the prosecutor had an airtight case. Ultimately, Jeff Jackson was convicted on all counts. Domestic assault, burglary, strangulation, and attempted assault on a police officer, and sent to prison.

As Harper left the courtroom after sentencing months later, Ashley approached him, eyes clear and voice steady.

"Thank you," she said simply.

Harper met her gaze, nodding gently.

"I just did my job," he said quietly. But both of them knew it was more than that.

It was a promise kept.

● ● ● ● ●

CHAPTER 21: THE FORGOTTEN

Now.

Harper and Foster pulled into the lot of the Neskatah Tribal Police Department just after 10 a.m. The building was modest, tan brick, one story, with clean lines, and out front, waiting with arms loosely crossed, stood Detective Kalama.

He looked like someone who didn't miss much.

Athletic, maybe six feet tall and solidly built, about 200 pounds, with the kind of strength that came from functional training, not ego lifting. Dark hair, buzzed short. Striking blue eyes that stood out against his warm complexion, watchful but not unfriendly. He wore jeans and a fitted polo, a star-shaped badge clipped to his belt next to a well-worn sidearm.

Harper clocked him instantly as someone who moved with quiet confidence, with no wasted motion, no need to posture.

After introductions, Kalama led them down a quiet hallway to the department's briefing room. At the center stood a stunning hardwood table. It was thick, polished, and clearly handmade. Surrounding it were well-worn but sturdy chairs, each tucked in with military precision.

Inlaid in the middle of the table was the badge of the Neskatah Tribal Police Department, a seven-pointed star with the tribal seal at its heart, carved directly into the wood and stained a rich, dark hue.

Kalama noticed them staring.

"Inmates from the nearby prison made it," he said, stepping around the table. "Part of a vocational program, teaching them woodworking, furniture-making, that kind of thing. We paid the program for the table."

He paused, hand brushing the edge of the inlay.

"Win-win. We got a beautiful custom piece at a fraction of the price, and the money goes back into giving those guys a trade. Something to carry with them when they're out. Cuts recidivism. Gives them purpose."

Harper ran a hand across the smooth surface. "Hell of a table."

Kalama nodded once. "And a hell of a second chance."

As they settled around the table, Kalama didn't waste time.

"So," he said, leaning forward, "you said on the phone all of our cases tie together?"

"Yeah," Harper replied. "Does the name Raul Estrada mean anything to you?"

Kalama nodded slowly. "Raul, yeah. We looked into him a little back then. Before my time, though."

Harper opened the case file Kalama had sent over and flipped to the oldest report, tapping the section he'd highlighted. "Here, a witness remembered a girl calling out Raul's name."

Kalama raised an eyebrow but stayed quiet, listening.

Harper turned a few pages. "And here, a partial plate. White panel van. Then this case: gray Camry. Sound familiar?"

He laid out the Cottage Grove files next, one by one. "Same patterns. Gray Camry. White van. Matching suspect descriptions. It's consistent across three counties."

Kalama leaned in, eyes narrowing. "Estrada drove a gray Camry. And a white van."

Harper nodded. "And the van's plate ended in H498."

"Christ," Kalama muttered. He sat back for a beat, taking it in. "So what's next?"

Harper glanced at Foster, who picked it up smoothly.

"That's where we come in. There's a compound in Blackridge County—goes by Redhaven. We've linked it to shell corporations, off-books finances, and missing persons across the region."

"We believe girls are being trafficked there," Harper added. "Women, too. Sold to wealthy clients—politicians, execs. Estrada's connected."

Foster laid out the map and some of the printed photos. "If your witnesses ID Estrada, we've got our probable cause. We bring him in, pressure him to flip. If he talks..."

"We get names," Kalama said, finishing the thought. "Locations. Chains of command."

"And maybe," Harper said quietly, "we get some of them home."

"I already have the lineups ready to go, generated from DMV photos of Estrada and similar individuals," Harper said.

Kalama stood. "Then let's not waste time."

Harper and Foster followed Kalama out to their vehicles. Kalama climbed into a black unmarked pickup, and the detectives got back into the Durango, pulling in behind him as he led the way. They drove down a quiet street bordered by pine trees and scattered tribal housing developments. Dogs lounged in driveways. Children played in open yards.

Eventually, they turned onto Black Pine Lane and pulled up to a weathered apartment complex. Kalama parked and got out, moving with purpose toward the exterior stairs. Harper and Foster followed him up to the second floor.

He knocked firmly on the door of unit 2B with a sharp, unmistakable knock that said *police*.

"Heather?" Kalama called. "It's me. Taylor."

A few quiet seconds passed. Then the door cracked open. A woman peered out cautiously, one hand still gripping the edge of the door.

"Who are they?" she asked softly.

"They're friends of mine," Kalama said, his tone gentle but direct. "Can we come in?"

Her eyes narrowed slightly, measuring them. Assessing risk.

Then Kalama added, more quietly, "It's about Kailey."

Something shifted in her expression. With a quiet sigh, she opened the door wider and stepped aside.

Harper took her in quickly, instinctively cataloging detail. She was beautiful—Native, like Kalama—with long raven-black hair that fell down her back. Her eyes, an arresting ice-blue, mirrored Kalama's almost exactly. She wore jeans and a fitted t-shirt, tattoos curling up one well-muscled arm, showing stylized lines and shapes that looked traditional, intentional. She looked strong. Not gym-fit, but capable, like someone who'd been through some things and come out tougher for it.

The apartment was small but clean, the light dimmed by heavy, handwoven blankets hung over the windows. Their vibrant patterns gave the space a lived-in, almost sacred feel.

"Heather," Kalama said, gesturing to his colleagues, "this is Detective Jake Harper and Sgt. Foster."

Harper stepped forward and offered his hand. "Jake," he said simply.

Heather shook it, her grip firm, her gaze sharp. "Heather Stonewood," she replied, her voice low but steady.

Foster gave her a small nod. "Thank you for letting us in."

She said nothing in return, just gestured toward the couch. "Talk fast," she said. "I've got to pick up my niece in an hour."

Once they were seated, Kalama leaned forward, resting his forearms on his knees. His voice was soft, but steady.

"Heather," he began, "we're taking a second look at Kailey's case. Some new information came up, connections that tie what happened here to something they're working in Stonehaven."

Heather's eyes snapped to him. "Let me guess," she said, voice tight. "Some white girl went missing, and now suddenly everyone gives a damn?"

Foster shifted in his seat, raising a calming hand. "I get how that sounds, and I don't blame you for thinking it. But this isn't a PR thing. We're here because there's a real, direct link. And we're not walking away from it."

Heather crossed her arms, eyes sharp and angry, but beneath the fire was something older, something tired. Hurt. "You know how many times I've told Kailey's story? How many times I've handed over photos, begged for follow-ups, and gotten nothing but polite nods and empty promises?"

Kalama's tone sharpened, not unkind, but firm. "Heather, I wouldn't have brought them here if this was performative. Harper found the connection. He's the one who came to us. Not the other way around."

All eyes turned to Harper. He met Heather's gaze head-on.

"I know I'm late to this," Harper said quietly. "But I'm here now. And I'm trying to bring your sister home. That's not a sound bite. That's real."

Heather stared at him for a long moment, reading the lines of his face. Whatever she saw there softened her expression just slightly.

"Then start talking," she said. "Tell me what you found."

Harper retrieved a folder from his bag, laying it gently on the table. "We'd like you to look at some photographs," he said, his tone measured. "There are eight in total. The person who took your sister may or may not be among them. If you recognize anyone, please let us know."

Heather's gaze hardened with determination as she nodded.

One by one, Harper presented each photograph, allowing Heather a few moments to study each face before moving to the next. With each image, she shook her head, her expression unchanging.

Upon the fifth photograph, Heather's breath caught audibly. Her eyes widened, and she leaned closer, her hand trembling as she pointed. "That's him," she whispered, her voice thick with emotion. Then, more forcefully, she repeated, "That's him!"

Harper leaned forward. "You're sure?"

Heather nodded, her jaw tightening. "That's the guy Kailey was seeing. The one she was in love with." She swallowed hard, fighting the memory. "She never told us his name. Just said he was older. Said he understood her. Promised her the world."

She shook her head. "He never came to the house. Refused to meet the family. Would only pick her up down the block. My parents thought he didn't exist. That she was just acting out. But I saw him. Once."

Her voice dropped to a bitter whisper.

"They were in his van. White. Parked behind the community center. I caught them kissing, and, God, she was still in high school. And he was a grown man. I told her it was wrong. That it wasn't love."

Harper stayed silent. Let her keep going.

"But she didn't listen. A few weeks later, she said they were going to leave together. Said he was taking her somewhere better. Somewhere he'd take care of her." Her voice cracked. "That was the last time I saw her."

She looked back down at the photo. Estrada's face frozen on glossy paper.

"I didn't know his name until now. But I never forgot his face."

Harper exchanged a glance with Kalama and Briggs, a shared understanding passing between them. They had him.

Heather's eyes filled with tears, a mixture of relief and anguish. "You found him," she said, choking. "After all these years..."

Harper reached across the table, his hand hovering near hers in a gesture of support. "We're going to bring him in, Heather," he assured her. "And we're going to find Kailey."

Heather nodded, her resolve returning. "Do whatever it takes," she said, her voice steady. "Just bring my sister home."

• • • • •

Harper, Kalama, and Foster spent the remainder of the morning diligently reaching out to witnesses connected to the missing persons cases. Navigating the winding roads of the reservation, they conducted personal visits, managing to interview five families. Each conversation added weight to their suspicions.

One by one, the witnesses examined the photo lineup presented by the investigators. Without hesitation, all identified Raul Estrada.

"That's him," one middle-aged woman said softly, her finger trembling slightly as she tapped Estrada's photograph. "I'll never forget that face. He's the one that took my little girl."

These confirmations solidified their lead, transforming suspicion into certainty. Armed with compelling evidence, they returned to the Neskatah Tribal Police Department's briefing room, their collective determination palpable.

Kalama was the first to break the silence. His voice was steady, authoritative. "I want in."

Foster glanced at him, immediately nodding in agreement. "Absolutely. We're planning to apprehend Estrada tomorrow morning. Will that timing work for you? We'll need to clear it with your chain of command."

"Already done," Kalama replied swiftly, a resolute glint in his eyes. "My lieutenant gave me the green light. I'm fully cleared and ready."

Harper leaned forward, his gaze firm and resolute. "Then it's settled. Let's do this. We'll head back to Stonehaven, brief our team thoroughly, and finalize our operational plan. No mistakes."

"HSI could possibly provide additional resources," Foster said, tapping a finger thoughtfully against the tabletop. "They'll have extra tactical support and surveillance ready."

The trio shared a determined glance, acknowledging the gravity of their mission. With the framework of their operation now firmly set, they rose from their seats, energy revitalized by the tangible progress they'd made. Stepping outside into the cool air, each felt buoyed by their breakthrough, driven by a shared resolve to see justice served.

• • • • •

A few hours later, they reconvened in the Stonehaven PD briefing room. Harper had called Special Agent Briggs on the drive over, and he was already there when they arrived.

"Team," Harper began, "this is Detective Taylor Kalama from the Neskatah Tribal Police." He gestured towards Kalama, who stood with a confident yet approachable demeanor. "Taylor, meet the team."

One by one, the team members stood to greet Kalama:

"Carrie," Hurst offered, her grip firm and professional.

"Ryan," Cho said, nodding as he shook hands.

When it was Briggs's turn, he stepped forward with a grin. "Austin," he said, extending a hand to Kalama. Then he turned to Foster, offered the same handshake and repeated, "Austin," as if he hadn't been a detective at Stonehaven just a year earlier.

The shared laughter that followed eased any lingering tension, setting a collaborative tone for the meeting.

Harper initiated the briefing, his tone crisp and authoritative.

"We'll convene here tomorrow at 0300 hours. It's a three-hour drive to Blackridge County, positioning us there by 0600. The shift change for the Blackrock neighborhood security is at 0700, which grants us an hour to establish our setup."

Briggs stepped forward, pinning a series of high-resolution surveillance photos and a detailed map of the Blackrock neighborhood onto the board.

"While you were in Neskatah, I coordinated with my team to conduct surveillance on the Blackrock neighborhood," he explained. "It's a gated community with a primary guard shack here." He indicated a spot on the map. "Fortunately, adjacent neighborhoods have access points where we can discreetly park our vehicles out of sight."

Harper took the lead again, outlining the operational roles.

"The takedown team will consist of Briggs, Kalama, and myself. We'll position ourselves in Briggs's van here," he said, pointing to a location on the map one street over, "monitoring for Estrada. He resides within the gated community, so the optimal time to apprehend him is just after the shift change."

Briggs elaborated on the strategy.

"We need to prevent him from triggering any alarms that would alert additional guards near Alvarez's residence. To achieve this, we'll employ a ruse to draw him out."

Harper turned to Hurst.

"Carrie, you'll be instrumental in this. You'll pose as a disoriented, wine-drunk soccer mom returning from a late-night bachelorette party. As you approach the gate, you'll feign passing out at the wheel. This should prompt Estrada to leave his post to check on you."

Briggs continued, "While Estrada is preoccupied with Carrie, Harper will approach on foot."

Kalama interjected, "And that's where I come in."

"Exactly," Briggs confirmed. "Harper will hold Estrada at gunpoint while Kalama and I exit the van, secure Estrada, and bring him into the vehicle. Harper will then join us, and Carrie will expedite our departure from the area."

Harper addressed the rest of the team.

"Foster, Cho. you'll serve as our backup and additional eyes and ears. If complications arise, you'll manage our exfil."

Both Detectives nodded in acknowledgment.

Briggs concluded the briefing.

"Once Estrada is secured, we'll transport him to our HSI facility just outside Blackridge for interrogation."

Harper added, "Our objective is to have him flip on Alvarez, Dunham, and the individuals detained at Redhaven."

Kalama inquired, "How do you plan to achieve that?"

Briggs responded with a slight smile, "You haven't seen Harper and I in an interrogation room yet. You'll see."

Foster concluded the op brief.

"Alright everyone, go get a few hours sleep. See you in a few hours."

• • • • •

Harper shut the door behind him with a quiet click. The house was dim, the only light spilling from under the kitchen hood, warm and golden. The scent of coffee lingered in the air, mingled with something sweet. Vanilla, maybe. He drew in a breath and let it out slow, dropping his keys into the bowl by the door.

"You're late," Alyssa called from the kitchen. Her voice was soft but steady, like she'd been expecting him to show up exactly this way.

"Yeah," he muttered.

She didn't turn around. Instead, she poured coffee into a ceramic mug and slid a takeout container onto the counter. "Rough day?"

He set his badge beside the food and exhaled through his nose. "Something like that."

"You forgot to eat again." Her tone wasn't accusing, just familiar, like someone who'd already resigned herself to the pattern. She turned and handed him the mug, arching one brow.

He took it with a nod. "Thanks."

"You know," she said, crossing her arms and leaning against the counter, "you'd make this a lot easier if you just let me install a feeding tube."

Harper smirked, eyes half-lidded. "You'd make one hell of a detective."

"You already bring the work home. I might as well get paid too." She nodded toward the takeout. "Eat before you pass out."

He grunted something that might've been gratitude and lowered himself onto the couch like his bones had aged fifty years in a day. The cushions sighed beneath him. Alyssa followed a few seconds later, sitting beside him, tucking one leg under the other.

"You working a case," she asked, "or trying to win the martyrdom Olympics?"

He looked over at her, a tired grin creeping across his face. "Is there a prize?"

"There is. A heart attack, bad knees, and three different kinds of ulcers."

"Sounds like my pension plan."

She rolled her eyes and leaned into him, resting her head on his shoulder. "Eat first. Then I'll let you complain about the state of the world."

He let the silence stretch for a beat, then wrapped an arm around her shoulders, pulling her in gently.

"I missed you," he said quietly.

"You always do," she whispered. "But you still come back. That's what matters."

•••••

CHAPTER 22: IN PURSUIT

Then.

Sweat dripped down Officer Harper's brow, the summer heat turning his patrol car into a stifling oven as he watched the passing traffic. Harper was hunting. So far, no vehicles matched the suspect description Harper was looking for.

Positioned discreetly between two brick buildings adjacent to a gas station, he had an unobstructed view of the highway slicing through Stonehaven. His eyes, shielded behind dark Oakley sunglasses, meticulously scanned each passing vehicle, diligently searching for a brown Toyota pickup with Montana plates reading 65T-467Y. The image of her battered face, swollen and discolored, haunted his thoughts. She was counting on him. *I can't let her down.*

An hour earlier, the Suburban barreled north on the rain-slicked highway, wipers beating in time with Melissa's pounding heart. Her fingers tightened around the steering wheel, knuckles pale. In the rearview mirror, she caught a glimpse of her daughter, curled in her booster seat, clutching a stuffed giraffe, too quiet for a five-year-old.

"Why the hell was it *him* again?" Tony snapped from the passenger seat, his breath thick with booze, sour and sharp. "You like that doctor, huh? Bet you couldn't wait to spread your legs when I wasn't looking."

Melissa flinched. "Tony, stop. Please." She kept her voice calm, measured, the way you talk to a bear sniffing your tent flap. "She's got a fever. That's all this is. We're going to the clinic."

Tony sneered, his eyes bloodshot and unblinking. "Don't lie to me. You think I don't see it? You put on that little smile for him. Bat your lashes like some desperate bitch."

"I'm not—" she started, then stopped herself. She'd been down this road before, in more ways than one. Logic never worked with Tony. Not when he was like this. And Tony was like this a lot.

He slammed his palm against the dashboard. The sudden crack of flesh against plastic made their daughter gasp. Melissa glanced in the rearview again. Her girl's wide eyes were filled with tears, bottom lip trembling.

"Tony, please," Melissa said again, quieter this time. "She's watching."

That did it. Something behind his eyes flickered, then snapped.

"You care more about her than me," he hissed.

His fist came at her.

She didn't even have time to scream. Just the sound—*thwap*—knuckles against cheekbone. Her head snapped sideways, vision exploding into sparks. The car veered left. She fought to keep control, one hand still on the wheel, the other shielding her face. Their daughter shrieked, high and panicked.

Thwap.

Another blow. Her lip split. Blood filled her mouth.

She didn't think. She just turned the wheel hard and swerved into a gas station. Tires shrieked against the pavement as the SUV jolted to a stop near the ice machines. She barely had the gearshift in park before Tony reached for her again.

Doors opened somewhere nearby. Shouts. Footsteps pounding the pavement.

"Hey! Get out of the car!"

Tony froze.

A group of teenage boys in FFA jackets swarmed the vehicle. The passenger door flew open and strong hands dragged Tony from the seat. One boy, barely eighteen by the look of him, held a pitchfork from a truck bed. Another cracked his knuckles.

"Run, asshole," the biggest one said. "See how far you get."

Tony's eyes darted, wild and cornered. Then he bolted.

By the time Officer Harper arrived, the parking lot was already cordoned off with flashing lights and yellow tape. EMTs were crouched beside Melissa, who sat slumped on the curb, her face a bruised kaleidoscope of purple, red, and swelling. Her jaw hung crooked, and her right eye was sealed shut.

Harper's gaze drifted to the little girl bundled in a blanket in the back of the ambulance. Her cheeks were tear-streaked, and her arms still wrapped around the giraffe.

He felt his jaw tighten.

"Kid was in the car during the assault," one of the medics said quietly. "Hell of a scene."

Harper nodded. That made it a felony. Mandatory arrest wasn't just policy. It was the right thing to do.

He approached Melissa and crouched beside her. "Melissa, I know this is hard. But I need your help to find him."

She didn't answer. She just stared at her lap, eyes dull with fear and shame.

She blinked slowly. A tear traced down her unbruised cheek.

"But you've got a daughter," he said. "And she just watched a man beat her mother. What do you think that teaches her? That love feels like fear?"

Melissa's lip quivered. She looked over at the ambulance and the tiny silhouette in the open doorway.

"She doesn't deserve that," Harper said. "And neither do you."

A long pause passed. Then Melissa whispered, through cracked lips, "His mom's house. On Jennings Street. A couple blocks east."

Harper stood. The air felt colder now, heavier with purpose. "We'll find him."

Tony was a coward. He'd run home to mommy.

Tony's mother was a well-known enabler within Stonehaven's affluent circles. An attorney with influence, she had a history of shielding her son from consequences. From high school drug charges that were dismissed after she got the school board to reassign the School Resource Officer back to patrol, to college DUIs she'd gotten reduced, she had always managed to manipulate the system in Tony's favor. Now, as an adult, Tony continued to exploit her protection, especially after his violent outbursts.

"She just bought a pickup from her brother in Montana," Melissa informed Harper, her voice strained from pain. "Whenever we fight, he runs to her. If they're not home, they're likely driving around in that truck."

Handing her his card with his cell number scrawled on the back, Harper urged, "Contact me if you hear from Tony. For both your sakes."

Harper's initial visit to Tony's mother's house yielded nothing; the brown pickup was absent, and his knocks went unanswered. However, a text from Melissa soon provided a lead: Tony was aware of the police interest and was attempting to flee town with his mother.

Strategically, officers were stationed near Melissa's residence should Tony attempt to return home. Harper positioned himself on the town's northern exit route, anticipating their escape. His vigilance paid off when, approximately ten minutes after pulling into his hiding spot at the gas station, the brown pickup cruised past.

Merging into traffic, Harper tailed the vehicle, radioing in his position and the unfolding situation. Officer Melbourne acknowledged, indicating his proximity and readiness to assist. Through the pickup's rear window, Harper discerned a female driver but couldn't confirm Tony's presence. He needed a legitimate reason to initiate a stop.

The pickup's driving was frustratingly impeccable. It strictly adhered to the speed limit, used turn signals right on time. However, upon entering a 25 mph zone, the vehicle maintained a steady 30 mph. *Minor*, Harper thought. *But it'll do.* Probable cause is probable cause. As Melbourne's cruiser drew near, Harper reached down and activated his lights, signaling the pickup to pull over.

The truck's response was methodical: right blinker, a turn onto a side street, then another into a residential area. Harper's instincts made the hair on the back of his neck stand up. *They're stalling.*

Finally, the pickup rolled to a stop along the curb. Harper threw his cruiser into park and stepped out, just as the passenger door of the truck swung open. Tony burst out and locked eyes with him. There was no hesitation in his stare, just pure defiance.

Harper recognized him immediately from the DMV photo. Same greasy hair. Same hollow stare.

"Tony! Stop right there. You're under arrest!" Harper called out, hand instinctively moving toward his belt.

"Fuck you!" Tony spat, and bolted, cutting across the front of the truck, then veering hard westbound across the street and into a row of front yards.

Harper didn't hesitate. He took off in pursuit, his boots hammering the pavement. Thirty pounds of gear weighed him down—duty belt, external vest, radio, handcuffs, taser—but adrenaline made him weightless.

"I'll cut him off!" Officer Melbourne shouted, veering north to circle behind the houses Tony was charging through.

Tony had a head start, but Harper was closing the distance fast. The guy was sloppy, drunk or coming down from something, and Harper was still in the kind of shape that made suspects underestimate him. Lawn after lawn blurred by as Harper ran, shouting, "STOP! POLICE! YOU'RE UNDER ARREST!"

One house away.

Then Tony juked left between two homes, vanishing from sight.

Harper slowed, pulse pounding in his ears. He pulled his Glock and edged forward, slicing the corner clean as he cleared the angle, careful not to walk into an ambush.

"33 Baker," he said into his vest mic, voice steady but sharp. "Suspect ran behind 4405 NW Cellar Drive. I'm clearing and continuing the pursuit."

"35 Baker, copy," came Melbourne's voice through the radio. "I'm one block north, five houses down. I'll catch him if he pops out."

Harper advanced down the narrow side yard, eyes scanning. He caught a flicker of movement as Tony scrambled over a backyard fence.

"He's coming your way!" Harper shouted into the mic, holstering his weapon mid-sprint.

Two strides and he hit the fence. Left boot, right boot, grip, and vault. He cleared the top cleanly and landed low in the backyard. Ahead, the gate swung open. Tony barreled through, cutting back into the front yard.

Harper ran harder.

Tony crossed the street, heading toward the neighborhood park. Open ground. No cover. Just a wide, grassy field.

Harper chased him into the open, boots chewing up the turf, breathing hard but controlled.

Then Tony stopped.

He spun around and crouched, arms snapping up into a shooter's stance. His feet planted, knees bent, hands locked out in front of him with something black gripped in both palms.

"Shoot me, motherfucker!" Tony screamed, his voice ragged with rage. "DO IT!"

Shit.

Harper's world narrowed.

Some part of his brain registered that his gun was in his hands, sights aligned on Tony's chest. He didn't remember drawing.

Trigger pressure. The wall. Just a whisper more, and—

Cell phone.

Tony was holding a phone like a gun.

He wanted Harper to shoot him.

Not today, motherfucker.

He holstered the pistol in one motion, dropped his weight, and surged forward again.

His shoulder slammed into Tony's midsection like a battering ram, lifting him off his feet and driving him to the ground. Tony's breath exploded in a strangled grunt as they hit the grass, limbs tangling.

Harper took a wild punch to the jaw, dull pain flaring, but he answered with a sharp elbow to Tony's nose. There was a crack, a spray of blood, and a howl of pain.

Melbourne arrived an instant later, dropping onto Tony's legs. Harper wrestled Tony's arms down, pinning them as Melbourne secured the cuffs.

It was over.

Tony writhed, bleeding and cursing, but the fight had drained out of him.

Later, back at the station, the patrol sergeants pulled Harper aside.

"You did good," one of them said. "Right call, all the way."

The use-of-force review came back, well within policy. The video told the story, and Harper's restraint spoke louder than any report.

As he sat alone afterward, sipping stale coffee from a paper cup, the weight of it all began to settle.

For the first time in years, he wasn't waiting for the other shoe to drop. No second-guessing. No sideways glances. No one trying to hang him out to dry.

I'm home.

•••••

"There is no hunting like the hunting of man, and those who have hunted armed men long enough and liked it, never care for anything else thereafter." - Ernest Hemingway

CHAPTER 23: THE ECHO OF SILENCE

Now.

The van hummed quietly along the highway, tires whispering rhythmically against the pavement beneath a slate-gray sky. Harper sat silently in the passenger seat, eyes fixed on the blurred streaks of white and yellow painted lines disappearing beneath them, his thermos balanced precariously on one knee, untouched and cooling.

Behind him, Hurst's soft, rhythmic breathing punctuated the silence, occasionally interrupted by a sleepy shift or muted sigh as she dozed, head resting gently against the window. Up front, Kalama spoke in low, measured tones to Briggs, their quiet conversation blending seamlessly with the muted hum of the engine, becoming little more than background noise to Harper.

The three hour drive to Blackridge had been uneventful, giving space for Harper's mind to drift deep beneath the surface of the road rushing by. Images and memories swirled restlessly, relentless in their demand for his attention. He saw Grant's frozen stare again. The once-powerful man's face twisted in agony, lifeless eyes fixed blankly toward the ceiling. Whitaker's blood-coated teeth flashed sharply in his memory, the man's desperate, choking voice forming Durham's name with the last breath he'd ever take, fear taking root in his eyes.

Harper's throat tightened involuntarily at the thought of Vanessa Whitaker, her stunned silence and then the wracking sobs, grief breaking her voice when he delivered the news that should shatter her world forever. The memory clawed at him, raw and unhealed.

A sudden sharp inhale escaped him as his mind flashed back to Holly and her wide eyes filled with terror, splinters of wood exploding violently around them, the sharp whistle of bullets slicing through air mere inches from their heads. His jaw clenched, knuckles whitening around the thermos as he fought down the vivid sensation of adrenaline returning, the phantom echo of gunfire reverberating through his bones.

Heather Stonewood's anguished face materialized next, a lifetime of sorrow etched deeply into her eyes as she recounted the abduction of her sister. The years of waiting, hoping, each day bleeding painfully into the next without answers.

And then Raul Estrada, and the cruel efficiency with which he stole lives. Women, children. The thought twisted in Harper's gut like a blade, sharp and unrelenting. His imagination ran unchecked, conjuring shadowy horrors inside the secretive walls of the Redhaven Compound. Unimaginable suffering concealed behind those gates.

Harper's eyes narrowed, breath catching as anger surged, hot and controlled. All threads led back to one place. To Dunham. To Alvarez.

The blurred lines on the road seemed to tighten, becoming clearer as his resolve hardened. They had escaped justice long enough. He shifted slightly in his seat, exhaled slowly, and stared out at the horizon with renewed clarity.

It was time to end this.

● ● ● ● ●

The van rolled into the quiet streets of the Blackrock neighborhood just before six. The engine was little more than a hum, swallowed by the early morning stillness. Inside, the tension was thick with focus.

In the backseat, Hurst stretched with a muted yawn, rubbing sleep from her eyes as she blinked at the soft glow of the dashboard lights. Up front, Harper caught the low whisper of Briggs's voice as he reviewed the plan with Kalama in short, clipped phrases heavy with finality. Every word felt like a countdown.

Two blocks away, Cho's newly repaired Bronco idled with its lights off, tucked into the shadow of a large pine. Foster sat inside, adjusting the straps on his bullet-resistant vest with methodical care, fingers brushing lightly over the cloth badge stitched over the chest. His face was carved in stillness, the look of a man who'd done this before, and knew exactly what was about to happen.

To their right, a dark SUV was parked low and quiet. Through the tinted glass, Harper could just make out the silhouettes of Briggs's tactical team. Their movements were crisp and economical—checking rifles, zipping gear, adjusting comms—each one a silent ritual honed by repetition and adrenaline.

Briggs eased the van to a stop a street away from the guard shack and killed the headlights. In an instant, they were part of the dark again.

"No chatter," Briggs said. "Hard in. Hard out."

Hurst climbed over into the driver's seat, smudging her lipstick with a thumb and cracking open an old bottle of Chardonnay just enough to let the scent spill out. She tossed a red Solo cup onto the floorboards, slouched low, and let her mascara run slightly at the corners of her eyes. Just another drunk suburbanite lost in the wrong neighborhood.

Harper stepped out onto the pavement, his Chucks landing soft on the cold asphalt. He adjusted the brim of his dark green ball cap, tugging his black hoodie lower to cast deeper shadows across his face. The familiar weight of his Glock pressed against his abdomen, snug in its appendix holster beneath the hoodie, his badge tucked out of sight. He moved quickly, slipping down a side street without a word.

He took a winding path through yards and alleys, weaving between fences and hedges. The neighborhood was still asleep, windows dark and the air damp with morning dew. He reached his vantage point four houses down and crouched behind the corner of a detached garage. Holding his breath, he waited.

From this angle, he had a clear line of sight to the guard shack. The small building sat at the bottom of the hill, the ornate steel fence washed in pale orange from an overhead streetlamp. It was quiet. Inside, a lone figure hunched over a cell phone, the screen's blue light reflecting off his too-young face. Barely twenty. High and tight haircut. Slack posture. Probably struggling to stay awake.

Harper's jaw tightened slightly. Not the threat.

He waited.

At precisely seven, Harper's gaze sharpened. A figure descended the hill, passing beneath a streetlight. It was a man in a guard uniform, broad-shouldered with a thick, unmistakable mustache.

Estrada. Right on schedule.

Harper quietly raised his phone, whispering sharply, "Target on site. Two tangos, will confirm when he's alone."

A pause. Then a soft double-click in his earpiece acknowledged the report.

Moments later, the young guard stepped from the shack, yawning as he walked to a beat up red Honda Civic parked at the curb. The engine sputtered to life, then rolled down the street, tail lights flickering out of view.

"Target alone. Green light," Harper whispered again, pocketing the phone as he stepped from shadow to shadow, closing the distance quickly.

Headlights sliced through the dark as the van approached from down the street, weaving slightly and deliberately across the road. Harper felt a small, appreciative smile tug at his lips as the left turn signal blinked once, then the vehicle turned sharply right. A little drunk-driving flair for authenticity.

"Nice touch, Carrie," he muttered quietly.

The van coasted to a stop outside the shack. Hurst leaned out the window, her voice exaggerated and syrupy. "Hello? Ish anyone here?"

From the shack, Estrada barked, "Private property! Turn around now!"

"I'm losssht," Hurst slurred, leaning harder, her words tangled and slow. Then, with a groan, she threw the door open and collapsed to the pavement with a heavy thud, limbs splayed unnaturally. Her hair was a mess, makeup smeared. She didn't move.

Harper drew his Glock with practiced silence and began to close the distance, hugging the line of hedges, keeping to the shadows.

"Private property, ma'me," Estrada barked again. "Leave now or I'm calling the cops."

No response.

"Ma'am?" A beat of hesitation. "Ma'am?"

His voice changed, irritation replaced by concern.

The moment he stepped out of the shack, Harper moved.

Harper surged forward from the darkness, crossing the distance and wrapping an arm around Estrada's neck, jamming the muzzle of his Glock against the man's skull. "Police. Do not move."

Estrada's hand twitched toward his hip. *I don't think so.*

Harper yanked the pistol from his holster and tossed it to Hurst, who was already on her feet, badge exposed on her belt.

The van door burst open, and Briggs and Kalama moved in tight and fast. Estrada was secured before he could finish a shout, flex cuffs cinched, arms pinned. They hauled him into the van and forced him face-down to the floorboard. A mesh spit hood dropped over his head.

"Quiet," Briggs ordered. "Police. Do not move. Do not speak."

Harper slipped in after them, and Hurst slammed the door shut, dropping back into the driver's seat.

The tires chirped against asphalt, and in seconds, they were gone—vanishing into the shadows they'd emerged from, leaving behind nothing but a guard shack and the echo of silence.

Briggs leaned forward from the passenger seat, typing something into a tablet. A beat later, he gave a satisfied nod.

"Video feed's wiped," he said. "Security camera loop scrubbed. When the next shift shows up, they'll assume he walked off the job."

• • • • •

CHAPTER 24: BREAK POINT

One hour later, Raul Estrada was dragged from the back of the van, the tight mesh of a spit hood still clinging to his face, muting sound and light alike. Rough hands pushed him forward, guiding him with sharp, wordless commands. His feet scraped concrete, then tile. Light bled faintly through the fabric, a dull gray haze behind the mesh.

A hard shove knocked him backward into a cold metal chair. The flex cuffs were sliced off, only for his left wrist to be immediately locked to a bolted steel ring on the tabletop with standard-issue handcuffs.

Then, silence.

A door opened.

Footsteps. Another chair scraping. Raul could see the outline of a man sitting down across from him. Paper rustled faintly over the dull roar of Raul's heartbeat in his ears.

"You can take the hood off, Raul," a calm voice said from the darkness.

Raul hesitated, then raised his freed right hand to peel the spit hood away. The light overhead stung his eyes. He blinked several times, adjusting to the sterile grayness of the room. Cinder block walls, a single surveillance camera in the corner, a battered metal table bolted to the floor.

Across from him sat a man in his mid-30s with hard lines around his mouth and a muscular build under a worn gray henley, sleeves pushed to his elbows. He was flipping through a folder, slow and methodical, like he had all the time in the world.

"Where am I?" Raul croaked. "Who the hell are you? Why am I here?"

The man didn't look up immediately. When he did, his gaze was sharp and cold. The kind of look that said he'd seen everything and wasn't impressed.

He set a leather badge wallet on the table with a crisp clink of metal. "Detective Jake Harper. Stonehaven Police Department."

Raul's mouth twisted. "Stonehaven? What the hell is this?"

Harper leaned back, casually flipping another page. "You're here because we need to talk."

"About what?" Raul said, posture defensive. "You got the wrong guy. I didn't do anything."

"Sure," Harper said evenly. "But before we get into all that…"

He pulled a small card from his wallet and began reading the Miranda rights. His voice was calm and deliberate, like reciting a bedtime story. Raul listened, but said nothing. He just watched, trying to read how deep he was in.

"You understand your rights?"

Raul gave a tight nod.

"Say it out loud. For the record."

Raul instinctively swallowed, his throat dry. His heart thudded faster. "…Yeah. I understand."

"Keeping that in mind, will you speak with me?"

"…Yeah."

Harper set the card down and leaned forward. "Good. Let's start simple."

He tapped the folder lightly. "You've been busy, Raul. Driving around, odd hours. Not exactly Lyft."

Raul gave a weak chuckle. "I've got a courier gig. Flexible schedule."

"Sure you do." Harper tilted his head. "So help me out. What were you delivering two nights ago? Near the river? Or last week, outside Redhaven?"

Raul squinted. "Red-what?"

"Interesting," Harper murmured. "You ever been to Clackamas? Welches? Cottage Grove? How about Neskatah?"

"You askin' if I've been to a whole county?" Raul leaned back, forcing a smile. "Man, I don't keep a logbook."

Harper didn't smile back.

He slid a photo across the table. A grainy aerial of a heavily wooded area, trees encircling what looked like a small compound.

Raul looked at it. "No idea what that is."

Another photo. This one was clearer, with trailers, fencing, and floodlights. Redhaven.

Raul's eyes narrowed. "Still nothing."

A third. Raul, standing beside a white van, parked outside the compound.

His jaw twitched, but his voice stayed cool. "Photoshopped."

Harper didn't react. Just kept laying photos down. Girls. Missing girls. Names and ages scrawled on white tape at the bottom of each. Some were smiling, some looked hollowed out by whatever came after the camera flash.

Raul stared, expression tightening, heat creeping into his face.

"These girls," Harper said, "are gone. Some for months. Some for years. Some were last seen in Cottage Grove. Some in Clackamas. All of them…ended up here."

He tapped the photo of Redhaven.

"And you were their ride."

Raul leaned back. "I don't know what you think you have, but I don't run anything. I'm just a driver. I don't know what they do in that place."

"You sure?" Harper asked, tone still calm. "Because I've got a folder full of witness statements, security footage, financials, and GPS data that all say otherwise."

Raul scoffed, but there was a flicker of panic in his eyes now.

Harper kept going.

"Let's talk about the charges. Human trafficking. Kidnapping. Rape. Drugging minors. Assault. State and federal. Each girl is a separate count."

He paused, letting the weight of the table between them feel like a mountain. Raul was sweating now, his chest rising and falling quickly.

"And that's not even including the children."

Harper laid out more photos.

"Seven years kidnapping, eight years for rape. Per count. Per victim. Consecutive sentencing. You're looking at sixty, seventy years. Minimum. And in prison, with those charges?"

Harper waited another beat. Let Raul sit in it.

"At your age, that's a life sentence. No matter how you look at it. And prison isn't kind to people with these types of charges hanging over them."

Raul looked away. His mouth opened, then closed.

"What do you want?" he asked, voice barely above a whisper.

"You're not walking out of this, Raul. You know that, right? Not unless you start talking."

"What do you want to know?"

"Everything," Harper said simply. "Tell me everything."

Raul hesitated, trying to summon another lie. "Even if I did know something… you think the big man gives orders to nobodies like me? I don't know names. I just drive. That's it."

Harper didn't blink. "Funny. The cameras say different."

Raul shook his head. "You don't get it. You don't know who you're dealing with."

"I think I do."

He slid one final photo across the table.

Thomas Alvarez. Smiling. Campaign fundraiser. Arms around two county commissioners.

Then another.

Alvarez stepping out of a black Escalade at Redhaven, eyes hidden behind sunglasses, a faint smirk on his lips.

Raul stared at the images. His mask cracked, his face paling and ashen.

"I know *exactly* who we're dealing with," Harper said.

Raul dropped his eyes to the table. His shoulders sagged. The sweat at his temples formed drops, moving down his neck to his shirt until his collar darkened with it. He rubbed his face like he was trying to wipe everything away.

Harper kept his voice even. "There are Homeland Security agents waiting outside. You're facing state and federal charges. But if you give us Alvarez, we'll work with the DA, tell them you cooperated. Otherwise? We take you. And I promise, no one will care what your reasons were."

Raul buried his face in his hands, his shoulders shaking in silent sobs.

Harper said nothing. He moved his chair in, set a hand on Raul's shoulder, and let the moment stretch.

"It wasn't supposed to be like this," Raul muttered.

Harper waited. Let the silence press Raul forward.

Finally, Raul spoke, his voice choked. "I had a gambling problem, I... I owed money I couldn't pay. A lot of money. The kind you can't get out from under. The guy I owed money to, he said if I drove for him, the debt was gone."

"And you said yes."

Raul nodded. "At first it was just packages. Drugs, I figured. Then the guy got picked up by the feds. Turns out he was a fucking cop. Sergeant Hale. Selling pills."

Hale. Harper's jaw tensed.

"Go on," he said.

"I drove stuff. I didn't ask what. I needed out. Then Hale got arrested. I thought I was free and clear."

"But you weren't."

Raul nodded. "Dunham pulled me over one night. Real calm. Said my debt was his now. Gave me a name, a photo of a girl in Welches. Said she owed, too. Told me how to grab her. Gave me syringes. Knock-out drugs."

Harper's skin prickled cold beneath his shirt.

"And after that?"

"No more names. Just types. 'Blonde, petite, maybe eighteen.' Orders. Then younger. Twelve, thirteen."

Harper steadied his breathing. "How did Neskatah come into play?"

Raul dropped his gaze. Harper slid the photo of Kailey across the table. Raul stared at the photo of the young, raven-haired girl.

"I was living out that way. He told me to start picking up girls on the 'rez. Said no one cares about missing native girls. No one would look for them."

Harper waited. Let the silence stretch.

Raul swallowed hard. "After that first girl—the one in Welches—someone showed me how to… *recruit*. They called it 'romancing the mark.' Said girls are easier to move when they come willingly. When they think they're choosing you."

Harper's voice stayed low, controlled. "Explain."

Raul rubbed the back of his neck, avoiding eye contact. "You start by noticing them. Really noticing them. You compliment their hair. Their smile. You ask about their dreams. Make them feel special. Then you listen. You find out what they need. What they hate about where they are. What they're running from."

He exhaled shakily.

"Then you become the escape plan. The boyfriend. The protector. You tell them you're falling in love. That you're going to build a life together. You keep it a secret. You say no one would understand your connection. Not their friends. Not their family."

Harper said nothing. Just stared.

Raul's voice grew quieter. "I'd tell them I got a new job. Across the state. That I wanted them to come with me. Start over. Buy a house. Get married. Some even picked the town. Picked the damn paint color for the house."

His hands curled into fists.

"When they got in the van, they thought they were starting their lives. But by the time we got to Blackridge, they were broke. Cut off. Had nothing. And Dunham would be waiting."

Harper's chest burned. He exhaled slowly through his nose, steadying his breathing. He dropped his voice, looking straight at Raul. "Where did you take them?"

"Warehouse in Stonehaven, first. Then Redhaven. They built it up. Big time. Guards, surveillance. Real setup. They were sold, pimped out, drugged. Men come to fuck 'em, live out their fantasies. Whatever kink you got, Alvarez lets you do to the girls."

"What kinds of kinks?"

"Whatever you want. You want a woman to tell you she loves you? She'll do that. You want to tie her up and have her beg you to stop? Beat the shit out of her? Stab her? Shoot her? *Kill her?* Nothing is off limits in Redhaven, for the right price."

Harper's voice dropped lower. "Even the kids?"

Raul's voice cracked. "All of it, man. All of it."

"They keep files," he added. "Photos, videos. Medical records. Preferences, client requests. The girls wear bracelets with color codes. Red means they fight. Yellow means compliant. Blue means drugged. Green means underage."

Harper's eyes gleamed like ice under the lights of the room.

"What happens to them when it's over?"

"Alvarez brings in a doctor. Patches up the ones who need patching up, gives them what they need to keep the dope sickness away. The ones who make it just get fixed up for the next round."

The ones who make it. Harper zeroed in on that phrase.

"What happens to the ones who don't?"

Raul's voice faltered. "I take care of 'em. Bury them. Out in the woods. Same place every time. I can show you."

Harper nodded, pulled out a map. Raul pointed at a spot on the map. Harper followed his finger, locking the spot into memory. He didn't write it down. He wouldn't forget it.

"Tell me more about Alvarez."

"He's the boss. Never dealt with him directly, but everyone knows. He inspects the girls. Spends time with them. When he's there… it's different. Colder. The men who come to play, they all owe favors to Alvarez."

Harper's jaw tightened. "Yeah," he murmured. "That sounds like him."

Raul looked up. "You know him?"

"I know him," Harper said flatly. "Where's his office?"

"Main building. Top floor. Has cameras inside."

"How many girls are there now?"

"Ten, fifteen."

"Ages?"

"Youngest, maybe twelve? Oldest is maybe twenty-five. He doesn't like them older than that."

Harper's voice dropped. "Is Kailey there?"

Raul hesitated. "She mouthed off to Dunham. Three weeks ago. I was told to take her to the woods."

Silence fell. Harper stared at the photo. His jaw tightened, the muscle near his temple twitching.

He looked back at Raul, and when he spoke again, his voice was quiet, cold enough to make Raul flinch.

"You buried her?"

Raul nodded once. "Near the others."

Harper didn't blink. "Then I'll dig her up myself."

His words landed like a hammer.

The door opened. Briggs stepped inside, face unreadable. "Time to go."

Raul looked up, panicked. "Wait! I gave you everything!"

Harper stared him down. "And we'll let the DA know. But you're still facing murder, trafficking, the whole thing. That doesn't mean you're walking. And we can't risk you making a call."

Briggs moved forward. "Federal hold. Ninety-six hours."

Raul started yelling as he was hauled out of the chair.

Harper didn't look back. He stepped into the observation room where Foster and the team waited.

Foster folded his arms. "Well?"

Harper exhaled. "We've got enough. Let's get the warrant."

He turned, walking toward the door.

"Time to hit the compound."

Fucking showtime.

• • • • •

INTERLUDE: THE ARCHITECT

Thomas Alvarez learned early that power wasn't seized. It was *granted*, offered in whispers and handshakes, traded in favors, and cloaked in legality.

He had started as a patrol officer in the small town of McKenzie, nestled at the base of the Cascades. Known as the "gateway to Blackridge," it was a dusty Western holdover with a population just north of two thousand and architecture that hadn't changed since the '60s. Alvarez—clean cut, well-spoken, fluent in English and Spanish—quickly became a favorite among locals. But like many small towns, McKenzie faced an existential crisis in the late nineties: not enough money to keep the lights on, let alone fund a four-man police department.

When the town voted to disband its force and contract with the Blackridge County Sheriff's Office, the sheriff offered spots to the displaced officers. Alvarez was the first to raise his hand.

He barely spent a year in patrol before angling for a position on the county's underfunded Search and Rescue team. It wasn't glamorous, but Alvarez saw the angles. When a missing hiker or runaway kid turned up—usually thanks to patrol grunt work—he was already on scene to take the credit. Posing for newspaper photos. Giving interviews. Consoling grateful parents. He built a reputation not as a cop, but as a savior. One who solved cases with a smile and a handshake.

Internally, those who worked with him knew better. He was rarely first on scene. Rarely in the woods or at the staging areas. He had a knack for showing up just as the work was done, making sure the cameras saw his face before the patrol guys even put away their radios.

From there, Alvarez slid into the detective bureau, hand-picked for high-profile, low-effort cases. Media-friendly assignments. Home invasions with obvious suspects. Political graffiti that made good headlines. Nothing messy, nothing unsolvable. He wasn't good at detective work. But he was excellent at *looking* like he was.

It was during those years that he built alliances. Strategic ones. Sgt. Hale, who was then a patrol sergeant working the rural south end of the county, was running pills behind the scenes, using seized property and bogus evidence logs to move product with impunity. Alvarez didn't just look the other way. He insulated it. Protected it.

Dunham, already promoted to sergeant by then, became Hale's unofficial enforcer. Brash. Unquestioning. Loyal to a fault. The kind of guy who could "lose" dash cam footage and lean on a witness without blinking. Alvarez pulled the strings from above as patrol lieutenant, ensuring complaints died in inboxes and audits got "deprioritized." In return, he took his cut, quietly, through shell companies and PACs.

The operation might have stayed buried if it wasn't for Harper and Deputy Nolan Warren stumbling into the operation all those years ago. For a brief moment, it looked like everything might unravel.

Alvarez acted quickly. He bought Warren's silence—promises, pressure, veiled threats—and then turned the full weight of the department against Harper. Warren helped fabricate misconduct. DUI paperwork. Missing evidence. A questionable use of force turned into an IA death sentence. By the end of it, Harper was fired, disgraced, and dragged through the mud.

The message was clear: dig too deep, and we'll bury you in it.

With Harper gone and the story buried, Alvarez was promoted again, this time to Undersheriff, with a clean record and glowing endorsements. He stayed out of sight, letting the uniformed Sheriff take the spotlight while he handled "internal affairs" from behind the curtain.

Years later, when the feds finally caught up with Hale on a trafficking charge, Alvarez didn't panic. He sent Dunham to remind both Hale and Warren exactly how far the sheriff's office reach still extended. Whatever was said in that backroom conversation, it worked.

Warren flipped on Hale, but only Hale. The case never reached higher. Alvarez stood behind the podium a week later, somber-eyed, delivering soundbites to the press.

'We are shocked and saddened by Sgt. Hale's betrayal of public trust. This department does not tolerate corruption. We will rebuild stronger."

No one asked why Hale had operated so long without oversight. No one asked why the paper trail ended just short of command.

The Redhaven compound—the real operation—remained untouched. Built with seized assets. Staffed not by deputies, but by military contractors, all recruited through Dunham's old Marine Corps contacts. Private. Loyal. Off-the-books. It wasn't a safe house. It was a black site.

And when Michael Grant came offering expansion through money and digital infrastructure in exchange for political capital, Alvarez didn't hesitate.

Grant was ambitious. But Alvarez was *inevitable.*

When things went wrong, Alvarez didn't panic. He delegated.

Dunham was more than a loyal soldier, he was a blunt instrument, a man who didn't ask why. And Estrada? A street rat with ambition and no conscience, easy to bribe, easier to discard.

What Alvarez never saw coming—what men like him *couldn't* see—was someone like Harper. Not because Harper was better, or louder, or more connected. But because Harper *cared.* Because Harper would keep digging long after the cameras went home. Long after it stopped being convenient.

Alvarez's only mistake was assuming no one would look too closely.

But now Harper was digging.

And the thing about architects?

They don't go down without collapsing the building on top of you.

• • • • •

CHAPTER 25: ASH AND IRON

Now.

Harper tightened the side straps on his plate carrier, the nylon whispering beneath his fingers. The warehouse was quiet but tense, like a held breath. Around him, the sounds of preparation filled the space. Rifle bolts racked, radios chirped, Velcro tore, gear settled with dull thuds on concrete.

He rolled his shoulders, stretching out the weight, then reached for his duty belt.

Across the room, Austin Briggs was locking down the rear of the van, issuing last-minute adjustments to Kalama and the HSI entry team. Even now, after transferring out of Stonehaven and into a federal role, Briggs had stayed in the fight with him. Had picked up the phone when no one else would. Had vouched for him when Harper needed a second chance.

"You land this job in Stonehaven," he'd said, *"you make it count. I know what they did to you in Blackridge. Prove 'em all wrong."*

And Harper had. Because someone believed in him.

Nearby, Foster was pulling his vest over his head, adjusting the Velcro with calm precision. No speeches. No posturing. Just quiet readiness, the kind that steadied a room without trying. The kind that made younger officers stand a little straighter without knowing why.

He had always carried himself that way. Steady. Grounded. Unshakable.

Back when Harper was still in patrol, Foster had been his sergeant, the one who took him under his wing without making a show of it. He didn't coddle. He didn't chase praise. He just taught. He had shown Harper how to be thorough, how to follow his instincts, and more importantly, when not to back down.

Most supervisors told you when to let something go. Foster was the one who told Harper to pull the thread.

"See where it goes," he'd say. "And if it leads somewhere bad, go anyway."

He had encouraged Harper to chase leads to the end. To trust his gut. And when Harper had tried to explain why it mattered so much, why he couldn't let things slide, why he couldn't let wrong be ignored, Foster had helped him find the words.

Right is right. No matter the cost.

It had started as a conversation. Somewhere along the line, it became a principle.

Now, years later, Foster wasn't just a mentor. He wasn't just the sergeant who'd helped Harper become the detective he was.

He was more than that.

Foster was family now. A brother in every way that mattered.

Across the room, Hurst was checking her mags and organizing case folders in her bag like she always did. Meticulous. Efficient. Unflinching. She and Harper still partnered often in the bureau, and over time, they'd developed a quiet rhythm. A glance. A single word. That was all it took.

She never questioned why he pushed so hard. She just matched him, step for step.

There were days when her clarity pulled him back from the edge. Days when she reminded him, without saying a word, that justice didn't always follow a clean path, but it still had to be pursued.

They weren't just colleagues. They were a team. The kind that didn't need reassignment forms or formal titles to make it official. The work spoke for itself. And so did the trust between them.

And Cho.

Cho was newer to the team, still learning, still finding his footing.

Harper saw a lot of himself in the kid. Not just the work ethic, but the fire underneath. That need to make things right. That refusal to look away, even when the truth hurt.

Lately, Harper had started mentoring him, though he'd never use the word out loud. Not by hovering or preaching. Just by being there. By backing him up when it mattered and letting him find his own way when it didn't.

It was strange, sometimes, to see the shift.

To feel the weight pass into his hands.

He wasn't the one reaching for the lifeline anymore.

Now, he was the one handing them out.

Harper exhaled, slow and steady, letting the memories fall away like spent brass.

The ghosts still flickered at the edges. Quentin Everstone, Nolan Warren, Thomas Alvarez. Names that used to mean something.

Now just echoes.

There were false brothers.

But there were true ones too.

And tonight, he was going to war with the right kind.

Harper slid the last mag into his vest and gave it a pat. He drew his Glock with his left hand, pulled the slide back just enough to see brass in the chamber, a quick press check. The weapon light blinked steady. Red dot burned bright. He holstered it with a firm click, then clipped his radio mic to his shoulder strap and slipped the earpiece into his right ear.

He repeated the motions with his rifle, an FN AR-15 variant, red dot, mounted light, zeroed and ready.

The gear felt heavier tonight. Maybe it always did before the unknown.

Briggs approached, nodding once. "We're set. Kalama, you'll be with the Stonehaven dicks. My team is in place at the rock quarry, ready to roll in with you. Ten total in the stack. We're green across the board."

Harper gave a short nod. "Any word from the eye on the ridge?"

"All quiet," Briggs said. "Lights on in the main house, but no movement in the barn or outbuildings. They're either asleep, gone, or waiting."

Foster stepped in beside them, wearing his game face. "My money's on waiting."

Harper smirked faintly. "How'd I know you'd say that?"

Foster shrugged. "Because we've seen too much to believe in luck." He gave Harper a pointed look. "You good?"

"Yeah," Harper said. "Better than I should be."

Foster studied him for a beat. "That's what I like about you. You show up anyway."

Kalama looked over, rifle slung, a quiet intensity in his gaze. "Briggs, your guy with the eye wants final positions confirmed. We're locking in thirty."

Briggs gave a sharp nod and turned to go, but paused to clap Harper once on the shoulder. "We bring 'em in, Jake. Clean. Precise. No cowboy shit."

Harper gave a dry smile. "I'm not the one you have to worry about."

From the rear of the room, Cho raised an eyebrow. "I heard that."

The team chuckled, just for a second. Just enough to breathe.

Foster looked at them all. "Alright. Last check. Gear tight. Comms hot. Once we roll, there's no reset button."

Harper tightened the last strap on his vest and looked around the room, at the agents, the cops, the men and women willing to follow him into darkness.

"I've got your backs," he said quietly.

Foster nodded. "And we've got yours."

Harper's voice was steady now. "Let's bring those girls home."

He gave the nod.

"Roll out."

•••••

CHAPTER 26: REDHAVEN

The woods were quiet on the approach. *Too* quiet. No wind in the trees. No rustle of deer in the brush. Not even the rhythmic chirp of frogs that usually owned the night. It was the kind of silence that settled deep in your chest, like the world itself was holding its breath.

Harper had secured the state warrant while Briggs locked down the federal one. Both included rare provisions authorizing a night raid, a legal exception justified by the imminent danger to the women and children believed to be held inside. Harper had run through the affidavit with the state judge over the phone. She didn't interrupt. She didn't ask for clarification.

She just gasped.

The line went quiet for a moment. Then a quiet, trembling, "Stand by."

Ten minutes later, she called back and swore him in. Her voice cracked as she read the approval aloud, every syllable laced with fury and heartbreak.

"Go get those girls," she said.

"I will, Your Honor," Harper replied.

Now, the convoy pulled out from the warehouse in practiced formation.

Engines rumbled to life, headlights carving sharp beams through the dark. No sirens. No chatter. Just a quiet, surgical resolve.

Harper led in his gray Durango, fingers tight on the wheel. Behind him came Briggs and Kalama in the beat-up minivan, the kind of vehicle no one gave a second look to. Then Cho's Bronco. Hurst's Camry. Foster's matte-black F150, steady and familiar, anchored the rear.

They rolled down the highway like a shadow stretching across the asphalt. Controlled. Deliberate.

No one spoke. No one sped. The tires hummed low against the pavement as they neared the gravel turnout that led to the rock quarry, steady as a war drum.

As they turned onto the gravel cutoff leading to the quarry, the terrain shifted beneath their wheels. Crunching stone and soft snow muffled their approach.

Up ahead, two Homeland Security vans sat dead in the tree line, lights off, moonlight glinting faintly off steel. Retrofitted for transport, two had cages installed in the back for any arrests they made tonight. Reinforced locks. They weren't here to make friends, and they couldn't trust the Blackridge County Sheriff's Office to make the arrests for them. That much had been clear for a long time.

The survivors, if they found any, would ride out in the investigator rigs. It wasn't right. They deserved better. But for tonight, *safe* would have to be enough.

The air outside was cold. The kind that snuck beneath collars and gloves. Snow drifted down, silent and persistent, clinging to hoods and windshield wipers.

Harper sat still, one gloved hand gripping the wheel, the other resting on the rifle across the passenger seat. His breath fogged the glass as he watched Briggs step out to confer with his agents. No shouting. Just hand signals, quick nods. Everyone already knew their roles.

A moment later, Briggs slid back into his seat and keyed the mic.

"Eye says all is quiet."

Harper exhaled slowly and picked up his radio. "Copy. Let's hit it."

He eased the Durango forward, leading the convoy once more. The wheels crunched softly over the gravel, snow accumulating in the dips between ruts. His pulse quickened, not frantic but sharp, steady and hard. He could feel the adrenaline rising in his chest. He drew in a slow breath through his nose, held it for three seconds, then let it out through his mouth. Again.

The breathing drill had carried him through countless boardings and blacked-out operations with MSRT. When your body needed calm but your instincts screamed otherwise. Tonight, it was keeping him centered.

His gloved hands gripped the wheel tighter as they neared the turnoff to Redhaven. The trees opened to a winding approach, the compound still hidden beyond the final bend. Harper reached over and flipped the headlights off, plunging the convoy into darkness.

One by one, the vehicles behind him followed suit. Darkness swallowed the road. No sound beyond the low grind of tires on gravel and the ticking of engines cooling behind the vans.

Just before the last bend, Briggs's voice came over the radio, a crackle of quiet authority.

"Cell phone jammer is active."

Harper lifted the mic one last time. "Greenlight. We are a go."

He hit the switch.

The Durango's lights snapped on, red and blue slicing through the trees. Harper floored it. Tires shrieked. The SUV launched like a beast unchained.

Behind him, the convoy erupted. Sirens wailed.. Lights tore through the dark.

The stillness shattered.

Ahead, floodlights, a chain-link gate. A guard shack. Two silhouettes sprinting into view, rifles raised.

Harper hit the brakes. The Durango fishtailed, gravel and slush flying as he spun it sideways, engine block towards the threat. He was already moving, door open, boots hitting gravel, rifle up, cheek to stock.

"DROP 'EM! POLICE! ON THE GROUND! NOW!" Harper shouted.

The guards didn't hesitate. They opened fire.

Rounds ripped into the vehicles. Bullets sparked off steel. Windshields fractured. Someone shouted. Glass exploded above Harper's head as he ducked lower, rifle raised, cheek to stock.

Then—

CRACK. CRACK.

Two precise shots echoed from the hills. The guard's heads snapped back, red mist blooming in the cold night air. Rifles dropped from limp fingers. Blood drops scattered into the falling snow.

Their bodies hit the gravel with dull, lifeless thuds.

Harper didn't need to look. He already knew. Overwatch had made the shots.

He sprinted forward, boots sliding on the snow-dusted gravel. He passed the bodies and slammed his gloved fist into the gate control box. The old mechanism clicked and hummed to life, the gate groaning open, its power drawing from a generator.

He spun back to his vehicle, heart hammering, surprised to see it still running despite the bullet-riddled front end.

Detroit engineering at its best.

Behind him, the convoy surged forward. Vehicles fanned out across the compound yard, tires skidding on gravel, engines snarling under the wash of flashing red and blue. Doors flew open. Boots hit the ground.

The team moved fast, carbines up, slicing through the dark with mounted lights.

"MOVE! MOVE!"

Cho, Hurst, and the four HSI special agents peeled off toward the barn and outbuildings. Shadows darted between sheds as the team fanned out, sweeping through the outer edges.

Harper charged toward the main building, flanked by Briggs, Kalama, and Foster.

The front door loomed ahead, a plain wood slab reinforced with metal trim. Harper reached it first and gave the handle a quick twist. Locked.

Foster was already moving. "I got it!" He planted one boot, leaned back, and drove his heel forward in one clean motion. The frame cracked hard, splinters flying, and the door burst inward with a hollow slam.

Harper moved in immediately, rifle up, eyes scanning. The entryway opened into a wide hallway lined with closed doors on both sides. Bedrooms, most likely. Shadows pooled beneath the doorframes. The smell of mildew and cheap cleaning supplies hung in the air.

Briggs fell in behind him, Kalama close behind, with Foster sweeping in last to secure the rear.

They pushed forward quickly, clearing room to room in tight, practiced rhythm. Each door they passed was locked.

"Stack up. Push past for now, we'll come back for them," Harper ordered. No time to breach each one yet. They kept moving, feet pounding across stained laminate, rounding corners as they aimed for the central office on the second floor.

At the end of the hallway, the floor forked. A staircase curled upward to the right. Another corridor stretched forward.

Harper turned toward the stairs. "I've got the office," he said, voice clipped through his comms.

No hesitation. No argument, Foster falling in behind him without a word. Harper adjusted his grip and started climbing, rifle angled high, eyes on the landing. Briggs and Kalama moved forward into the next hall, vanishing around the corner as the team split.

The stairwell echoed faintly with each footstep. Plaster flaked along the railing. Shadows clung to every corner. Halfway up, the sharp stutter of gunfire erupted from below and ahead. A tight burst of automatic fire. Then silence.

Briggs's voice in Harper's earpiece, steady and calm. "Two tangos down. Clear."

Harper and Foster reached the landing. The second-floor hallway stretched out before them. Empty. Still.

Harper scanned left, then right. No movement. No sound.

They moved quietly, the hallway stretching ahead in dim silence. The floor creaked beneath their boots, but nothing stirred. As they reached the office door, Harper glanced at Foster. Foster raised one hand and held up five fingers. He brought them down one by one.

Five. Four. Three. Two. One.

At one, Foster turned the knob and threw the door open wide.

Harper stepped in fast, rifle up, sweeping the corners. His eyes moved with the barrel, clearing instinctively from left to right.

"Clear," he called out.

He lowered the rifle and slung it over his shoulder. The room was empty. There was a cheap desk, filing cabinet, and the windows were covered with blackout curtains. A security monitor blinked faintly on the wall, its feed cycling slowly through a handful of angles from outside.

Harper keyed his mic. "Second floor secure."

"First floor secure," Briggs replied a moment later.

"Outbuildings secure. Two tangos in custody," came Hurst's voice, clipped but calm.

"Alright. Get the custodies secured, then get over here. We've got about two dozen rooms to search," Harper said.

•••••

CHAPTER 27: WHERE THE SILENCE ENDS

Within minutes, the team had regrouped in the main hallway. Their footfalls echoed now as they moved together in pairs, moving methodically from room to room.

Knock. Announce. Open. Clear.

"Police," they called, again and again, voices calm but firm. "You're safe. We're here to help."

But the words felt fragile in the air, like paper lanterns in a storm.

What they found behind those doors hollowed them out.

The women were scattered across rooms like forgotten memories. Some crouched in corners, arms wrapped tight around themselves. Others sat motionless on stained mattresses, eyes vacant and wide, as if time had stopped for them and never resumed. Most were barefoot. Their clothes were mismatched, some in oversized T-shirts, others in torn leggings or nothing but thin slips. Arms riddled with bruises, some fresh, some fading. Tracks snaked along the veins of a few, their skin yellowed and paper-thin.

It was the silence that struck hardest. Not one of them cried out.

Some didn't respond at all. They blinked slowly, mechanically, when officers entered. Others recoiled instinctively, shrinking from even the softest voice.

And then the children.

The children were worse.

They didn't scream. They didn't cry. They simply stared. Small bodies curled beneath threadbare blankets, clinging to each other like shipwreck survivors. One girl, maybe ten, flinched when Foster crouched and offered her a water bottle. She shrank away like it was a trick.

Foster didn't push. He just set it down and backed off, eyes stinging.

Harper stepped into a room with Hurst and Cho, the scent of sweat, bleach, and something metallic hanging thick in the air. A teenage girl sat beside the bed, knees drawn to her chest, face buried in a tattered fleece blanket.

He crouched slowly, keeping his voice gentle. Soft. Like you might speak to a frightened animal.

"Hey," he said. "You're safe now. What's your name?"

She looked up.

She looked through him, not at him. Her face was streaked with tears, freckles dotting the bridge of her nose. Her pupils were blown wide, her eyes empty, as if whatever used to be there had long since disappeared.

She opened her mouth, but stopped. Then she shook her head. Her voice barely surfaced.

"I don't remember," she whispered. "I only remember what the big man called me."

Harper's throat tightened. He swallowed hard.

"What did he call you?" he asked softly, already knowing he'd hate the answer.

Her voice cracked.

"Freckles."

The word shattered something in the room. She broke down into quiet sobs, her small frame shaking with each breath. Hurst knelt beside her, one hand on her shoulder. Cho looked away, his jaw clenched so tight the muscles pulsed.

Harper gently unfolded a wool blanket from his pack and draped it around her shoulders. She leaned into it like it was the only real thing in the world.

"You're safe now," he repeated, barely above a whisper. "Come on, let's get you out of here."

He helped her to her feet and guided her out into the cold. The snow was still falling, a light dusting already forming on the blacktop as he led her to one of the waiting vans.

She didn't speak again. She didn't need to.

Harper closed the van door behind her and stood there for a moment, the weight of everything pressing down on his chest. His eyes burned, but he blinked the sting away. Even from outside, Harper could hear the sound of a girl crying in another room.

There were more rooms to search.

And more girls to bring home.

The hallway again. Room by room.

Each door opened into another version of the same nightmare.

In one, a woman screamed at the sight of light and bolted under the bed. She kicked and clawed at the air until Briggs crouched low, murmuring to her like one might calm a dying bird. It took minutes, long minutes, for her to trust his outstretched hand.

When she finally emerged, eyes red and shaking, she asked if she was in trouble.

"No," Briggs said gently. "You're going home."

The word "home" didn't seem to register. She just stared at the floor, her shoulders sagging.

In another room, Hurst found a woman curled up on a bare mattress. Her face was swollen, one eye nearly shut, a deep bruise trailing down her jawline. She wouldn't speak, wouldn't even look up.

Hurst sat beside her and simply waited. She didn't press. Just stayed, waited in silence.

Minutes passed. Then the woman spoke, voice small and raw.

"Do I have to go back?"

"You never have to go back," Hurst said. "Not ever."

Cho and Kalama moved through a row of smaller rooms in the west wing. Most were empty now, abandoned. But in one, they found two girls, no older than ten, huddled together under a stained comforter. Their clothes were thin, and their feet were purple from the cold. One clutched a plastic fork like a weapon.

Cho took off his jacket and wrapped it around them both.

They didn't cry. They didn't speak. But they didn't let go of his jacket either.

in one of the final rooms, Harper and Foster found a girl lying on the floor. Barely twenty. Her lips were blue. A syringe lay on the table. Her pupils were blown wide. Her chest barely moved.

"Narcan," Harper said.

Foster moved fast, clearing her airway while Harper injected the dose. Seconds crawled by. Then—

A gasp.

She lurched upright, coughing, eyes wide in confusion and fear.

"I thought I was dead," she said.

"You're not," Harper told her. "Not tonight."

Outside, the vans filled. One by one.

Blankets. Water bottles. Gentle hands and whispered reassurances.

Quiet voices guiding survivors out of the dark. It was a scene of organized chaos, but this wasn't triage. It was rescue. Each step out the door was a defiance of what had been done to them. Each survivor a flicker of light, still burning. And for each one, someone knelt beside them. No uniforms. No orders. Just presence.

The girls ranged from about eight to maybe twenty-four. Most of them had stopped crying. Some hadn't started yet. Haunted expressions. Vacant eyes. Shoulders that flinched at sudden movement. No one spoke unless spoken to. They had all learned to be invisible. Harper saw Hurst helping one of the teenage girls tie her shoes, the girl's hands too shaky to do it herself.

Harper stood near the gate and watched it all unfold. He felt the cold now, the snow soaking through his sleeves, but he didn't move.

They had found them.

He stood alone for a long moment, his breath fogging in the cold. His gloves were wet from tears. His breath fogged in the cold. Snow gathered on the brim of his cap. All he could see were their faces. The girls. The youngest ones. Eight. Nine. Ten. Too young for any of this.

He felt his stomach turn.

Estrada's voice echoed in his mind, defensive in the interrogation room.

"We never went that young. We weren't monsters."

Harper's jaw clenched. His fingers curled into fists.

You lied. You bastard. You knew. You lied with a straight face.

His hands curled into fists. Jaw locked. The rage settled in his chest like coals on a bed of ash. Controlled. Contained. But burning just the same.

Harper stood outside the main building as the last of the vans pulled away. Their tail lights glowed faintly through the snow, then vanished behind the trees. Inside those vehicles were girls who had been caged and sold, who now sat wrapped in blankets, unsure if the nightmare was truly over.

He had watched each one of them leave. Silent. Shattered. Alive.

Now the quiet returned.

• • • • •

Harper turned back toward the building, boots crunching in the fresh snow, and stepped inside. The air was still thick with the scent of mold, bleach, and sweat. The hallway was empty. The doors stood open behind them now, memories still clinging to the doorframes. The office waited at the end of the hall, untouched.

He entered and shut the door behind him.

The office was cold, but sweat clung to the back of his neck beneath the collar of his vest. The walls seemed to close in. Dust floated in the beam of his flashlight. The air stank of mildew, sweat and something metallic beneath it all. Blood maybe, or old fear soaked into the walls. The kind of scent that didn't come out.

He started with the desk. The top drawer slid open with a soft creak. Inside were loose papers and folders, organized in a way that felt almost surgical. Harper flipped one open.

Names. Names of women. Names of girls.

Each page listed identifiers. A first name, or sometimes just a nickname, followed by age, a photo, and status. Some had check marks beside them. Others were crossed out. Living. Deceased. Sold.

He turned to the next file. More lists. This one was labeled "Clients." Some entries were initials. Some were masked behind shell companies, PACs, or acronyms. But a few? A few were unmistakable.

State senators. Judges. Tech moguls. Public figures. Mostly men. A handful of women. All of them scum.

Beside each name, notes in small, neat handwriting. Preferences. Requirements. Limits. Some had none. Others were worse.

"Ages 12–14. Must cry. No tattoos. No permanent injuries."

His stomach twisted. He kept going.

At the bottom of the drawer were thumb drives, bundled in rubber bands. He grabbed one at random and inserted it into the computer. The monitor glowed to life. Files loaded. Folder after folder, each labeled with a name or code.

He clicked one at random.

The footage was grainy. A girl, maybe sixteen, tied to a bed frame. She was screaming. Someone off camera laughed. The video continued. Harper hit pause, breathing through his nose, hand tight on the mouse.

He found another folder. This one was labeled *Kaylie Stonewood.*

He hesitated.

Then he clicked.

The screen flickered. The video began without a preamble.

Kaylie sat on the floor of the very room Harper now stood in. Her clothes were torn. Barely hanging on. Blood matted the side of her face. She was crying, the kind of deep, panicked sobs that came from someone who knew no help was coming. Hyperventilating.

A man entered the frame. She tried to crawl away, sobs shaking her shoulders. He grabbed her by the hair and yanked her to her knees. *Dunham.* He was unmistakable. Clean-shaven. Calm. Detached. And in his right hand was the Kabar.

He ripped what little clothing remained from her body and shoved her to the ground. She screamed and kicked, but he didn't flinch. He undid his belt, pulled his pants down just enough, and climbed on top of her. The knife stayed pressed against her throat the entire time.

Kaylie's voice was ragged, pleading. "Please stop. Please. Please."

He said nothing. Just grunted.

The sound of it. The violence. The quiet cruelty. Harper watched, jaw locked, every muscle taut as piano wire.

Watched as Dunham raped her. Watched as she screamed, begging him to stop. When it was over, she lay there, crying, her ribs shaking with each breath.

Dunham looked down at her like she was nothing, contempt burning in his eyes.

"Shut the fuck up already," he said.

He didn't raise his voice. Didn't blink. He just pulled the knife back, placed the tip above her breastbone, and drove it in.

Straight. Hard. Deep.

No hesitation. No warning.

No other words.

Her eyes flew open, shock crashing through them like a storm. Her mouth parted in a choked cough, the breath stolen before it could escape. Her back arched violently, muscles seizing against the cold floor. Blood pulsed out around the blade as he yanked it out, bright and immediate.

Then, stillness. Her body dropped like something unplugged. Her head lolled back with a hollow *thud*, eyes frozen on nothing. Final tears tracking slowly down her cheeks in perfect, unbearable silence.

Dunham stood over her a moment. Then he reached down, wiped the knife clean on the fabric of her jeans, slow and methodical. He adjusted his belt, turned, and walked out of frame.

Harper reached for the trash can and vomited. He dropped to one knee, bracing against the desk as bile burned the back of his throat. He didn't move for a long time. When he finally stood, he wiped his mouth with his sleeve and went back to the drawer, his face pale. There was more.

He pulled out a second folder. This one thick. Legal documents. Real estate records. PAC donations. Transfer papers. Layers of holding companies and LLCs, all woven together like a spider's web.

He flipped through contracts and transfer agreements, scanned through shell accounts and lobbyist filings. It was all carefully constructed. Every page clean, notarized, official.

At the back of the stack was the one he was looking for.

Redhaven Compound – ownership registered to Shellmark Holdings LLC.

And underneath, another name.

Thornewood.

Then another. Aegis Forward PAC. Attached to each was a trail of wire transfers and board authorizations. He flipped one more page and found what he expected.

Banking records. Profit shares. Land use agreements. Each document trailed into the next: land use agreements, campaign donations, offshore deposits. It all tied back to one name.

Thomas Alvarez.

Harper stared at the signature on the last page. Neat. Bold. Proud.

He kept digging. A paper-clipped stack near the bottom caught his attention. Emails. Printed. Clipped together. Dozens of them. Internal memos. Encrypted correspondence. He skimmed, then stopped on one near the middle of the stack.

FROM: T. Alvarez
TO: J. Dunham
SUBJECT: Grant

Grant is going to be a problem. No one blackmails me.
Once he's out of the picture, ownership reverts under clause six.
Make it look personal.
Use the penthouse. No cameras.
And for God's sake, clean the damn boots this time.

A timestamp. Two days before Michael Grant was killed. Harper's pulse jumped. He turned the page. Another, dated a day before Whitaker's murder.

FROM: T. Alvarez

TO: J. Dunham

SUBJECT: Loose ends

Whitaker's been asking questions. Take care of it. Keep it quiet.

Same play as last time. Tell Estrada to sit tight.

No blowback.

Another email. This one made Harper's jaw clench, dated a day after Grant's murder.

FROM: T. Alvarez

TO: J. Dunham

SUBJECT: Welches

Get up to the cabin. Grant left something there—files, maybe media.

If the cops find it before we do, we've got a problem.

I want it cleaned out by tonight.

Burn everything you can't carry.

Another line. Just two sentences, but they hit like a hammer.

FROM: T. Alvarez

TO: J. Dunham

SUBJECT: Caldwell

Take care of Holly Caldwell. No more loose ends.

Make it look like a robbery gone wrong.

Harper's hand gripped the edge of the desk so hard the wood creaked beneath his fingers. He turned to the last page in the stack. An email dated just three days ago.

FROM: T. Alvarez

TO: J. Dunham

SUBJECT: Harper

Time to finish it. He's getting too close.

I should've clipped his wings when he worked for us.

That was a mistake.

Take care of it. Make it look clean.

He can't walk away from this.

The files included internal memos from Grant Technologies showing the expansion project, fully funded by Grant himself in exchange for partial ownership of the Redhaven property. But Grant never filed the ownership claim.

There was a note scribbled in the margin, in Alvarez's handwriting:

"Kill the deal. Keep the land. Get the files."

Grant thought he could outplay Alvarez. Thought blackmail would keep him safe. Thought the expansion would give him leverage. It gave him a grave instead.

Harper turned to the next page. More emails. This time between Alvarez and Estrada. Direct orders.

"Two new girls before the commissioners arrive. One blonde. One Native. Preferably under sixteen."

"We need the new batch clean. Tell the supplier no tattoos. I want them afraid."

"Remind Dunham that fear sells better than consent."

Harper's fingers tightened on the edge of the folder. The man didn't just run the operation. He designed it. Funded it. Turned human lives into a business model.

He closed the folder slowly, the edges worn and curling in his hands. This was no longer about theories. It was truth. It was evidence. It was premeditated. It was *power*.

Murder. Trafficking. Fraud. Conspiracy.

It was war. And Harper had the enemy's playbook.

•••••

The sun was just starting to bleed through the trees when Harper and Kalama stepped out of the Durango. The forest was quiet. Not the same silence as the night before, but something heavier. The kind that settled into the soil.

They walked side by side, boots crunching through frosted leaves, the stillness broken only by the distant caw of a crow. Harper carried a shovel over one shoulder. Kalama held the printed map, the corner still damp from the condensation inside the console.

Estrada had marked the spot.

Just north of the property line.

The place he said they buried the ones who didn't make it.

The path opened into a clearing, ringed by pine. The ground was uneven here, churned and soft. Fresh.

They didn't speak.

A mound of dirt waited ahead, barely disguised beneath scattered branches and dry grass. Harper stopped at its edge and planted the shovel in the soil. The blade sank in easy. Too easy.

He started digging.

The earth gave way quickly, dark and loose. After only a few shovelfuls, the metal edge struck something solid. Not stone. Plastic.

He cleared it with gloved hands, revealing the edge of a tarp. His breath fogged the cold air. Slowly, he reached down, grabbed the folded corner, and pulled.

The tarp peeled back with a quiet rustle, and a hand slipped out. Pale. Still. The fingers delicate, frozen mid-curl. Her nail polish was pristine, sky blue with a single glitter stripe on each nail, like it had just dried.

Harper's jaw clenched. He reached forward to brush a strand of dirt-caked hair from her face. Around her neck hung a small silver cross. Kalama stepped closer. He stopped suddenly, eyes fixed on the necklace.

"I know that cross," he said quietly.

Harper turned to him. Kalama swallowed hard, his voice barely audible. "She was my girlfriend in High School. When she disappeared," he choked out. "Kaylie."

He knelt beside the grave, one hand hovering above the girl's arm, not quite touching. Harper didn't say anything. There was nothing to say. They stood there in silence, the early morning wind cutting through the trees. A crow called once. Then again.

And slowly, Harper looked up.

Across the clearing, the shapes came into focus. Not shapes. Graves. Uneven patches of sorrow, stretching into the tree line. Each one a secret buried beneath pine and silence. There were dozens of them. One after another.

Kalama's breath caught in his throat. He turned away, tears brimming his eyes. Harper didn't. He stared at them, Righteous anger burning his eyes more than the tears.

●●●●●

CHAPTER 28: GRIEVANCES

The sun had barely crested the eastern ridgeline when Kalama pulled his pickup off the gravel road and onto the weathered lot on Black Pine Lane. The complex loomed ahead, gray concrete, old siding curling at the edges, a place forgotten by developers and politicians alike. Apartment 2B sat on the second floor, its paint faded, the railing outside rusted in patches.

He turned off the engine and sat in the silence, his hands resting on the wheel, breath tight in his chest. The fog had lifted with the dawn, but inside of him lingered a haze of exhaustion and fury, his heart heavy.

He climbed the stairs slowly, his boots thudding softly on the worn wooden steps. The door to 2B hadn't changed. Still the same faded dream catcher hanging from the peephole. Still the chipped paint around the frame. Still the threshold of a life paused.

He didn't knock.

Heather opened the door before he could raise his hand. She stood in the frame like she'd been waiting all night. Maybe she had.

She was barefoot, wearing sweats and a t-shirt, her long black hair up in a pony-tail. Kalama looked at the tattoos curling up her arm, stylized, traditional lines that spoke of heritage and pain, roots and defiance, once again shocked at how much she looked like her sister. Her ice-blue eyes locked onto his, hard as stone.

She didn't speak. Just stared.

"Heather," Kalama said, quietly. "Can I come in?"

She stepped aside. Inside the apartment, once Heather had shut the door, Kalama spoke.

"It's Kailey," he said softly. "We found her."

Heather's face didn't change. Not at first. Her eyes searched his, looking for hope. Finding none, her shoulders dropped, just slightly, and the breath left her body.

"Where?"

"A compound. East of Blackridge. We found her grave this morning."

She stepped back slowly, hand reaching for the edge of the wall as if the room had tilted. She didn't cry. Not yet. Her voice was flat, almost distant. "How do you know it's her?"

Kalama swallowed. "She was buried under a tarp. With a small silver cross around her neck. That cross she always wore."

Heather's knees buckled. Kalama caught her before she fell.

"No," she whispered, over and over again. "No, no, no—"

Heather's breaths came in shudders, her hands curled into fists in her lap. "I gave her that necklace," she said. "It was…it was mine when I was little. I told her it would keep her safe."

Kalama sank onto the floor in front of her, his voice barely above a whisper, tears glistening in his eyes. "I know. I remember."

Heather stared at the floor, eyes vacant. "She was only sixteen."

"She was older now," Kalama said gently. "She'd been gone a long time."

Heather closed her eyes, face crumpling but still holding the flood at bay.

"She fought," she said. "I know she did."

"She did," Kalama said. "And now… she's not alone anymore."

For a long time, they sat in silence. Then Heather's breath hitched, and the tears came. Quiet at first, then sharp and wracking. Kalama didn't speak. He just sat beside her, letting both of their grief run its course.

• • • • •

Cho pulled a length of yellow crime scene tape tight between two trees, securing it with a zip tie. The plastic snapped in the cold air as it stretched across the edge of the gravel turnout. Hurst stood a few yards away, camera in hand, snapping wide shots of the compound exterior. Every door, window, and corner logged in sequence.

He took a long sip from the thermos Harper had handed him hours earlier. It was lukewarm now, but strong enough to cut through the fog in his mind. Sleep was not something anyone here could afford.

They worked in silence, the only sounds the click of the camera shutter and the steady flap of crime scene tape in the breeze. Pine needles crunched beneath their boots. The early light filtered through the trees in slanted shafts, catching on disturbed dirt and broken branches where the firefight had erupted hours earlier.

"The teams are still an hour out," Hurst said, lowering the camera. "Maybe longer with this terrain."

Cho glanced toward the treeline where the burial mounds waited, undisturbed. "We should flag the path before they get here. We don't want anyone stepping on evidence."

Hurst nodded, already unspooling another roll of tape. "Start from the cabin to the treeline. I'll mark the grid once I finish the exterior photos."

Cho moved toward the narrow footpath where they'd found the graves, his breath visible in the morning chill. Twenty-six shallow depressions in the forest floor, each one a secret someone had tried to bury. He knelt beside the first and placed a small orange flag beside it, then the next, and the next. By the time he reached the sixth, the quiet was starting to wear on him.

Back at the main house, Hurst finished photographing the shattered front door. Splinters from the doorframe still littered the porch. She paused for a moment, brushing windblown hair from her face. Her fingers hovered over the shutter again.

"Feels like something out of a war zone," she said quietly.

Cho returned to her side, dropping a final marker into his pouch. "It is," he replied. "We just didn't know we were fighting one."

They exchanged a glance. Both knew what was coming once the teams arrived. Dozens of bodies to exhume. A compound full of forensic evidence to catalog. A case that would haunt them for years.

Hurst looked down the driveway. No sirens. No dust trail. Just the woods and the wind.

"They're taking too long," she muttered.

"They're bringing everything they've got," Cho said. "It'll be worth the wait."

"I hope so," she said. "Because this place needs to speak. And we need to listen."

Cho looked down the road toward the parked vehicles near the gate. Harper's Durango waited there, idling quietly in the morning haze.

"They're not staying," Hurst said, following his gaze.

"No," Cho answered. "They're going after the ones who started all this."

• • • • •

Harper stood by the front bumper of the Durango, arms folded, his expression unreadable. His clothes were the same from last night. Dusty. Wrinkled. Blood along one cuff from digging in the dark. He hadn't changed. There hadn't been time. But it wasn't exhaustion in his face now. It was focus. The kind that only came at the end of something long and hard.

Foster was talking quietly with Briggs over the hood of an unmarked SUV. Briggs tapped through messages on his phone, likely updating someone at the federal level. Coordination was key, but this moment felt like something beyond jurisdictions or chain of command.

Foster looked over. "We need to move."

Harper nodded. "Dunham and Alvarez?"

Foster confirmed. "We hit them before they hear about the raid. Once they find out, they'll either disappear or dig in."

Harper opened the driver's door. "They won't get that chance."

Briggs slid his phone into his jacket pocket. "I've got a U.S. Attorney prepped if we need to push federal. We can charge them six different ways."

Harper shook his head. "We don't need six. We just need one. Murder."

Foster moved to the passenger side. "Let's go. Before anyone has a chance to tip them off."

Harper started the engine. Gravel crunched beneath the tires as the Durango pulled away from the compound. The morning sun glinted off the hood and windshield, catching the still-visible impact marks from the rifle rounds the night before.

They didn't talk for a while. The road ahead stretched east, winding toward Blackridge.

But the reckoning had already begun.

•••••

A low rumble echoed down the road.

Hurst looked up from the clipboard just as the first Clackamas County van came into view, tires grinding through loose gravel. Behind it followed two more vehicles, one marked with Stonehaven PD's evidence response unit, the other towing a mobile command trailer. The convoy slowed and rolled to a stop in the clearing near the cabin.

Cho exhaled slowly. "Finally."

Doors opened. Crime scene technicians stepped out, some already in masks, others snapping on gloves as they scanned the scene. Their jackets were marked with bold white lettering: EVIDENCE, FORENSICS, STONEHAVEN, CLACKAMAS COUNTY. They moved with quiet purpose, each one trained for moments like this, though none of them had expected it here.

A lead tech from Clackamas approached, carrying a tablet. "We're staged and ready. Which site do you want processed first?"

Hurst handed him a marked map. "Split into two teams. This area is the main compound. Start with the upstairs bedroom and the hidden office. Full biological and digital sweep. We believe it was used for trafficking."

She turned to the next team already unloading gear. "You'll head into the woods. Follow the flagged path. Orange markers identify each grave."

Cho stepped beside her. "We've located twenty-six so far. Shallow mounds. Nothing's been touched since we arrived."

The tech nodded without comment. His face remained neutral, but his hands moved faster as he keyed notes into his tablet. The response teams began to fan out. Tents went up. Perimeter tape was reinforced. Cameras and portable lights hummed to life. The clearing shifted from eerie silence to quiet coordination.

In the forest, one tent was raised over the gravesite. Cho walked the line, keeping track as the techs dropped to their knees and began clearing topsoil with brushes and gloved hands. Every movement was slow and deliberate. The ground gave way with ease. The earth had never truly settled.

The first tarp was uncovered just before noon.

It peeled back with a soft snap, revealing the form of a young woman curled beneath it. Her skin was pale and drawn. Her hair remained braided. A silver cross rested against her collarbone, dulled by time but intact.

The crew fell silent.

A tech stepped away and marked a location on his digital log. "One of… twenty-six," he said. His voice was calm, but his expression told the rest.

The next grave revealed another woman. Then another. Then yet another. They continued down the line, working without interruption. Most of the bodies were wrapped in fabric, blankets, bed sheets, and discarded coats. Some had bracelets or rings. One wore a hoodie with a faded cartoon logo still clinging to the fabric.

The odor of disturbed soil and decay grew stronger as the work continued. The only sounds were the scrape of trowels, the click of cameras, and the gentle rustle of wind through the trees.

By midafternoon, the number was confirmed.

Twenty-six bodies. All women. Estimated ages ranged from twelve to early thirties. Several showed signs of physical trauma. One had a fractured wrist. Another bore visible marks around her neck. Most were found with something personal left with them, as if whoever buried them had wanted to pretend it meant something.

Hurst made the final notation at the top of the scene log. Her pen hovered over the number. For a moment, she did not move.

Cho stepped beside her, watching the techs work beneath the tent. "You alright?"

She kept her eyes on the graves. "I've processed deaths. Scenes with kids. But this..." She swallowed, her voice tightening. "This is something else."

Cho nodded once. "Yeah. It is."

They stood together in the growing quiet, the compound behind them and the forest ahead. Between them and the truth lay twenty-six graves. Each one a life stolen, hidden, and nearly forgotten.

Not anymore.

•••••

CHAPTER 29: INTO THE ASHES

Harper's hands gripped the steering wheel tight, his knuckles pale on the leather of the wheel. He flexed his fingers, once, then again, then again, trying to shake the tension building in his forearms. The muscles wouldn't relax. His jaw clenched hard enough to ache.

Beside him, Foster sat silent, one elbow resting against the door, gaze fixed on the dark blur of pine trees outside the passenger window. He hadn't said a word since they left the compound. He didn't need to. The silence between them was heavy enough to make the cabin feel smaller than it was.

Only the tires made a sound, low and steady on the pavement, humming like a distant warning.

They were heading south. Back to Blackridge County. Back to the Sheriff's Office.

Back to the place where it had all started.

Harper knew the road by heart. Every turn, every sign, every tree line where the shoulder narrowed. He had driven it a hundred times in his former life, back when he wore the Blackridge star on his chest instead of the Detective's shield on his belt.

It hadn't changed much. But he had.

This time, his thoughts didn't drift to old memories or faded mistakes. He wasn't reliving the past. He was grounded in the present. Focused. Cold.

There was a cold fire burning in his chest, but it wasn't rage.

It was purpose.

Kaylie.

Her name surfaced first.

The image of her curled on the floor of that office, her voice raw with pleading, blood matting her hair while Dunham brutalized her. Her small body, broken and used. The look in her eyes, like she knew exactly what was coming and no longer had the strength to fight it.

Harper blinked hard. The memory didn't fade.

He could still hear her scream.

Still hear the sound she made when Dunham stabbed her.

Still feel the weight of her body beneath that tarp. Cold. Fragile. Forgotten.

He saw again the cross around her neck. The one Kalama had recognized. The one that had once been a gift, back when she was still someone's daughter. Someone's first love. Before she became a victim. A number. A secret grave.

Those were sights and sounds that would follow him for the rest of his days.

Then came the faces of the others. The women and girls they had pulled from Redhaven. Faces that didn't blink. Eyes that didn't cry. Hollowed-out expressions, like the light had been scraped from behind their eyes.

He remembered the girl who called herself Freckles, because she had forgotten her real name.

He remembered how she clung to the blanket like it was the only solid thing left in the world.

His mind moved to Alan Whitaker, bleeding out on that country road, trying to speak around the blood flooding his throat. *Dunham,* he had said. That dying whisper echoing through Harper's mind now like a ghost.

He saw Vanessa Whitaker again, her shoulders shaking as he delivered the news. Her sobs cutting through the living room like broken glass.

He saw Michael Grant. Arrogant. Ambitious. Obsessed with power. Slashed open like a piece of meat in a penthouse no one could save him from.

So. Much. Death.

So many lives torn apart. So much stolen. Futures, childhoods, peace. The raw, grinding toll of greed left behind like wreckage after a storm.

Not just a few victims. Not just one compound. A system. Dozens of girls. Dozens of families. Years of rot and silence. The raw human *cost* was staggering. So much pain, born from the malice of two men.

John Dunham. Thomas Alvarez.

He clenched the wheel tighter. The pain helped him stay sharp.

Foster cleared his throat softly. The sound cut through the silence, grounding Harper for a moment.

"You good?" Foster asked, his voice low.

Harper didn't answer right away. His eyes stayed on the road, on the faint silver line of highway stretching ahead through the dark. Pines crowded both sides like silent sentinels. The snow on the shoulder reflected the occasional headlight glare, streaking the world in pale white ghosts.

They were closing in on the Blackridge county line. Closing in on the men who had built this horror.

"I will be," he said finally, the words clipped, like they cost him something to say.

"You did good, Jake."

Harper gave a half shrug. "Sure, boss."

"I mean it. You really did. This case..." He paused, exhaled through his nose. "This case was bigger than anything we imagined. Bigger than anything we were ready for."

Harper said nothing. His jaw worked slightly, a quiet grind of tension. He flexed his fingers against the wheel again, letting the pressure bite through his fingers. The rhythmic hum of tires on asphalt was the only response.

Foster continued, his tone steady but softer than usual.

"Listen, Jake. I've been doing this a long time. I've seen some shit. Murders, suicides, drug houses with kids in the next room. Stuff that sticks with you."

He paused again. Not for effect, but because he needed to.

"But nothing like this. Nothing close. Redhaven wasn't just criminal, it was evil. Anyone would understand if you were shaken."

Harper's silence was a wall. But his breathing had changed. Slightly shallower. A little less even.

"I know I sure as hell am," Foster added.

Harper nodded once, still staring straight ahead. His throat moved as he swallowed, hard.

"You didn't back down," Foster said. "Not once. You chased every lead. You fought like hell. For Grant. For Whitaker. For those girls."

Harper's voice cracked when he finally spoke. "It didn't help Kaylie," he said. "Didn't help the ones buried in the woods."

He gripped the wheel tighter again, eyes burning now. The road blurred at the edges of his vision. Foster didn't rush in with a platitude. He let it settle. Let the ache have space.

"Some things are beyond our control," he said gently. "You know that. Doesn't make it easier. But you have to let go of what you couldn't stop. You have to hold onto what you *did*."

He turned toward Harper, his voice firmer now.

"Fifteen women and girls are alive because of you. Because you kept digging when others would've given up. They're going home, Jake. Or somewhere safe. They're going to sleep in real beds. Eat real food. Start over. And they won't end up in the ground somewhere with no name."

Harper blinked fast, trying to clear his vision. He didn't speak, but the shake of his shoulders gave him away.

"Thanks, Sarge," he said after a long pause, voice rough.

Foster nodded. "You're a hell of a detective. Hell of a cop. I'm damn proud to work with you. To call you friend."

Harper gave another small nod, lips pressed tight, throat too thick to speak.

The silence returned, but it felt different now. Not as heavy. Not as cold.

They kept driving.

The county line sign flashed past them in the dark.

And ahead, the Blackridge Sheriff's Office waited.

•••••

"We are each our own devil, and we make this world our hell."
- Oscar Wilde

CHAPTER 30: THE RECKONING

As the Durango turned into the parking lot of the Blackridge County Sheriff's Office, Harper found himself staring at the building like it was a ghost from a former life. Same cracked concrete. Same fading yellow paint curling at the corners like old parchment. Patrol cars sat neatly in a row near the far end of the lot, parked with military precision. Personal vehicles filled the other side, just as they had back when he was one of them.

Some things never change.

Harper eased into a space marked VISITOR and cut the engine. He sat for a beat, the silence settling heavy around him. Then he stepped out, walked to the back hatch, and popped it open. The blood-stained camo shirt came off in one motion, tossed into the back next to his plate carrier. He grabbed a fresh flannel—green and soft from years of washes—and shrugged into it, buttoning it slowly, methodically.

The cold air bit at his skin, but it didn't matter. His hands worked on autopilot.

He kicked off his boots, the soles thudding against the bumper, and slipped into his battered Converse. Laced them tight. Reached for his badge chain and draped it around his neck, the cold metal hitting his chest with a quiet finality.

Briggs pulled in behind him. The van hissed as it stopped, and a moment later, the Homeland agent stepped out without a word. Foster exited Harper's Durango and fell in step beside them.

They walked toward the entrance together.

Three men.

One mission.

The lobby was just as Harper remembered. Dim overhead lights, scuffed linoleum, and vending machines humming in the corner. The front desk sat behind a thick pane of plexiglass, its corners stained yellow with age and tape residue. A woman sat behind the window, typing without looking up.

Harper stepped forward.

"Detective Harper, Stonehaven PD. Here to see Undersheriff Dunham," he said, sliding his worn leather badge wallet under the slot in the glass. As he glanced at her name tag, his mind registered it automatically.

Helen. A new name. A new face.

Some things do change.

Helen looked up, blinking as she reached for the wallet. "And you are?" she asked, nodding toward the others.

"Detective Sergeant Foster, Stonehaven PD," Foster said evenly.

"Special Agent Briggs, Homeland Security," Briggs added, flashing his badge with one hand while the other rested near his hip.

Helen's posture straightened. "Oh, okay. Can I ask what this is about?"

Harper's gaze didn't flinch. "No, you may not."

The words landed like a dropped weight. Helen blinked, taken aback, then looked toward Foster, perhaps expecting a gentler tone or clarification. She got neither.

Foster just stared back, expression unreadable. Silence stretched.

Helen's discomfort grew visible. She shifted in her chair, typing something half-heartedly into her terminal. "Uh… well, he's not here right now. He went to the county commissioners meeting this morning. Supposed to testify on the budget. They've been trying to gut us for years," she said with a nervous chuckle.

Harper turned toward Foster, then Briggs. He shrugged.

"Fuck it," he said quietly.

He reached into his jacket and pulled out a folded document, slid it across the counter.

"This is a probable cause affidavit for the arrest of Undersheriff John Dunham," he said. "Twenty-eight counts of murder. Three counts of attempted murder, including two against sworn officers."

Helen's face went pale.

Briggs stepped forward and produced a second document. His tone was calm. Cold.

"This is a federal arrest warrant. It includes a gag order," he said, setting it gently atop Harper's. "If you notify Dunham, you will be charged as an accessory to obstruction of justice. Minimum five years."

Helen's mouth opened, but no words came at first. Her eyes flicked between the three men. Between the badges. Between the papers that made the blood drain from her cheeks.

"I… I wouldn't do that," she said quickly. "He's really at the meeting. The commissioner building. Feel free to check."

Harper didn't respond. He and Briggs were already walking away.

Foster stepped closer to the glass.

"We will, ma'am," he said quietly.

Then he turned and followed.

● ● ● ● ●

Back in the Durango, Harper and Foster sat in silence as the vehicle rolled down the two-lane stretch of road that led to the County Commissioner's Office. The engine hummed beneath them, a steady rhythm that matched the tension still coiled in Harper's chest.

Behind them, Briggs followed in his government-issued van, headlights catching on patches of wet asphalt as the sun began to break through the thinning clouds. The storm had passed, but the cold hadn't gone. Snowmelt trickled in streaks along the shoulders of the road, glinting in the midmorning light.

Harper adjusted his grip on the wheel. A hairline crack snaked through the upper left corner of the windshield, a scar left over from the night before. Light caught the fracture and scattered across the dash like broken glass.

No music. No radio. Just the low hum of tires and the echo of everything they had seen.

As they neared the turnoff for the government complex, Harper finally broke the silence.

"Hey, Sarge?"

Foster turned his head slightly. "Yeah?"

"Thanks."

Foster looked at him, brow raised. "For what?"

Harper's voice was quieter this time, rough around the edges.

"For earlier. For backing me when this thing got hard. For sticking by me. I remember what it felt like not to have that. Being back in Blackridge like this...I used to drive these streets with a target on my back. Now I'm here with you and Briggs, and we're doing this the right way. I guess I just wanted to say thanks."

Foster gave a faint nod. The corner of his mouth tugged upward into something halfway between a smile and a grimace.

"You've got it, kid," he said.

Harper pulled into the parking lot and shifted the Durango into park. The building ahead was newer than the sheriff's office but only slightly less worn. Long, squat, and lined with tinted windows. County seal by the front doors. Flags fluttering in the breeze above the entrance.

He stepped out and closed the door behind him. The slam echoed across the lot. He stood still for a moment, letting the wind nip at his cheeks, then drew in a deep breath that filled his chest.

Foster's voice called from behind him. "Jake. Hold up."

Harper turned, eyebrows raised.

"Let's vest up," Foster said. "These guys are dangerous. And cornered animals don't always go quietly."

Harper nodded once and walked back to the rear hatch. He popped it open and reached inside, pushing past the blood-stained plate carrier to grab his soft armor vest. It was still cold from the night air, stiff in places where moisture had frozen along the seams. He shrugged it on, the fabric settling over his shoulders like weight made tangible.

He zipped it closed and adjusted the collar. The badge patch sat square over his heart. Beneath it, the words "Stonehaven Police." His name, "Harper," was stitched across the other side. Across the back, bold white letters spelled one thing.

POLICE.

Foster grabbed his own vest and pulled it over his flannel, tightening the side straps before running a hand down the front to smooth it. Briggs joined them, pulling a matching vest from the back of his van. His was nearly identical, but instead of a department name, the bold lettering on his chest read HOMELAND SECURITY.

They stood there for a second, the three of them side by side. Snowmelt trickled into the gutter nearby. The wind carried the faint flap of the American flag above the building, along with the hum of traffic from the nearby road.

No sirens. No shouting. Not yet.

But there'd be no mistaking them now.

The reckoning had begun.

The three men walked through the double doors without hesitation. Their footsteps echoed against the tile, steady and sure. Heads turned as they passed reception. A woman behind the desk blinked at them, confused.

"Gentlemen? Can I help you? Gentlemen? Hello...?"

None of them answered. Harper's eyes were locked ahead, his focus unshakable. Foster followed close behind, scanning the hall. Briggs trailed a step behind them, his hand brushing the edge of his vest.

They reached the wooden door just outside the commission chamber. A heavyset man in a stretched polo shirt stood to intercept them, rising awkwardly from a folding chair. The word "SECURITY" was printed across his chest in faded white letters.

"What can I do for you gentlemen?" he asked, his voice uncertain but trying to sound official.

Harper didn't slow. His eyes fixed on the door like it had already opened.

"You can stand aside. Police business," he said, voice low and sharp.

The guard caught a glimpse of the badge on Harper's chest and the sidearm holstered at his waist. Then he saw Briggs's vest. He stepped back without another word. The door creaked open, the noise inside washing over them like a wave.

Fluorescent lights buzzed above rows of plastic-backed chairs filled with local citizens. A few were leaning forward, taking notes. Others sat with arms folded, listening but skeptical. At the front of the room stood John Dunham, dressed in full Blackridge County Sheriff's Office uniform. Two silver stars gleamed on his collar, denoting his rank of Undersheriff. Alvarez sat near the end of the dais, flanked by fellow commissioners. His nameplate read "Thomas Alvarez – Board Chair."

Dunham was in the middle of a speech, gesturing to a PowerPoint behind him that displayed bar graphs and pie charts. His voice was loud and confident, echoing through the small chamber.

"...and if we want to maintain a safe and responsive department, the public safety levy must—"

He froze mid-sentence.

His eyes landed on Foster. Then on Briggs. And finally, on Harper.

He turned fully, slowly, like his body couldn't keep up with his mind. The room went quiet. The sound of shuffling paper stopped. A cough died mid-throat.

Harper walked straight down the center aisle, each step deliberate. His left hand dropped to his holster. He drew his pistol slowly, the metal whispering free of the kydex. The muzzle remained down, but the intent was clear.

Briggs mirrored the movement beside him. Foster did the same. Gasps rippled through the crowd. Chairs creaked. One woman reached for her phone, fumbling with the screen.

Harper's voice cut through the silence like a blade.

"John Dunham. Thomas Alvarez. You're both under arrest. Murder. Human trafficking."

The entire room froze. Someone gasped in the back. Phones were pulled out, cameras on the front of the room. Alvarez's eyes widened. His jaw slackened, but no sound came out.

Dunham's expression changed slower. From disbelief, to confusion, to something colder. Something darker. Harper stepped forward. His voice did not rise, but it carried.

"Raise your hands. Slowly. Turn and face the wall."

Dunham didn't move. Neither did Alvarez. Briggs shifted his stance and raised his pistol higher, no longer pointed down. Foster's hand tightened on the grip of his weapon. The moment stretched thin.

Harper watched Dunham's eyes. Saw the flicker of calculation. The tension building in his shoulders. The slow inhale through his nose.

Harper took another step forward. "Do it. Now."

But Dunham's hand twitched. And everything exploded.

POP! POP!

The first two shots rang out like thunder. In the chaos, Foster's head snapped back, and he dropped. Harper didn't even see Dunham draw the weapon. It had been hidden behind the podium, waiting. Now it smoked in his right hand as he bolted for the back of the room, Alvarez right behind him.

Screams erupted across the chamber. Chairs clattered. People ducked and scrambled for cover. A baby cried. Somewhere, someone was sobbing. Briggs dove to the side, already firing, his sidearm barking as he tried to hit them before they slipped away.

Dunham and Alvarez burst through the emergency exit behind the dais. The door slammed shut behind them with a hollow bang. Harper couldn't move. His ears were ringing. His brain hadn't caught up to what had just happened.

Then he heard someone screaming. It took him a second to realize the voice was his own.

He rushed forward, stumbling over fallen chairs and terrified civilians. His knees hit the floor beside Foster.

"Sarge? CRAIG?!"

Foster lay face-down on the carpet. Blood spread in a growing halo beneath his head. Harper turned him over and recoiled. There were two holes in his face. One between his eyebrows. The other just beneath his right cheekbone. Blood leaked slowly from both, and his eyes were wide open, glassy and lifeless.

Harper dropped to his knees fully and reached for Foster's throat, fingers trembling as he searched for a pulse. There was nothing.

"No no no no—come on, come on—" Harper muttered, tears flooding his vision. He pressed his hands to Foster's chest and started compressions. One. Two. Three. Hard and fast. His shoulders shook as he worked, breath ragged, grief pouring out with every pump of his arms.

Behind him, Briggs's voice roared into the radio.

"OFFICER DOWN! OFFICER DOWN! Gunshot wounds to the head! Send everyone!"

But Harper wasn't listening.

He just kept pressing.

The blood soaked through Foster's shirt and into Harper's sleeves. His hands slipped. His vision blurred.

"I've got this," Briggs said, suddenly kneeling beside him, voice low and urgent. "I've got this. Go."

Harper didn't respond.

"Jake." Briggs grabbed his shoulder. "*Go*. Don't let those bastards get away."

Harper's hands froze.

He looked down at Foster one last time.

At the man who had believed in him. Who had stood by him when no one else did. Who had just taken a bullet to the face before Harper could even react.

His throat tightened. His mouth went dry.

Then he stood.

His legs felt like stone, but they moved.

His weapon came up.

And he ran.

•••••

"And I looked, and behold a pale horse: and his name that sat on him was Death, and Hell followed with him."
- Revelation 6:8

CHAPTER 31: RUNNING OUT THE DEVIL

Harper's ears pounded as he exploded through the back exit, boots slamming against the pavement. His heart thudded in his chest, fast and uneven, but his grip on the pistol was steady. He came through the door with the muzzle up, eyes scanning, ready to return fire.

A few hundred yards ahead, he caught a flash of movement.

Alvarez was diving into the passenger side of a black SUV. Dunham was already behind the wheel. The Suburban's engine roared to life, tires squealing as the vehicle lurched forward. Harper didn't hesitate. He sprinted after them, chest heaving, legs burning. He raised his weapon and fired.

The pistol barked three times in rapid succession. The rear windshield shattered, glass spraying across the asphalt. The bullets punched into the vehicle, but it kept moving, fishtailing as it tore down the access road and out of the lot.

The SUV disappeared around the corner, tires howling.

Harper didn't slow. He turned on his heel and sprinted back across the parking lot toward the Durango. Gravel crunched underfoot. His breath came in sharp, ragged bursts.

He yanked open the driver's door and threw himself behind the wheel. The engine was still warm. He shoved it into gear and slammed the gas pedal to the floor. The Durango surged forward. His lights flicked on. Sirens screamed to life. The red and blue strobes lit the street as he tore onto Highway 27, the black Suburban already half a mile ahead.

Harper snatched the radio from its cradle and keyed the mic, voice loud over the wail of the sirens.

"This is Detective Harper, Stonehaven PD. I'm in pursuit. Black Chevy Suburban, license plate two-two-four-Echo-Papa-Yankee, southbound on Highway 27. Two homicide suspects. Armed and dangerous."

The radio crackled. Dispatch hesitated.

"Confirming plate two-two-four-Echo-Papa-Yankee?"

"Affirm. Suspects are Thomas Alvarez and John Dunham. Dunham just shot a police sergeant inside the county commission chamber."

There was a beat of silence.

Then another voice came over the air.

"This is Special Agent Austin Briggs, Homeland Security. Confirming we have probable cause for homicide. Paramedics have called it. Time of death, twelve thirty-seven p.m."

Harper swallowed hard. His throat burned. His grip tightened on the wheel until his knuckles turned white.

The line stayed quiet for a moment. Then dispatch returned, her voice clearer now. Steadier.

"Roger that, Detective. We've got units rolling from every district. Air support is on standby. You're not alone out there. Go get 'em."

Harper didn't answer. He leaned forward in his seat, eyes locked on the taillights in the distance. He wasn't letting them get away. Not after Foster. Not after everything.

The Durango's engine roared as Harper kept the accelerator pinned. The gears shifted beneath him, the vehicle growling louder with every second. Up ahead, the black Suburban weaved through traffic, tires screeching, struggling to maintain control.

Sixty.

Seventy.

Eighty.

Ninety.

Harper's eyes narrowed. The Suburban was close now. Too close to escape. The Durango was eating the distance with every second.

Then—flashes from the rear window.

POP POP POP. TSH TSH TSH.

Three rounds slammed into the windshield. Glass spiderwebbed instantly, spraying fragments across the dash. Tiny shards glittered in the sun as they scattered across Harper's vest and arms.

He blinked once, checked himself. No pain. No blood.

He was still in it.

Harper gritted his teeth and pressed the pedal harder. The Durango surged forward, chasing the scream of the Suburban's tires as it swerved wildly in front of him.

CRACK. CRACK.

Two more shots tore through the windshield. The passenger seat exploded in a puff of foam and fabric, torn open by the rounds.

He didn't flinch. Didn't let up. The Durango closed the final gap like a freight train.

He slammed into the back bumper of the Suburban. Metal crunched. The Suburban jerked sideways, tires skidding as it lost traction. Harper stayed on it, pushing again, harder this time. The SUV began to fishtail.

Its brake lights lit up, glowing red across Harper's cracked windshield. He yanked the wheel and stomped on the brakes, tires screaming in protest as the Durango swerved to avoid a collision.

The Suburban veered sharply into the ditch, its right side lifting off the ground. Then it flipped.

Once.

Twice.

Three times.

A fourth.

The heavy vehicle crashed down hard, landing on its side in a cloud of dirt and snow, glass and debris tumbling through the air. And everything went still. Steam hissed from the engine block.

Harper didn't wait. He threw the Durango into park and flung open the door. Pistol drawn, boots hitting the dirt, he ran toward the wreck. As Harper neared the wreck, steam curled from the crumpled hood of the Suburban. The metal hissed, ticking as it cooled in the winter air. One rear wheel was still spinning, slowly, like the vehicle hadn't realized the chase was over.

Then he saw movement. Alvarez was dragging himself through the shattered windshield, glass crunching under his knees and palms. Blood streaked down one side of his face, but his eyes were sharp, locked on Harper with pure hatred.

Dunham was gone. The driver's seat was empty. Harper's eyes scanned the tree line, the ditch, the field beyond the fence. Nothing. No movement. Just wind and the distant hum of traffic.

"Put your fucking hands up, Alvarez!" Harper shouted, pistol raised.

Alvarez froze halfway out the windshield, breath ragged, arms trembling. He looked up at Harper, eyes wide, lips curled into a sneer of contempt.

Then—

Muzzle flashes.

From deep inside the SUV.

THWACK. THWACK.

Two rounds slammed into Harper's vest. The impact knocked the air from his lungs like a punch from a heavyweight. He stumbled back, legs giving way, and tumbled into the icy ditch beside the highway. Rocks dug into his back. Mud soaked into his jeans.

Another shot snapped past his ear. Then another, hissing overhead. Gasping, Harper rolled onto his stomach and crawled low, pressing himself into the dirt. He gritted his teeth and dragged in a shallow breath, chest screaming from the hits. He felt the burn beneath the armor, bruises already forming across his ribs.

He raised his pistol slowly, just high enough to clear the edge of the ditch, and fired blind into the Suburban's cabin.

Crack. Crack. Crack.

Glass shattered. Plastic popped. The vehicle rocked slightly from the return fire.

Alvarez scrambled sideways in a panic, hands flailing as he crawled through the gravel, slipping in the melted snow. His bravado vanished, replaced with raw fear. He tripped, scrambled again, and disappeared behind the back end of the overturned SUV.

Harper dragged himself upright, still using the ditch as cover. His hands were shaking. His chest was bruised, but the vest had done its job.

"Dunham! Alvarez! It's over!" Harper shouted, voice ragged, echoing across the field.

From behind the overturned Suburban, Dunham's voice came back sharp and venomous.

"Go fuck yourself, Harper! Should've gutted you when I had the chance!"

Harper kept his pistol steady, muzzle pointed at the downed vehicle.

"Last chance, Dunham!" Harper yelled, as sirens could be heard in the distance. Sirens wailed in the distance now, growing louder with every second. A figure shifted behind the SUV.

Dunham crawled out, hands empty, chest rising and falling. His uniform was torn, blood streaking one sleeve.

"I'm empty anyway," he said, lifting his hands slowly and standing upright.

"You too, Alvarez! Come out, NOW!" Harper barked.

Alvarez hesitated, then crept around the far side of the Suburban, eyes flicking between Harper and Dunham. His hands rose above his head.

"Keep those hands high," Harper ordered. "Palms out. No surprises."

Alvarez stepped in line beside Dunham, his expression a mix of defiance and panic. Harper got to his feet, his knees stiff, chest still sore from the impacts. He raised his pistol again, arms steady despite the tremor in his muscles.

"Don't you *fucking* move."

Dunham just smiled.

"I'm the goddamn Undersheriff. You really think those deputies are coming for me?" His lip curled. "You're nothing but a disgraced deputy. You think anyone's backing you now?"

"And I'm the Commissioner!" Alvarez snapped, eyes wild. "You realize who the hell I am?"

Harper didn't flinch.

"That's where you're both wrong. We have everything, Tom. The files. The videos. Redhaven got hit last night. We've got the compound. We've got the victims."

Alvarez's face drained of color. His mouth opened slightly, disbelief flickering in his eyes. Dunham didn't blink. His expression just darkened.

"Like men then," he said, voice low. "Let's finish it."

His hand dropped to his belt in one swift motion. The Kabar flashed in the light as he pulled it free and charged. Harper didn't hesitate.

Pop. Pop. Pop. Pop. Pop.

Five rounds tore into Dunham's chest, hammering into the center mass. He staggered, but didn't fall. He screamed as he ran, a primal roar tearing from his throat. His boots tore up the dirt as he closed the gap.

He was wearing a vest.

Harper's eyes locked on it. He pivoted hard to the right, stepping out of the line of attack. His right hand yanked a fresh magazine from his belt. The empty one dropped to the ground as he slammed the new mag home and racked the slide. Dunham was almost on him, the Kabar raised.

Harper brought the pistol up again, breathing steady despite the surge of adrenaline.

Pop. Pop. Pop. Pop. Pop. Pop.

Each shot traced upward. One struck Dunham's throat. Another split his lip. The third clipped the bridge of his nose. The final three buried themselves in the center of his forehead.

Dunham's momentum carried him forward for another half-step. Then his body went limp. The knife slipped from his fingers, and he collapsed face-first into the dirt, skidding to a stop at Harper's shoes.

Silence settled around them. The sirens still howled in the distance, but Harper barely heard them. He stepped forward, pistol still raised, and turned it on Alvarez.

"Don't!" Alvarez cried out, stumbling back. "I give up! I give up!"

He dropped to his knees, hands raised, eyes squeezed shut. Harper stood over him, blood splattered on his vest, chest heaving. The sirens grew louder.

Alvarez remained on his knees, arms above his head, chest rising and falling in shallow, panicked breaths. Dirt clung to his suit, his hair matted with sweat. He flinched as Harper stepped forward.

Harper pulled handcuffs from his belt.

"Wait! Wait! Please," Alvarez said quickly, voice cracking. "Don't do this. I can fix it. I'll make a call. I've got money. Connections. Whatever you want. Name it!"

Harper holstered his gun, grabbed one of his wrists and twisted it behind his back. The cuffs snapped into place, metal biting into Alvarez's skin.

"Come on," Alvarez begged. "You don't have to do this. You can walk away. Just say the word."

Harper tightened the cuffs, then looked down at him, calm, steady, resolved.

"No," he said. "I can't live with what you've done."

Alvarez froze. For a moment, he stopped breathing. Recognition flickered in his eyes.

Because he had said those exact words once—years ago—when he fired Harper without warning, without cause, with Dunham standing at his side. Harper stepped away, leaving Alvarez kneeling in the dirt.

Red and blue lights washed across the trees, the wreck, and the blood-stained dirt. Engines roared as vehicles skidded to a stop along the highway. Doors slammed. Boots hit pavement.

Briggs was the first to arrive, rifle in hand, eyes wide as he scanned the scene. He saw Dunham's body, the Kabar beside it, and Harper standing over Alvarez.

"You good?" Briggs called out, voice sharp, but steady. Harper gave a slow nod.

Blackridge deputies followed behind him, at least six, vests on, weapons drawn. For a moment, their eyes flicked between Harper and the wreckage, unsure. Then one of them lowered his rifle.

"We got you, Detective," he said.

One by one, the rest followed. Harper turned away and walked toward Briggs, leaving the commissioner kneeling in the dirt, surrounded by the flashing lights and the weight of everything he had built.

And everything he had lost.

• • • • •

"Right is Right. No matter the cost."
-Detective Sergeant Craig Foster

CHAPTER 32: JUSTICE IN THE WAKE

One week later.

Harper stood motionless in his Class A dress uniform, the brim of his cover shadowing his eyes. The sky above was thick with dark clouds, low and churning, a quiet threat of rain hanging in the air.

The cemetery was filled with rows of officers in uniform, black bands across their badges, standing shoulder to shoulder. Behind them, members of the public stood in silence. Members of his family, friends, and the city Foster had spent his life protecting.

The Honor Guard stepped forward in unison.

Harper, Hurst, Cho, Officers Garcia and Thompson, and Special Agent Austin Briggs—dressed in his old Stonehaven uniform—moved as one. Six men, six sets of polished shoes crunching softly on the gravel path. Their gloved hands gripped the casket's silver handles, the weight of it settling into their shoulders.

Nothing Harper had ever carried felt heavier.

They marched with precision, each step perfectly timed, their grief hidden behind disciplined movement. The world was quiet but for the creak of the casket and the breeze moving through the flags.

They reached the raised platform and carefully set the casket down onto the dais. Once it was secure, they stepped back and stood at attention, shoulders squared, eyes forward.

The silence was broken by the sharp command of the rifle detail.

"Ready."

"Aim."

Harper flinched with each crack of the rifle fire, the reports echoing across the cemetery like thunder.

CRACK.

Pause.

CRACK..

Pause.

CRACK.

Twenty-one shots. Seven officers. Three volleys.

When the last shell casing hit the grass, the notes of "Amazing Grace" began to rise, soft and mournful, played on a single set of bagpipes at the crest of the hill. The sound carried over the crowd like a lament carried on the wind.

Harper stared straight ahead, but the tears came anyway. He didn't wipe them away.

Chief Merrick stepped back to the podium, voice steady.

"Detective Sergeant Foster was everything we ask a police officer to be. He wore the badge with pride, but not ego. He served with strength, but also compassion. He made this department better, not just with his actions, but with the kind of man he was when the uniform came off.

"He didn't just train good cops. He trained good people. He didn't just solve cases. He changed lives. And for those of us lucky enough to know him as more than a colleague, we carry a hole in our hearts that no uniform can fill."

Merrick looked out over the officers gathered.

"He stood with us. Now we stand for him."

When the service ended, Harper joined the Honor Guard once again. They moved to the casket one final time and reached for the flag.

Each movement was exact, deliberate. Folded corner to corner. Red and white tucked into blue. Harper could feel the tightness in his chest as the last fold formed a perfect triangle, stars outward. He took the flag into his hands, turning slowly toward the front row.

He marched toward Heidi Foster, her face pale but composed. Her hands trembled slightly as she stood, their two children clinging to her sides, eyes wide and confused.

Harper knelt in front of her, holding the flag against his chest before extending it toward her with both hands.

His voice broke as he spoke.

"On behalf of a grateful city, and the Stonehaven Police Department, we thank you for your husband's service, and for his sacrifice."

The words caught in his throat. The tears came faster now, and he didn't stop them.

Heidi reached for the flag with shaking hands. She held it close, lips pressed tight, tears running silently down her cheeks.

Harper rose slowly, gave her a final nod, and stepped back.

Behind him, the honor guard snapped to attention.

A bell rang out three times from the ceremonial detail. One ring for each of the final calls.

End of Watch.

Harper didn't move. Didn't speak.

But inside, something cracked open.

And the weight of what they had lost settled in for good.

As the final notes of the bagpipes faded into the wind and the crowd began to disperse, Harper remained still, staring at the polished casket one last time. Rain finally broke from the clouds, soft at first, then steady. It soaked into the grass, into the stone, into the flag still clutched in Heidi Foster's arms.

Harper stood in silence until the last patrol car pulled away.

It wasn't over. Not really. The dead were buried, but the truth had only just come to light.

●●●●●

The news came fast.

In the days following the Redhaven raid, headlines swept across the state. Words like *trafficking ring, mass graves, murder conspiracy,* and *public corruption* were on every station. Photos of the Redhaven compound ran on every front page, the drone footage showing rows of evidence tents, tarped remains, and crime scene tape fluttering in the wind.

Investigation into Redhaven Compound's Shocking Deaths Continues, read the Oregonian's front page. *Blackridge County Sheriff Resigns Amid Scandal,* announced the Fox affiliate. *Governor Calls for Independent Review of Rural County Oversight,* followed another.

But Harper didn't pay much attention to the headlines. He had work to do. The detective's bullpen at Stonehaven PD was quieter than usual. Half the lights were off. The overhead hum of fluorescent bulbs was softer than he remembered.

Harper sat at his desk, scrolling through the final arrest packets. One for Thomas Alvarez. One for John Dunham, marked "Deceased." One for Raul Estrada. Case files thick with evidence, chain of custody records, and recorded statement transcripts. Forensic analyses. Bank transfers. Hard drive logs. Ballistic reports. High profile suspects, politicians, actors, senators, culled from the client lists.

He flipped through a signed affidavit from one of the rescued girls. A young woman, barely eighteen, who had identified her trafficker from a photo lineup and cried when she saw Dunham's face. Her signature was shaky, the ink smudged.

Across the room, Hurst stood with Cho and Officer Garcia. They were gathered near the sergeant's desk, still empty. Still untouched. A framed photo had been mounted on the wall above it just that morning.

Sergeant Craig Foster.

In the portrait, he wore his class A blues, eyes steady, a quiet confidence in his expression.

No one said anything as they looked up at it. They didn't have to.

●●●●●

Harper's inbox pinged.

He clicked it open, expecting more court notifications or follow-ups from the DA. Instead, he saw a name that stopped him for a second.

Holly Caldwell.

The message was simple. A thank you.

> *Detective Harper,*
>
> *I wanted to say thank you. Not just for protecting me, but for believing me when others didn't. You never judged me. You treated me like a person, not a case file. I don't know how to explain what that meant to me.*
>
> *I know things with Michael were complicated. He wasn't perfect. Neither was I. But he's gone, and I'm not afraid anymore. I'm free.*
>
> *Thank you for giving me that.*
>
> *—Holly*

Harper read it twice. Then again.

He leaned back in his chair, the hum of the room fading for a moment. Outside the window, the rain tapped against the glass, soft and steady.

Some wounds still lingered. Some would never close completely.

But others?

They were healing.

●●●●●

The headlines shifted again as the legal process moved forward.

Alvarez Indicted on 28 Counts of Murder, One Capital. State Trial Set.

High profile senator indicted in Redhaven Conspiracy. Governor's office declines statement. Feds take over Redhaven list investigation.

It had taken weeks of grand jury testimony. Harper had been in and out of the courthouse, called more than a dozen times to testify. Each session peeled back another layer of the nightmare. He spoke under oath about the murders of Grant and Whitaker, about Dunham's ambush and the bullets that had nearly killed him. He walked them through the compound. Through the discovery of Kaylie's body. Through the 25 other graves.

And then there was Molly Parker.

The girl who could only remember her nickname. *Freckles.*

When Harper spoke her name aloud, his voice cracked. He'd tried to hold it together, but the tears came anyway. None of the jurors looked away. They listened. And they believed him.

By the time the indictments were handed down, the list of charges was staggering.

Thomas Alvarez had been formally indicted on 28 counts of murder, and one count of capital murder: Detective Sergeant Mark Foster. Even though Dunham had pulled the trigger, prosecutors made it clear: Foster's death was the result of Alvarez's conspiracy. His enterprise. His evil.

He was also charged with human trafficking, rape, kidnapping, and dozens of related felonies under both state and federal statutes. The state trial was scheduled for six months from now. The federal case would follow a year later.

If convicted, Alvarez would never walk free again. He was facing the rest of his life, and then some. More than 300 years in total sentences. And in Harper's eyes, it still didn't feel like enough.

Raul Estrada wouldn't be testifying.

Three days after the indictments were unsealed, guards found him hanging in his cell. They discovered a suicide note in his bunk, though its authenticity remained in question. Some suspected he had been silenced to keep buried secrets from reaching trial.

But that investigation belonged to another agency now. Another case file. Another detective.

•••••

Harper drove home in silence that night, headlights stretching down the dark rural road towards Stonehaven. The rain had passed. A breeze swept through the evergreens. The weight of the last few months clung to his shoulders, heavier now that the adrenaline had long faded.

He thought about the victims. The ones who had been found. The ones still missing. The ones who were learning how to live again. And he thought about Foster. About the way he had looked in the Class A portrait now hanging over his empty desk.

Harper gripped the wheel and turned onto the street that led to his home. The porch light was on. He thought about those words. The ones Foster had said so many times, until they belonged to all of them.

"Right is right. No matter the cost."

•••••

EPILOGUE

Laughter still echoed down the hallways of their home.

Adelyn's fourth birthday party had gone off without a hitch. Her preschool friends had taken turns swinging wildly at the piñata, shrieking with delight as candy exploded across the backyard. Harper's heart swelled as he watched her blow out the candles, her eyes wide with wonder, her cheeks flushed with excitement. Later, she tore into her presents with unfiltered glee, squealing as she pulled stuffed shark toys and princess figurines from beneath layers of wrapping paper.

That night, they tucked her into bed after one more story, her favorite kind, the ones she made up herself. Tonight, it was about princesses and dragons building a castle together. One with rainbow towers. And a waterslide. Her imagination had bloomed lately, always carrying her to bright, happy places.

"I love you, Daddy. I love you, Mommy," she whispered, eyes fluttering closed as they kissed her forehead.

Harper pulled the blanket up to her chin and shut the bedroom door behind him. In the quiet of the hallway, Alyssa reached for his hand, her smile playful.

"I have something to show you," she said, tugging him toward their bedroom.

Harper raised an eyebrow, but let her lead him in.

"Sit down. Close your eyes," she said, gently pushing him into the overstuffed chair in the corner.

He did as he was told, grinning.

"Okay," she said softly. "You can open them."

Harper blinked. Alyssa stood in front of him, holding out a white stick.

He took it, glanced down.

Two blue lines.

He looked up, his breath catching. "Oh my god. Really?"

Alyssa nodded, eyes shimmering. "Ready for another?"

Harper was on his feet before she could finish the sentence. He scooped her into his arms and spun her in a tight circle, laughter bubbling up from his chest. He kissed her like a man coming back to life.

"You bet," he said between kisses. "I. Cannot. Wait."

Outside, the stars had come out. Inside, the house was full of warmth. Of life. Of the future. And for the first time in a long time, Harper didn't feel haunted.

He felt whole.

•••••

One Month Later

The squad room had settled into a new rhythm.

It was quieter now, a little more grounded. The sting of Foster's absence hadn't faded, but the team had learned how to carry it. The chair at the end of the bullpen remained empty for a week before Chief Merrick made it official.

Hurst had earned the stripes.

She wore them well. Steady, sharp, and unapologetically herself. The promotion hadn't changed her much, except maybe the coffee she drank. Stronger now. No time for the sweet stuff.

Garcia had moved up, too. Officially a detective now, he sat two desks over from Harper, tackling cases like he had something to prove. He did. But he was a damn good cop, and everyone knew it.

Harper was back at his desk, the clutter more organized than usual. A small photo of his family sat next to his monitor. Adelyn's birthday drawing, something about unicorns and a rainbow starship, was pinned to his corkboard. Next to that, an ultrasound of their unborn son, due in May.

The overhead lights buzzed faintly, filing cabinets clicked in the background, and the printer coughed out copies in slow bursts.

It felt normal. Almost.

He was reviewing a robbery case, logging notes into the system, when Hurst walked over holding a manila folder. She dropped it onto his desk with a dull *thud.*

"Another doozy," she said. Her tone was dry, but her expression wasn't casual. Not for this one.

Harper raised an eyebrow and flipped the folder open. Sex assault. Minor victim. The suspect's last name stood out before he even read the first sentence. A familiar one, local.

Son of City Councilor Eli Worthington. Twelve years old. Repeated abuse. Harper scanned the report. The kid had only just spoken up. The case was going to be ugly, political, and high-profile.

Harper already knew one thing. He wasn't letting it go.

Before he could turn the page, his phone rang. Not his department cell. His personal one. The number was unlisted.

Harper picked it up. "This is Harper."

The voice on the other end was calm, clipped, professional.

"Petty Officer Harper?"

That name, that *rank*, hit different. It wasn't a Stonehaven matter calling. It was the uniform. The other one.

Harper straightened slightly in his chair. "Yes. Speaking."

"This is Special Agent Keira Lawson with the Coast Guard Investigative Service. I understand you're currently drilling as a reservist, an ME1?"

"That's correct," Harper said cautiously, already feeling the shift in tone. This wasn't a courtesy call. It was official. The use of his military rank wasn't just protocol, it meant jurisdiction. It meant they were involving him as a sailor, not a cop.

"We'd like to speak with you about a case. Several, actually," Lawson continued. "They involve someone you may be familiar with. An active duty member, Chief Petty Officer Logan Cross."

Harper's pulse ticked up.

"Yeah," he said. "I know him."

They'd served together. Deployed together. Cross had been there when Harper nearly unraveled, and when he started putting himself back together again. He hadn't heard from him in months, but that wasn't unusual. Cross had a way of going quiet when things got complicated.

And they usually did. Because Cross, like Harper, had a tendency to step on toes that protected ugly truths.

"What kind of investigation?" Harper asked.

Lawson paused. "That's part of what we'd like to discuss. Several joint operations. Some overseas. Some close to home. Chain of custody issues. Unexplained asset movements. He's either improvising under pressure… or working a deeper angle."

She paused. "We're not suggesting misconduct. But there are questions."

Harper stayed silent.

Lawson hesitated, then added, "Here's the thing. He asked for you. Said if anyone could help us figure out what's really going on, it's you."

That made Harper sit up straighter.

"And what are you asking?"

"We'd like to bring you on temporary active-duty orders," Lawson said. "Six months. Transition from ME1 to Investigator First Class. You'd be assigned to CGIS Northeast Region, effective immediately. Full clearance. Full access. We'll brief you in person."

Harper glanced across the squad room. Hurst was scribbling something on the whiteboard, half on the phone. Garcia was knee-deep in an interview packet. His own desk held the Worthington case, still open, still raw. The kind of case Harper would usually fight to keep.

But this time, someone else would have to take it.

Because Cross had asked for him. And if Cross was caught in something deeper, something that required a steady hand and a familiar face, Harper wasn't about to leave him twisting.

"I'll coordinate with my chief."

"We've already started the conversation," Lawson said. "They're willing to support it, if you are."

Harper tapped the edge of his desk once. Then again. "Alright. I'm in."

"We'll be in touch tonight," Lawson replied. "And Detective, thank you. In advance."

The line went dead. Harper lowered the phone, staring at nothing for a long moment.

Logan Cross. Still in uniform. Still pushing limits. And now Harper was being asked to chase shadows through the corridors they used to run through as brothers in arms.

Harper stood up, grabbed his jacket, and stepped outside.

The clouds were rolling in again.

The end.

•••••

To read more about Detective Harper's friend from the Coast Guard, Logan Cross…

Dive into *Cold Front: A Logan Cross Thriller* by D.M. Webber:

He left the shadows of special operations behind… but the storm was waiting.

Boatswain's Mate First Class Logan Cross wanted peace. After years serving on the Coast Guard's elite Maritime Security Response Team, he traded covert raids and near-death missions for a quiet post in Gloucester, Massachusetts—and a future with his wife, Melanie.

But when a routine search-and-rescue call leads his crew to a blood-soaked crime scene adrift at sea, Cross is pulled into a chilling conspiracy. A known trafficker executed. A suspicious cover-up ordered by his own command. And a silent warning whispered through the ranks: Don't ask questions.

As the body count rises and trust within the chain of command erodes, Cross must confront a terrifying truth—this wasn't a murder of opportunity. It was an opening move.

Now, with only his instincts and the loyalty of a shaken crew, Cross must navigate deadly currents of corruption, deception, and betrayal… before the storm breaks over everything he swore to protect.

Integrity has a cost. Logan Cross is about to pay it.

Coming soon.

ABOUT THE AUTHOR

J.K. Wolfe is a seasoned police officer with years of experience in criminal investigations, including homicide, sex crimes, child abuse, and financial crimes. He is also a U.S. Coast Guard veteran, bringing a disciplined, mission-focused perspective to both his service and his writing. His crime thrillers are grounded in real-world cases and written to reflect the reality of police work, its weight, its cost, and its purpose. Wolfe writes to honor those who wear the badge for the right reasons, because justice is not just a job. It is a calling.

JKWolfeBooks.com

www.ingramcontent.com/pod-product-compliance
Lightning Source LLC
Chambersburg PA
CBHW050520110726
47899CB00005B/1537